Wings of Glass

AmberLee Kolson

THEYTUS BOOKS

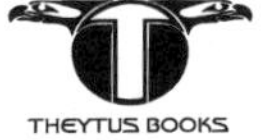

Library and Archives Canada Cataloguing in Publication

Kolson, AmberLee
Wings of Glass / AmberLee Kolson.

ISBN 978-1-894778-96-1

I. Title.

PS8621.O58W55 2010 C813'.6 C2010-901346-8

Printed in Canada by Gauvin Press

www.theytus.com
In Canada: Theytus Books, Green Mountain Rd., Lot 45, RR#2, Site 50, Comp. 8
Penticton, BC, V2A 6J7, Tel: 250-493-7181
In the USA: Theytus Books, P.O. Box 2890, Oroville, Washington, 98844

Patrimoine canadien

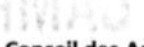
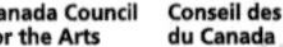

Theytus Books acknowledges the support of the following:
We acknowledge the financial support of the Government of Canada through the Canada Book Fund for our publishing activities. We acknowledge the support of the Canada Council for the Arts which last year invested $20.1 million in writing and publishing throughout Canada. Nous remercions de son soutien le Conseil des Arts du Canada, qui a investi 20,1 millions de dollars l'an dernier dans les lettres et l'édition à travers le Canada. We acknowledge the support of the Province of British Columbia through the British Columbia Arts Council.

Wings of Glass

AmberLee Kolson

To

Rob, Matt, Alex and Kate

You are all my favourites

Thank you to Melva McLean who guided me painlessly through the editing process. Thanks also to Joyce Spicer for the great picture.

CHAPTER 1

I was going to kill myself on the Monday after Gord's birthday but then I remembered I had to bake muffins for school and had to cancel. One thing led to another and there it was, the first week of October and I was still procrastinating. I'd better get a move on, I thought, as I gazed at the long sinewy oxtails piled high behind the glass at the Queen City Meat Market.

I had, until recently, enjoyed coming to the shop, hearing the bell tinkle as I opened the door. I liked the dark hardwood floor. It reminded me of saloons in classic westerns: the doors bursting open; the sound of boot heels on floorboards and the dull jangle of spurs against leather; the booze-soaked clientele startled into looking up slowly from warm beer in thick fingerprinted glasses, their pupils dilating in the unaccustomed light, just enough for them to see the cowboy toss back a shot of whiskey and spit a wad of tobacco onto the floor. I liked the old pictures on the wall: the original owners in their brown wool suits; smiling cashiers with arms crossed on their stomachs; meat cutters all standing in a crooked row outside the front doors of the market, their sleeves rolled up and their hands shoved into pockets hidden behind bloody white bib aprons. I liked the old-fashioned cash register at which an ancient-looking woman silently but pleasantly punched in the prices. Butchers carved up sides of beef on bloody tables, faces with blank expressions, and directly behind clerks who served customers in the order dictated by the number dispensing machine.

I walked over to the autumn bouquet of dried leaves and flowers set up on a small round table in the middle of the store. Eucalyptus branches mingled with purple stattice, pale pink roses, cornflowers and crispy baby's breath in a tall square steel bucket. An homage to Fall? Or was it mourning the death of vibrant and living summer, a formal acceptance of the slow and inevitable decline of life, exsiccated for our perennial pleasure? Like the carcasses strung up in the frozen meat locker, animals slaughtered for us in a rational manner devoid of all sentiment. It was the thought of the cold human calculation of it all, which I knew no butcher would dispute, and my increasingly vague state of mind that began to put me off the bloody pieces of meat behind the deli glass, literal shreds of their former animal selves, purge running slowly to the bottom of the meat tray.

"Eighty-three!"

I checked my number. If everything worked out, Vizula would wait on the chunky biker in royal blue spandex pants, matching windbreaker, a helmet pushed back on his head, and miss me. I liked all the clerks, except for Vizula. A wizened blonde, she spoke English with a thick European accent that defied all possibility of understanding. I looked around. I hoped Lou was working. She wore her name tag pinned smack dab in the middle of her gigantic bobbing breasts, which squished out the sides of her tightly tied apron. Short, dark-skinned, with frizzy salt-and-pepper hair pinned high on her head, Lou worked slowly but amiably. She chose my meat for me, pointing out why I should buy this steak, that piece of pork loin. She gave me hints on how to cook certain tough, cheaper cuts of meat. And she didn't look at me in a funny way that people do when they think you are one load short of a brick. Or was it one brick short of a load?

Clichés, clichés, I thought, as I peered into a cooler with a fluorescent pink and green sign above it proclaiming: "SALE!" Packages of spongy, pallid pork lungs were arranged in a pert fan-like design. The previous price of $1.09 a pound had been drastically reduced to a mere $.39 a pound. Just the thing for some taste-impaired alien who just happened to be buzzing by and had a yen to sink his fangs into the rubberized air sacs of a pig.

Had I sunk that low, I asked myself as I walked down the aisle toward the cheese case? Was I that far gone that the only way I could describe myself was by trite clichés? My shoulders suddenly seemed very heavy, and I felt tears well up in my eyes. Drat, I thought, looking up under my lashes, hoping the tears wouldn't completely fill my eyes and spill down my cheeks. I envisioned someone coming over to me, sympathetic, and asking me if anything was wrong.

"It's nothing," I would say as tears poured down my face. "I'm just a little upset at the rise in the price of chorizo sausage."

I blinked. The tears ran down my cheeks. All the items in the cheese case were a blur. I bent down, pretending to look at the cheeses and quickly wiped my face with my hand. I stared at a display of Stilton, the featured cheese of the month. Through my tears, I read from the information card that Stilton was a hard cow's milk cheese made in England's Leicester, Derbyshire and Nottinghamshire counties. I read, and noted, while blowing my nose, that Stilton had a pale yellow interior with blue-green veins, a wrinkled, melon-like rind, a rich, creamy, yet crumbly texture, and a pungent tangy flavour.

I also noted, with a slight start, that a black cockroach appeared to be slowly plodding its way down the right side of the cheese. I tried to catch the eye of a clerk but all were busy. I looked at the Stilton again. The cockroach had paused in its journey and I saw that, in actuality, what I had seen rolling down the cheese was a black olive that had escaped from a lettuce cup not far away. I looked up, glanced furtively around and sighed. No one had noticed a thing. I had gotten away with it again. I seemed completely normal.

"Eighty-four!"

I shot up my arm and walked toward the meat counter. Vizula, looking more than ever like she had just been to the crypt to consume a few litres of cow's blood, squinted at me, and said, "Keen eye chelup yew?"

I drove home through the river valley to escape the 3:15 traffic jams around the junior high school near our home. I cursed myself for the lack of control I had over my emotions. Lately, I started crying in the most peculiar places with absolutely no warning, like mowing the lawn, playing Whac-a-Mole at the Klondike Days Exhibition, or even just standing in the kitchen waiting for the kettle to boil for tea. The weekend before, I had taken Stevie and Clare to see *Ernest Scared Stupid*, a movie about an evil tree which disgorges trolls and goblins who turn children into wooden statues, and Ernest, the adult innocent who saves them.

The pop slurping, popcorn crunching adolescent audience around me guffawed delightedly at each prank and pratfall. I sat in the dark sucking sour soothers and staring at the screen trying to make out the words through all the noise. The sour citrus made my eyes water and my throat constrict. I watched as Ernest dispatched his own personal brand of justice: that of love. I found it particularly poignant that he simply "loved" the stinky little goblins to the hereafter.

I realized I was crying for real, overwhelmed by the enormous amount of effort it was going to take me to get out of my seat and go home. I could only think of how peaceful it would be to already be at home, in bed, lying under my quilt, still, listening to nothing. A week before that, one evening after the kids were in bed, I lay on the couch eating toasted bagels and cranberry sauce and watching the country music station on television. I burst into tears when George Jones launched into his hit single, "I Don't Need Your Rockin' Chair." Gord came home late from work and saw me, red eyed and teary, blowing my nose. He grabbed the remote and switched the channel to highlights of the hockey game. This afforded a fresh outbreak of tears as I saw that the Oilers had lost again.

The late afternoon sun shone through the trees lining the road at such precise intervals that it seemed I was driving through some kind of optical illusion. The feeling was intensified by the flashes of red and orange and faded yellow from those leaves still clinging to life. Indian summer heat blew in through the driver side window, and I wanted to refresh my hot feet on the cool tiles in my Mexican-style kitchen.

I had a sudden thought that my emotional troubles had begun the past spring. Clare's kindergarten teacher had sent a note home requesting parental help to stitch and sew one hundred hand puppets. The school planned to sell the puppets at the local farmers' market to raise money to buy a computer for the school. I had blithely tossed the volunteer request note into the garbage, expecting that to be the end of it. I was caught unaware when Cindy Morton's mother, who was head of the kindergarten phoning committee, refused to take "no" for an answer.

I showed up at the specified time and place clutching scrap pieces of wool and coloured materials we the friendly helpers had been asked to bring. I didn't volunteer often and had to endure the sanctimonious greetings of a group of women who measured their worth as devoted mothers by the number of hours they hung around the school laminating dried leaves or putting books away in the library. These were smooth-faced women who, when in their forties, would have firmly etched lines above their eyebrows as a result of a life spent looking out at the world with censorious disapproval.

Maureen, a pear-shaped woman given to wearing mauve sweatsuits with black leggings and clumpy Doc Martens, eyed me disdainfully as I entered the kindergarten room, and pushed her way, wheezing, to a chair as far away as possible from me. Stevie, my ten-year-old, had punched her ten-year-old son Caleb in the mouth several years earlier, causing loose teeth, and she had never forgotten the incident. Raised eyebrows and pursed lips now greeted me every time we met, and she had even suggested to the principal that Stevie might benefit from psychiatric counselling.

"You should be pleased," Gord had said when I complained to him about Maureen. "You don't have to listen to her rail on about the teachers anymore. She can bitch all she likes. I'll bet some of the mothers envy you."

I was glad she had chosen to sit far away from me. I didn't have the energy to deal with her childish snubs. I resolved to sit, sew, and go home. I saw Mrs. Smiley, the kindergarten teacher, arranging donated fabric, spools of thread and needles at her desk. I flinched. Her name was a misnomer. No one had ever seen her crack a smile. Her first name was Dolores. Gord called her Dolorous, which described her personality perfectly. Mrs. Smiley inspired fear, in the parents, but not the children, who uniformly adored her. I was afraid of her because when she looked at me I felt that she could see right through me, and that her eyes were two searchlights boring into my brain, finding the flaw, and yet pretending there was none.

Mrs. Smiley dispatched each mother with an anaemic puppet made of various donated materials. My puppet was made out of a long lime green sock with button eyes. I put it on my arm and looked at it.

"What do you think?" I asked Cindy's mother, whose name I could never remember. "A snake or an alligator?"

"Snake," she said. "Maybe with a hat."

I decided on a lady snake, one with a hat and a frilly pink dress. Other mothers gathered their materials and settled their widening bottoms into hard metal chairs and began to cut and sew.

Sewing hand puppets with seven other women that I saw occasionally at Christmas concerts and hot dog lunches was not an activity that I would rate as one of my favourite things to do with my already non-existent free time, so as I sewed, I mused. I had dabbled in acting in my early university days, scoring small parts in plays directed by hopeful drama majors. I had been cast as one of the women in the Chorus in T. S. Eliot's *Murder in the Cathedral.* Basically, it was our job, as the Chorus, to follow everyone around in the play and nag and make snide comments about what was happening. The fellow going for his Bachelor of Fine Arts in directing "really, really" wanted the Chorus to be seen as an integral part of the play, and I found myself rolling dramatically on the floor and sweeping majestically within an arm's length of a captive audience, performing the silent scream out loud, while looking directly into the astonished eyes of someone's blue-haired grandmother.

I sewed and listened as the red polished claws shot out and drew first blood as pecking order was established. I didn't play the status game and so was on the fringes of the conversation, sewing and listening. The topic was childhood. What a marvellous, wonderful, joyful time, it seemed, was had by all. A one-upmanship began, with descriptions of Barbie dolls, summer cottages and the makes of bikes that were ridden down tree-lined streets in front of houses that, within the memory of each teller, became just a little bit better than the house of the last one.

I was startled by Cindy's mother's elbow poking mine.

"What?" I asked, looking up.

"Tell us about your childhood," she said, smiling. "You've been so quiet."

"My childhood?" I asked, taken aback. An image of my bedroom flashed before my eyes. It exploded, bursting out of the top of the house in an enormous blast of silver and blue sparks.

"It was great," I said. "Just like everyone else's."

"What is the one thing you remember?" she pressed. "Above all else. Everyone has one memory that stands out above every other one. What's yours?"

The rectory, I thought. It was where my young life had changed forever.

"Hard to say," I said. "There are so many."

The bell rang. I was spared. But it had bothered me that I couldn't think of one happy childhood memory. I was sure if

I thought hard enough I would find one.

The next two times we met to complete the puppets the conversation turned to other things. I finished the snake, made an alligator, and an androgynous bear while listening with half an ear to the mindless chatter in the room.

I brought my attention back to driving the car. Traffic had slowed going up the hill. I looked in the rear-view mirror and counted at least ten cars in both lanes behind me. I looked ahead. I couldn't see around the bend at the top of the hill. I shook my head to clear it. How long had I been sitting in this tie-up daydreaming?

Something nagged at me. I had forgotten to do something. What was it? I thought of Gord, and my stomach began to churn. I fervently hoped it wasn't something I had promised to do for him. I mentally went over several tasks he had assigned me for the week. I tried to get the things he wanted done finished first. It was easier than having to listen to the lectures about my forgetfulness, my thoughtlessness.

"What is your problem?" he would ask. "Is sitting around the house all day too much for you?"

I would be punished by a withdrawal of affection for a few days, with sidelong glances of disappointment and the cold shoulder. I was getting tired of his pompous manner and secretly welcomed his having to work late or go out of town. I didn't like to hear myself described as brainless and hated myself even more for cowering inwardly at the rebuke. I had a dream once of stabbing Gord with a potato peeler, but it was dull and only made him angry. And yet, I felt guilty because, dimly, I could sense that something had changed. I was usually so meticulous about making sure that everyone was happy. And now I felt anger and despair at having to be responsible for the peace and inner contentment of all within my radar.

The line of cars began to move slowly up the hill. Cars from the left-hand lane were starting to put their blinker lights on, edging into the right-hand lane. I was glad I didn't have to change lanes. I didn't have the energy.

My head ached. I imagined my brain expanding, seeping through eyes, ears, and nose cavities, yet still contained within the rock hard skull. My brain was a pork lung, thawing slowly underneath the tightly wrapped plastic, ever expanding, ultimately contained by the refrigerated case that displayed it. I wondered if the pork lung would explode if the Styrofoam tray were taken out of the open-ended freezer and set on a counter, the plastic giving way with a "pop." My body felt heavy, too heavy to remain upright in my seat. I imagined, not for the first time, the substance of which my body was made: the organs, bones, tissues, skin, vessels through which blood coursed, unendingly. It dawned on me now why I didn't enjoy going to the meat market any more: it was the meat, the results of the slaughter, the flesh within the hide, and skin laid bare, in neat packages for eyes to see and judge.

I thought of my meditation book and a technique designed to rid the body of physical discomfort, where one visualized the body to be hollow, imagined the solid, concrete parts dissolving into light and then into empty space. This exercise supposedly rid the body of physical tension brought on by continuous thoughts and feelings; waves of the mind rising and falling, but I could never get the stale and somewhat rancid flesh that was my body to dissolve. It was upsetting to see it hanging, brownish and dry, on my splintered bones, and I'd quickly given up the notion that I was capable of understanding and transforming my mind through the magic of meditation.

Traffic edged up the hill. As I approached home, I heard the school bell signal the release of little captives for another day. I stopped at the four-way stop near the corner store and allowed Alastair, the simple-minded son of a crabby old woman who lived in the neighbourhood, to ride his bike haphazardly through the intersection, not once looking up to check for traffic. He was oblivious. I envied that about him, but not the reason why. I turned right and slowly drove the five blocks to home. You never knew who or what would come flying across the road or out from between parked cars at this hour of the day. I knew I would feel terrible if I came whizzing down the street, thunked into some small being, and sent them flying up onto someone's lawn. People in this neighbourhood were very particular about their lawns.

I pulled into the drive just as my two children came traipsing down the sidewalk, loud as usual. My children had been blessed with strong, muscular vocal chords and they exercised them daily at top volume to keep them in shape. I always knew where they were. Gord and I misplaced them once at a country fair. We stopped, cocked our ears to the wind and tracked our way quickly to the two of them enthusing at megawatt level about the gigantic nostrils of a huge bull penned in the middle of the midway.

"What's for supper?" Stevie, my eight-year-old asked as he opened the car door for me.

Stevie's first words were "lunch" and "supper." His first attempt at walking was a stagger into the kitchen, trying to get the refrigerator door to open.

"I have no idea at this moment," I replied. "But it will be something good because I went to the meat market this afternoon." I handed him a plastic bag of meat.

"Steak?" Drool formed at the corners of his mouth. "Or how about spareribs?"

"We'll see," I said. "Help me get this stuff into the house."

"Okay," Stevie said and shifted his backpack that I could see was full of books. "Report. Due Friday. Wolves. We have to do a bibliography this time. I'm going to do it tonight."

"Shouldn't you do the report first?" I asked.

"Mom!" Stevie shook his head and laughed. "Do you think I'm going to carry all these books home every day?"

"Aren't you going to use them?" I asked, confused.

"No. My report would be a million pages long if I used all these books."

"It appears I'm missing something here. I'll talk to you about it later," I said to his back and the slamming screen door.

"Mom! Mom!" Clare ran up and hugged me around the waist. "Kaitlynn said she hated me and so I said I hated her and then she hit me and I tripped her and she fell and got up and kicked me and *then* she started to cry and told the teacher that it was *me*!"

"Did you tell the teacher it was both of you?" I asked as I kicked the car door shut with my foot and walked quickly to the side door, three bags of meat, heavy and pulling on my wrenched shoulder. I had worked out too hard at aquafit and pulled a muscle in my upper arm. It seemed to be taking a long time to heal. I reached the door and put everything down with a grunt. Clare slipped in through the screen door and let it bang in my face. I sighed.

Stevie reappeared at the door and held it open for me. "Can we barbecue the steak?" he asked.

"Sure," I said. "If you get the barbecue out and set it all up."

"Yum-me!" Stevie yelled, pushing by me and running into the backyard.

The heat of the day had not yet dispersed to the upper atmosphere and it was quite warm in our sheltered backyard. Tall, elderly pines, evenly spaced with aged mountain ash trees, shaggy Elizabeth Skinner rose bushes in dire need of a ruthless prune, and fine-leafed gooseberry bushes whose berries were picked off by busy birds the instant they were ripe, surrounded the yard. Shasta daisies, whose seed had blown over from the invisible Japanese couple that lived next door and were only seen when walking their three dignified malamute huskies, erratically spotted the yard with their white blooms. A small circle of grass in the middle of the yard was patchy and brown due to the shade provided by the pine and mountain ash branches.

Stevie dragged an old table from the garage and set it on the grass near the back gate. Clare helped Stevie set the table with plates, cutlery and four cans of Cokes while I barbecued one large inside round steak, made a salad and heated up some curly fries in the oven. Gord called to say he would be working late, so we sat down to eat. As I ate my steak, the sounds of the neighbourhood provided a pleasant accompaniment to the happy chatter of my children as they swung their legs under their chairs and noisily chewed their steak.

I could hear the faint strains of a car radio. I knew that it came from the 1969 Volkswagen Bug that the tenant of the retired woman directly across the alley from us continually worked on. I had never seen his head, only his feet sticking out from under the car. I had never seen the car run for any appreciable length of time either, but had heard it cough, hiss and backfire as it tootled down the alley.

I strained to hear the melody. He listened to the same old-time sixties and seventies station that I did. The song seemed familiar. The singer crooned on about a sun and unending love and dreams. I was thirteen, I remembered, when this song was a hit. I was in love with the drummer in a local band. He had long black hair and that arrogant manner that teenaged girls always seem to find particularly appealing.

I watched Clare hop off her chair and skip over to the wily black cat that often sunned itself on the bricks of the small, round, do-it-yourself brick fireplace Gord and Stevie had built as a Mother's Day present for me several years earlier. The cat always managed to evade Clare's clumsy efforts to capture it and, now, as I watched, it sidestepped and danced away in a bored manner while it stretched its neck to see what tidbits on the table might be left for him.

The music reminded me of my junior high school years and a boy I was particularly fond of. It hadn't turned out well, at least for me.

Julian. That was the name of the drummer. I was walking home early from school one day and found myself standing opposite him on the sidewalk outside my house. He said "hello" and we talked about nothing, but which seemed like everything. I felt as if my world had been transformed. Wrapped in a cocoon of adolescent love I'd floated up to my front door. I remember being hot and breathless as I shut the front door and leaned against it.

"Slut!"

The familiar knot in my stomach was roused from its place of rest and began to twist and turn and cramp in anticipation of the onslaught to come. My adoptive mother Marie was sitting in the rocking chair by the front window in the living room. Her legs were crossed. One arm was folded across her chest; the hand held a cigarette up in the air. Smoke wafted up into oblivion, as I wished I could, from the lighted tip. The foot of her crossed leg tapped agitatedly against the air.

"Did you know that?" Marie asked. "Did you know you were a slut? Standing outside my home telling all the world you are a slut." She took a deep drag from the cigarette and blew the smoke out the side of her mouth, all the while staring at me. "No wonder I get calls from people around town telling me that my daughter, correction, my adopted daughter, is a slut. It's no news to me. I've known it all along. Are you sleeping with him?"

"What?" I asked disbelievingly.

"How long have you been sleeping with him? Do you like it? Do you like sleeping with him?

I wondered why she was home at this time. It was only three-thirty, and she didn't usually get home before six.

"Didn't think I'd be home, did you?" she asked, as if reading my mind. "Thought you could sneak around behind my back. Well? Don't you have anything to say for yourself? Slut."

"No."

What could I say? What could I do when Marie went on one of her raves except stand there and take it. I had learned that very quickly. Try to be meek. Try to act cowed. She liked that. If she could make you cry, she was happy. In the past, I had tried defending myself but it had sent Marie into a rage. She would circle me, screaming, poking and prodding my arms and my back. She would pinch me where it wouldn't show, big purple bruises forming overnight.

"Do you know why I pinch you there, and here and here?"

she had asked once. "So it won't show. I could slap you right across the face. I want to slap you right across the face. Do you know that? Slap that stupid look right off your face. But I can't. It would show. So I pinch you," she would say, savagely twisting hidden skin between shaking fingers.

I didn't say anything now. I waited. I thought about the smile the drummer had given me and the smile I had given him, unaware I had been spied upon.

"I'm going to tell Curtis that you are a slut," she said, still not done. "As if your father, no, your adopted father, didn't already know."

I was banished to my room, a barrage of words hurled at my head. I hoped she would have a nap on the sofa after supper so I could eat. If not, I would have to wait until she went to bed at ten so I could leave my room without being verbally set upon.

A scream of delight from Clare snapped me out of the past. I smiled at her. She was holding the black cat, which was straining to get away. The cat squirmed out of Clare's grasp and pawed its way to her shoulder from which it sprang onto the grass, shook itself in relief and then, without a backward glance, pounced its way to the edge of a gooseberry bush and disappeared.

I could hear the sound of a basketball bouncing in the driveway and Stevie laughing. Clare rolled over and over in the grass and then lay still, her arms and legs outspread, looking up at the sky. I looked at my cold steak. A few curly fries and a piece of celery from the salad lay next to it.

Dusk was settling in, filtering through the warmth, colouring it a soft mauve. Strains of the Beatles hit "Ob-La Di, Ob-La-Da" wafted from the radio. Was it on the ground beside the tool box or was it perched on the front hood, as it so often was, sending little streams of sound down the alley and into backyards and up into the silent atmosphere where it gently reminded listening ears of places and events of so long ago?

That was a happy memory, wasn't it? At least part of it was. Did that count? Or did it have to be happy from beginning to end?

I lay in bed that night staring at the red glow of the digital clock on Gord's nightstand: 11:42. Gord had called and said he would be very late, not to wait up. He would get his supper at the Greek restaurant across the street from the office.

The mountain ash tree outside the bedroom window scratched against the house. I could hear it creak heavily back and forth. The branches scraped the wood siding fleetingly and tapped on the overhanging metal shutters that shrouded the bedroom window. A spatter of rain swept across the shutters. I had wanted to cut the branches off the tree because the incessant scritching and scratching bothered me and made it difficult to get to sleep. Gord had been too busy at work to get around to it and I, afraid of heights, had been unable to climb up high enough on a shaky ladder to saw off the offending boughs. I had gotten used to them, eventually, and hardly heard them anymore, until lately, when my days had become punctuated with waves of an urgent restlessness and increasing intervals of weird behaviour.

The feeling of some great impending disaster began to lurk threateningly once again. The feeling as if I was being pushed from behind, my heels dug firmly into the earth, by some great black amorphous shape of such magnitude that I dared not look behind to see what it was. I knew only that I must not give into it. I must fight it, though sometimes I was bent over by the force of its thick and heavy, rubbery choking mass. Many times I was suspended to the very tips of my toes, about to fall. It was only at night, in the dark, cocooned and warm in my bed and unable to sleep, that I began to listen for the rasping of the branches against the wood, finding comfort and focus in the sound. I tucked the covers around me, glad to be cozy and warm in bed, listening to the storm.

I mentally checked that all the bikes were in the garage and the car windows rolled up. Clare and Stevie had played road hockey in the driveway after a game of basketball. They had dragged the hockey net from the backyard. Stevie had played goal. I hoped they had remembered to bring in the catcher's mitt. It was second-hand, but real leather. Clare had gone together with Gord to buy it for Stevie's birthday. It had been too stiff and hard for him to manipulate, so I had taken the car and run over it a few times to soften it up, much to his horror.

Small sheets of rain popped on the metal shutters like popcorn in a microwave. Wind forced the boughs of the pine to slap the house. I opened my eyes and glanced out between the half-open blinds. A great flash of lightning lit the patch of sky that was visible over the roof of the house next door. In the zigzag remnants of light imprinted on my retina, I saw the image of the glass doorknob of the closet in my room in Marie and Curtis's house. It was a glass knob with sharp, deep ridges. The fixture on it was loose, and anytime I opened the closet door, it clicked a bit. I would touch it as I paced the room. I felt my stomach tighten as the scene played out in my mind.

I needed to pace the room. I had to pace the room. I

had to pace it exactly right. Start on my left foot and end on my right foot. Forty-two steps brought me to the beginning again. It was urgent at first, the need to follow an outline, to go around and around and around. To start again and again. To establish that rhythm, to get into that groove. And after a while I felt better, somehow the walking soothed me. I breathed easier. I felt calmer.

But sometimes the pacing didn't work. I couldn't sleep. I lay in bed awake, staring at the ceiling, watching the swaying patterns of the birch tree outside my window reflected on the ceiling by the street lamp at the corner of the street. Some nights, windless nights, I could see the elongated outline of the tree, with its myriad of branches and leaves stamped black on the plaster. As I stared up at it, it became a highway, millions of roads, some ending abruptly, some meandering, long and winding, ending in a profusion of leaves clustered together, overlapping, a city asleep.

I took trips. I usually stuck to the main road, the trunk, but allowed myself short trips off into unknown but interesting looking territory of secondary branches. Sometimes it would be a disappointment, the looping curve that showed so much promise, ending straight and barren, pointing down. Sometimes my forays brought me to the end of a branch that looked like a rabbit or a witch or a cat licking its paw. But my main objective always remained the same; to trace my way slowly and surely upward, upward to the very top of the tree, where I would sit in the curve of a huge leaf, safe, warm, calm. On windy nights, when the silhouette of the tree swung wildly back and forth on the ceiling, I clung to it, inching my way to the top, inching my way to the leaf, holding tightly to the rough bark.

The hardwood floor in the bedroom creaked, and a drawer

unstuck. Gord cursed in the dark and flung a piece of clothing on the floor. He sat on his side of the futon.

"You awake?" he whispered.

I pretended to be asleep, watching him through slit eyes. He sighed, picked up the small portable digital clock, set it, and quietly placed it on the nightstand. He crawled under the covers and lay facing me. I could feel his breath on my hair and neck. I breathed in and out regularly to feign sleep. He reached out and gently pulled the quilt up around my neck.

In the not too distant past, I would have cuddled up to Gord when he came home late, fitting myself into the curve of his back or hugging his side. I would find his face with my hand and stroke his cheek, feeling the stubble of the day on his face rough against my palm. I couldn't do that anymore. I was always too angry. I closed my eyes, holding them still under the lids, feeling the tears roll down my cheeks.

CHAPTER 2

I thought about the tree and branch images from my past the next day as I sat in the F.S.R. The Franklin Stove Room was an eight-by-twenty-foot room that had been added on to the back of the house by the previous owners. Gord named the room after the old black cast iron Franklin stove that occupied the entire west wall. A cement pedestal, painted white, sitting eight inches off the floor, with a twelve-inch border all around the stove provided the base for the stove. A large black stovepipe reached up and disappeared into a hole in the ceiling. The walls had been finished with white clapboard panelling, the floor in a rose-coloured linoleum. One large picture window, framed by heavy drapes, looked out into the backyard. The room was freezing in the winter from inadequate insulation and shoddy workmanship.

I had installed a fish tank in the F.S.R when we moved in twelve years earlier. It seemed a good place to keep the fish until the rest of the house had been unpacked and settled. I had always kept fish. They were the ultimate low-maintenance pet. Death would occur almost instantaneously if the owner of fish attempted any the following: taking them for a walk, petting them or letting them sleep at the foot of your bed. You could even forget to feed them for weeks and they would merely root around the bottom of the tank looking for food or nipping the fins off the wimpy angelfish that brought new meaning to the word languid. One could even question if fish were pets. Gord often did. I would reply that fish were beautiful and soothing to look at.

The fish lived in the F.S.R. until one flash blizzard in early fall. The temperature dived to unheard of depths overnight, winds howled, and little hard pellets of frozen rain hailed from the sky. The morning after the storm, I stood in the F.S.R. watching my breath puff out of my mouth in frosty waves. The room had assumed the mien of a meat locker overnight, and I was dismayed to see the water in the fish tank frozen almost completely solid. One goldfish was preserved in ice, pressed against the glass, its eye bulging. A glass cat, never the most hardy of inhabitants in a community tank, lay half on and half off a thin pane of ice floating at the top of the tank, dead. I was reminded of Charlton Heston in *The Omega Man*, lying bug-eyed in the water fountain at the end of the movie with a twelve-foot spear jutting out of his abdomen. A red swordfish with black fins, one of the most neurotic additions to the tank, had committed suicide by leaping out of the tank and onto the rug. Its tail curled up in death, one last arrogant comment on the inadequacy of its habitat. I moved the tank into a corner in the kitchen that was too tiny for a table or an appliance. Gord built a bookcase above the tank for the telephone, my vast collection of cookbooks and several dozen pumpkin candles and candle holders, a particular fetish of mine.

In summer, the F.S.R. was hot. Sitting on the sofa or overstuffed loveseat, looking out into the backyard on a scorching summer's eve, was like sitting in a sweatbox with all your clothes on. In spring and fall, it was perfect. I liked to sit on the sofa and look at the dense foliage in the back yard. Vines, ground cover and ferns ran rampant. Clumps of tiny yellow flowers sat, faded, and dried on brown limbs. The previous owner's green thumb was in evidence everywhere and I bowed to his talent. Sometimes I sat near the window or the side French doors where I could see the sky through feathery pine boughs.

There were no ill effects that I could see in the backyard from the storm the previous night. I settled myself comfortably into the loveseat and watched two squirrels run nimbly over the telephone lines in the alley, hop onto a branch, swing down, ride the branch, and step lightly onto the back fence. They paused, the second squirrel bumping into the first. Tousling, churning around and around on the tiny ledge of the fence, they stopped, listened, their ears straight up. Then they streaked along the fence and up the big pine tree and into their home, the birdhouse Stevie had made at Cubs the year before.

I felt my thumb burning and looked down to see a mug of tea, forgotten, in my hands. I drank a cup of tea or hot chocolate in the morning after everyone had been sent, zipped and combed, off to school. I would read the paper at the table in the kitchen or sip it on the run as I threw clothes in the washer, made beds or vacuumed. This morning I had gotten out of bed feeling tired and shaky. I had crabbed at Clare because she was slow and sent her off with a surly goodbye. Labouring upstairs to get dressed, I'd seen dust motes swarming thickly in the shaft of sunlight beaming in through the tiny window on the landing. Standing there, with specks of dust flying past me in a gentle downward sweep, overwhelmed by a sense of futility, I'd wanted to scream at the unending absurdity of it all. Dust motes, forever floating to the floor. Vacuuming, only to vacuum again. Getting groceries, only to have them eaten and having to get more. The scene was tailor made for absurdist playwright Eugene Ionesco.

So I had gotten dressed, made some tea and sat myself down in the F.S.R. As I took a sip of tea, I shivered. I knew why I was so angry. The past was not allowed to intrude upon the present. Marie had said so. I didn't want to recall her words. But I did.

"Forget the past," she said. "It's over. Done. You belong to us."

I didn't want to belong to them. I didn't want to belong to anyone. My six-year-old mind could only think of going home. But images of the black and white police car pulling into our drive, the tall policeman stepping out of the car, and slowly walking up the drive to the back door, my mother gasping and crying, wouldn't go away. My sister Wynn and I were whisked away to the bedroom by my brother Ben. I couldn't hear what was being said but I knew all the commotion concerned my dad. He never came home again, and I didn't find out why until the next spring.

I was sitting at the back of the tool shed all by myself, chewing a piece of bubble gum I had taken from my mother's purse. Wynn and I were not allowed to chew bubble gum because we were, according to my mother, too young, would choke on it, and she would not be able to save us because she was unsure of just where to press on our sternums to effect the Heimlich manoeuvre, and then would have to go through life feeling guilty about killing us. Wynn and I had no idea what she was talking about but spared her feelings by chewing it out of her sight.

I peeked through the slats at the bottom of the shed where the boards didn't quite meet up with the floor, and saw Ben's legs and those of his friend Johnny. They also spared my mother's feelings by smoking their cigarettes behind the tool shed. Ben began talking about the time our father had gone fishing and never returned, about how he and his friend had been portaging their canoe and fallen over the falls. His friend had died immediately, but apparently our dad had lain on the rocks, suffering from a broken back and other injuries for several days before he had died.

I saw my father's face in a dream that night. The images of blood that framed his head and stuck in his hair as he blinked up at all of nature's silent splendour, the sun sparkling on the rushing waters of the rapids, dainty flowers growing out of cracks in boulders and between white foxtails, pink- and black-spotted butterflies flitting over his dying body as nature's final consecration, was so vivid I couldn't forget them.

I couldn't forget the last time I saw my mother either. She hugged me before she went to the hospital, crouching down to my level, enfolding me into her arms, holding the back of my head and pressing it into her neck, shaking a bit as she held me, and then walking away. The last thing I ever saw of my mother was the swish of her dress and the heel of her shoe as she disappeared through the door.

"Forget it," Marie would say when I asked where my brother and sister were. "That part of your life is over."

Once, when I asked Marie how I was to banish the memories of the first five years of my life, she said, "Pretend you are my daughter. Pretend that I gave birth to you. I would have been thirty-nine." She paused and looked at me sitting beside her on the sofa. I knew a response was required of me and I tried vainly to figure out what it was. "How old would I have been if I had given birth to you?" she prompted me.

"Thirty-nine?" I said, confused.

"That's right," she said, smiling at me. "Now, if anyone asks, that's what you tell them. My mom had me when she was thirty-nine. That's not too old to have a baby. Got that?"

"Yes," I said.

"Say it!" she commanded.

"My mom had me when she was thirty-nine," I said, thinking of my own mother, standing on a rickety wooden box to hang up sheets on the line in the backyard from an old faded turquoise plastic clothes hamper Ben had found at the dump. Did she have me when she was thirty-nine? I often wondered if she did.

Memories of my childhood intruded on my present life, constantly. How could they not? It was all there in my head waiting to pour out the second I let my guard down. I wanted to cry for my mother; walk arm in arm with Wynn in the bush looking for pussy willows; sit at the kitchen table and watch my father expertly fillet a white fish and sneak up on Ben and Johnny to try and hear what adventures they were plotting for the day behind the tool shed. I wanted to relive cracking the ice on the top of the water barrel in the back porch in the morning before I went out to play. But that was no longer allowed. So, at first I vigilantly monitored my thoughts, exorcising any reflections of past life transgressions. I tried to bar any remembrance from flashing before my inner eye. It was an exhausting battle that soon had teachers and friends alike asking why there was a permanent look of worry on my face.

I never understood why I had to hide the fact that I was adopted. I told a friend, in strictest confidence, when I was seven that I was adopted. It was in the hall at recess, both of us skipping, holding hands. We had stopped so my friend could tie her shoe. Feeling a swell of warmth and sisterhood with her, I bent down and whispered my deepest secret to her. My friend stood up and looked at me oddly.

"I know that," she said. "Everybody knows that. It was in the paper. Both when your dad was killed and when your mom died of cancer. Didn't you know? Come on, let's go, or all the best skipping places will be gone." And she ran outside, pushing the swinging doors open and disappearing into the bright sunshine. I saw the light flash back and forth between the doors, diminishing with every swing, until it was a small white line, still, between the doors.

I couldn't understand why I could tell no one about my adoption if it had been common knowledge. It had been in the papers. I began to look into the faces of people I met on the street wondering if they knew. And why was it all right for Marie to discuss the adoption on the telephone with her friends, when I was forbidden to talk about it, when I was forbidden even to think about it?

I asked Marie about it one day as I helped plant potatoes in a large garden plot in the backyard. Curtis had cleared the yard of the scrubby brush and stunted spruce trees as a first step toward the garden paradise that Marie envisioned. He had rented a tiller and ground the remaining roots and dirt to a fine powder. Several loads of odorous black dirt had been dumped and spread by two "Newfies" who were, according to Marie, "too familiar for their own good." I didn't know why she seemed so offended by them. They seemed very friendly, especially the one who kept wriggling his unibrow at her. The next step was to plant potatoes in the entire backyard, the idea being that potatoes gave off some kind of nutrients that fertilized the soil. Curtis dug the holes for the potatoes, and I dropped cut up seed potatoes from a gunnysack into the hole. Marie covered up the potatoes with a shovelful of dirt.

"Why can't I tell people I am adopted?"

"What brought this up?" Marie asked again, this time stopping and resting both her hands on the handle of the shovel and her left foot on the triangular blade.

"I don't know," I replied, wishing I hadn't asked.

"You must know. You asked," she said, waiting. I stood there, silent, squeezing cut potatoes inside the sack, my heart beating rapidly in my chest.

"Well?"

"Well," I said uncertainly. "You say I belong to you. You want me to say that you had me. But you didn't. My mother did."

"So?"

"So, it's not true," I said, my heart beating out of my chest. I wanted to sink into a potato hole and be covered up. "It's a lie."

There. I had said it. Panic now set in. But I needed to know what Marie would say. I needed to know on what foundation our relationship was based.

"Are you calling me a liar?" Marie smiled at me. I knew by then that when Marie smiled like that, she was very, very angry.

"No."

"Then what are you saying?"

"I don't know."

"You're not very smart, are you? You don't even know what you are saying."

"No."

"No, what?"

"No, I'm not very smart."

I wished that Curtis would look up, walk over to see how the planting was going, and save me.

"Who do you belong to?" Marie asked.

The panic spread. The world started to spin, and I felt like throwing up all over the ground. A hot flush rose from my chest to my head. I wanted to cry and yet knew I must not. I didn't belong to anyone. I was alone. The realization of that flooded me with fear.

"I can't hear you," Marie stated.

I wouldn't lie. Everyone knew I was adopted. If they asked and I lied, I was a liar.

"No one," I croaked haltingly.

"I think you can go to your room now," Marie said and turned away from me.

I had fled, dropping the sack but still clutching a raw potato in my hand.

"And remember," Marie called after me. "You can't come out until I say."

In my room, I'd sat, rigid, on the bed, waiting for Marie to come. But Marie hadn't come. I could hear her outside the bedroom door and in the kitchen and talking in the living room. I paced the room again and again, waiting for my punishment. I tried to cry but I was too frozen with fear. Afternoon turned into evening, and still Marie did not come. Finally, I hid in the closet and fell asleep. I woke abruptly when I heard the bedroom door open and Marie call my name. I pressed back against the wall of the closet and hoped that Marie would not think of looking there. The closet door opened and Marie stood there, looking at me.

"What are you doing in there?" she asked. She held out her hand. "Come on. Come out."

I couldn't come out of the closet. I couldn't take her hand. I didn't know what pact I was agreeing to, what contract I was signing. Marie reached into the closet, took hold of my arm and gently pulled me out. I held on to the glass doorknob, feeling its sharp edges bite into my hand. I held on until Marie put her hand on top of mine and peeled it off the knob. Panic set in and an immense horror overtook me. I began to wail and struggle to get away. Marie picked me up and carried me into the kitchen. She sat me down onto a chair. A sandwich and a glass of milk sat in front of me. Three Oreo cookies sat, piled one on top of the other, beside a glass of milk.

"Eat," Marie said and smiled at me. "You must be hungry."

I looked around for Curtis.

"I'm not hungry," I said, my mouth dry.

"Not even for a cookie?" Marie handed me an Oreo. I took the cookie and put the hand that held it in my lap.

"Eat it," Marie said.

I took a bite and chewed. My mouth was dry and the cookie stuck in my throat. I had to swallow twice to push it down my throat. I watched Marie watching me. I took a drink of milk and looked down the glass as I sipped. Chocolate cookie crumbs backwashed into the glass. I put the glass down and looked at Marie. She motioned for me to get up off the chair. Once again, a hysterical rush of wild fear coursed through my body. I wondered what violence Marie had in mind, but she merely took my hand and led me back to my room. She tucked me into bed that night and kissed me on the cheek. I still held the cookie and put it under my pillow for later.

Forget the past. Lord knows I had tried. I stared out the window. My memories had left me cold. The surface of my left cheek and temple felt numb. I tapped my left heel with my right toe and it was numb too. The numbness in my face and heel had been increasing lately. It wasn't quite bad enough to go to the doctor, but I often felt like a crotchety old sailor with a wooden leg and a bad eye tick.

The short burst of anger I had felt thinking of Marie had passed. I didn't feel angry. I felt weary. I watched a flock of tiny brown birds swoop and dart in unison in the middle of the yard before finally deciding to alight, en masse, on the bird feeder tacked to the big spruce. I envied their enthusiasm and calculated how much energy it would take to heave myself out of the sofa. I didn't have that much to do. Clean the house. Make supper. Return the videos that were at least a couple of days overdue. Go to aquafit.

I hadn't been to aquafit for several weeks. I had enjoyed going, hustling everyone out the door in the morning, stuffing my bathing suit and a towel into Gord's gym bag, and speeding down the freeway to the YMCA. Lately, it seemed to take forever to get going in the morning. I had taken to napping in the afternoon, throwing a quilt over myself on the sofa in the living room, dozing in front of the television, or lying in bed upstairs. I welcomed the silence of a deserted house and the oblivion that drowsing undisturbed brought. There was always too much noise in my world. Too many people or children talking at once. I couldn't concentrate. The only time I felt truly at peace was lying still, with my eyes closed. I could shut out the noises of the day. I could focus on the humming quiet, to the energy steeped in stillness. It was all I could handle.

I watched the birds feeding frantically, feverishly, their tiny heads popping up like miniature jack-in-the-boxes every second or so to check for danger, suddenly stopping, alert, and simultaneously streaking for the sky, gone.

I knew I was losing the tight control I had learned to keep of my thoughts, dreams and memories. That meant I could be ambushed emotionally at any time. The guerrilla warfare that had gone on within my head for the past thirty years over my secret family history showed every sign of escalating. I could no longer beat back the minor skirmishes that my jogged memory unearthed. I was encountering battle fatigue and I didn't know how much longer I could hang in there, or even if I wanted to.

Should I tell someone? Who would I tell? They wouldn't believe me. They would think I was being dramatic or neurotic, that I was ungrateful. If I could lay in bed all day listening to the furnace click on and off, listening to the house creak and hearing noises far off in the neighbourhood that had nothing to do with me and required no response; if I could just observe life as some sort of living inanimate being and never have to be directly involved in it, I could be happy.

"We picked you because you were the lightest," Marie told me once. "No one would know you were half Chipewyan with that blonde hair. I can't believe it myself."

It was true that of my brother and sister, only I had fair hair and blue eyes. Quite often my mother would take us down the hill to the sheltered bay, position us carefully into the front and middle parts of a big green flat bottomed canoe and paddle laboriously across the water to the village, a permanent native encampment sitting on the east point of the mouth of Yellowknife Bay.

A small group of my mother's aunts and uncles lived by

the edge of the bay in ramshackle huts and teepees, holdouts from the modern way of life that meant central heating, running water and electricity. My mother visited her relatives regularly, bringing them tea and bought cookies for their collective sweet tooth.

Being shy, my sister Wynn and I would hang back by a hut door or an entrance to a teepee, hoping to be ignored and yet still be silent members of the social group. But my aunts would ask about us in Slavey, a guttural slurring tongue that sounded to me like chickens clucking, and then swoop upon us, reaching out with weathered brown hands, grabbing us and crushing us against loose, smoky bosoms, and then, very much against our wills, planting moist kisses that seemed to last forever on our cheeks with gyrating pillowy lips.

They would centre me out and run their fingers through my yellow curls, scratching my scalp, making "oohing" sounds of delight. They would force several cookies into my hand, turn me around, spank my bottom and point to the door. I was dismissed and had permission to go outside and play so they could visit undisturbed with my mother.

"Don't ever tell anyone you are Indian. They'll never know," Marie would say. "Not like your poor sister Wynn. You can tell at a glance with her."

I didn't know what to do with this helpful advice because being "Indian" had never been a problem before. I wasn't going to lie about it, though, and I made Marie furious when she found out I had put my hand up when the teacher asked if anyone in the class was of First Nations blood. Our class was doing a social studies project on Louis Riel. As part of our study all students had to canvass the general public to see who might fall into the Métis category. I was surprised to see that the majority of Yellowknifers fit the bill, including my aunt Marilyn, whose face I often saw in the crowd.

"I don't want you talking to your aunt Marilyn," Marie said to me one evening. I was doing my homework at the dining room table, and Marie was reading the paper in the living room. She kept the paper up and spoke from behind it, as if she was reading an article aloud from it. "Lucy Codert told me she saw you talking to Marilyn on the street today outside her house. Is that true?"

"Yes," I said.

"She's not your aunt anymore," Marie said, giving the paper a shake. "And she's so . . ." She left the sentence unfinished.

I was silent. My stomach started to churn. I loved my aunt Marilyn. She was fun. She would come over to our house and do my mother's hair. Wynn and I would watch. After my mother's hair was done, piled into an improbable beehive on top of her head, Marilyn would do Wynn's and mine. My father came home during one of these sessions and opened the door to the four of us sitting at the kitchen table drinking tea, our hair sprayed and teased into stiff bulbs. After a startled second, he laughed until he cried. Wynn and I, insulted, had jumped up and began hitting him to make him stop. He wrestled us away from him and then grabbed me by one leg and Wynn by one leg and hung us both upside down, our fabulous hair inches from the floor.

Aunt Marilyn had a wonderful car with thick purple pile covers on the seats and big black and white spotted fuzzy dice hanging from the rear-view mirror. The outside of the car didn't look all that great what with the rust and missing front fender, but it was the motor that counted, Marilyn had always said. And it ran just fine, except when it stalled. She would take us to the local drive-in and buy us soft ice cream, then threaten us all the way home that she would skin us alive if we got so much as one drop of ice cream on the seats. She lived in a cramped trailer in the old town and would make us toast when we visited.

Aunt Marilyn cleaned houses for several women who lived by the school. She had cleaned houses for years, and once in a while, when my mother was still alive and had errands to do or an appointment to keep, Marilyn would take Wynn and I along with her. We would play in the school playground while she worked. She could keep an eye on us and we could have some fun at the same time. I saw her from time to time, and we would stop and chat.

"She's so what?" I finally asked.

"She's so Native. And she's a drunk." Marie tossed the paper on the floor. "I don't want you to have anything to do with her. You hear?" She looked at me. "Do you hear?"

"Yes."

The next time I saw Marilyn I slowed down on the street and told her I wasn't allowed to talk to her. I said I was afraid to stop in case someone was watching. They would tell Marie and I would be punished.

"The old bat," Marilyn had said. "Okay. I guess we can't talk anymore. But we can wink. I'll wink at you and you wink at me." She said. "Let's see if the old buzzard can see that."

We winked at each other for a while. Then Marilyn came less and less frequently to clean houses and then stopped altogether. I heard some years later she had met a man and moved with him to Fort Liard, where she worked in the local café.

I started to cry. The backyard was a blur. Tears filled my eyes and spilled down my cheeks in two rivers. I was powerless to stop them. Just as I was powerless to stop the memories, battering to be seen and heard, inside my weary head.

"Drat," I thought. "I'm losing it again."

What could I do? I needed to stop the barrage, and the only way I knew how to do that was to kill myself.

CHAPTER 3

Once you make a commitment to do away with yourself, you are free. Any other commitments, such as being a wife or a mother, are null and void. Potential suicides no longer have to watch their cholesterol levels, and those pesky diets they have been on for the last ten years can be pitched out. The fifteen pounds that sit snugly on hips and around waists are fleshy testimony that diets don't work anyway.

It's a liberating feeling knowing that you will soon be dead. Casually mentioning which dress you would like to be buried in should you suddenly meet face to face with a Mac truck elicits no reaction from anyone. You do feel somewhat claustrophobic thinking about being enclosed in a hermetically sealed coffin and stuck six feet under the ground, but the anxiety passes when you realize that the soul will have flown by that time and all that is nestled in that satin-lined casket will be a bunch of meaty bones.

I felt light-hearted once my decision had been made. I vacuumed cheerily and smilingly discussed the poor quality of cantaloupes with fussy senior citizens in the supermarket. I baked cakes and cookies, thinking that Stevie and Clare would not have much home baking once I was gone.

"Once I was gone." Who would have thought that those four little words could bring so much joy?

I looked at Gord in a new light. I felt sorry for him in a way. He worked hard and loved his family but he belonged to that assembly of beings known as males, the ones the aliens would reject when they came to Earth in a doomed attempt to seek out higher consciousness. He carried on as all males do, blithely unaware.

I spent a week in this new-found euphoria, experiencing true liberty. I could do anything, although I may have gone a bit overboard at a meeting of the food committee for the United Church that I attended, on occasion, with Gord.

Gord had volunteered my services for a law seminar he was giving in the basement, free, for any member of the congregation who was interested in hearing about environmental law. I resented his donation of my baking services without asking me, but consented after hearing that other women would be donating their time and baking as well. A meeting was scheduled in the kindergarten room in the basement of the church to iron out the details.

On October 14th, at ten in the morning, I sat on a pint-sized chair at a pint-sized table across from Brigit Olsen and Grace Peabody. Grace and Brigit were tut-tutting about a teenaged member of the congregation. I didn't catch her name, but heard that she had recently had her long hair cut. She now, apparently, sported two-inch spikes, the ends of which she had dyed red.

"But that's not all!" Brigit Olsen said, one eyebrow raised in that "wait-til-you-hear-this" look. She leaned forward and paused. Grace leaned forward slightly too so as not to miss a word. I stayed where I was so as not to appear to be eavesdropping. "She had her arm around another girl!" Brigit sat back and crossed her arms.

Grace, not understanding the implication, stayed leaning forward, her brow furrowed.

"She had her arm around another girl," Brigit repeated, verbally underlining the word "girl."

The implication sunk in, and Grace's hand flew to her mouth.

"You don't mean . . . ?" she queried.

"Yes. I do. The girl's gone and become a lesbeen."

"No!" Grace insisted. Grace's jaw dropped and her eyes bugged out.

"Well, her mother nearly fainted on the spot," Brigit continued, adjusting the coat she had slung on her shoulders. .

"She actually kissed her girlfriend right in front of her mother. To rub it in I guess," Brigit continued, satisfied at last at the effects her statements were having on Grace.

Grace's face turned red and her bottom lip quivered.

"Oh for heaven's sake, Grace, shut your mouth or you'll catch a fly."

Grace clapped her mouth shut.

"Don't you think that's just the limit?" Brigit asked. "I guess she said she'd been thinking about it for some time and had decided to come out of the closet. She's 'The Boy.'"

"What?" Grace asked.

"In the relationship. She's the boy. That's why the short hair."

Brigit finally turned to me and shook her head. "I guess she wanted the lesbeen experience."

I was feeling reckless. Maybe it was the way she spoke to me, so full of moral superiority, that made me want to put Brigit Olsen in her place.

"I had a lesbian experience once," I said. "More of a near lesbian experience," I continued. "When I was ten." Brigit gasped and her jaw almost hit the floor. I hoped I would be able to carry off my ruse. I could already feel the corners of my mouth wanting to curl up. Maybe I could make her faint.

"Yes," I said, placing a confidential expression on my face. "My mother was working and I went to spend the afternoon at the house of a new friend."

I fixed my eyes on the bulletin board after seeing Brigit's eyebrow begin to twitch. It was the only way I could keep from laughing. I had a fleeting flash of guilt at drawing her in so quickly and completely.

"Her name was Beverly, and she was quite nice at first," I added, foreshadowing. "We played Barbie and then talked about a book we were both reading. *Anne of Green Gables.*

"Beverly's mother gave us store-bought oatmeal cookies and Tang." I said the word Tang like there was some great significance to us drinking it. "Anyway Beverly's mother had to go to the store. When we were alone, Beverly asked if I'd like to see her mother's jewellery. So we go into Beverly's mother's bedroom. Beverly is busy closing drapes and plumping pillows, but I didn't think anything of it. Just as I didn't think anything of Beverly suggesting that I lie down on her parents' bed and relax while she got the jewellery."

"The little liar!" Grace spat.

"She brought a box of jewellery over from her mother's dresser and laid it at the foot of the bed. Then she told me to close my eyes. I thought maybe she was going to put jewellery on me and then have me look at it. But she didn't. She began to run her hand up my leg."

"Oh my God," said Grace, getting out a tissue and holding it to her nose.

"I asked her what she was doing. She said she was playing 'Mom and Dad.' I said I'd never played 'Mom and Dad' but I had played house. Beverly said playing Mom and Dad was much more fun. She said we got to make love."

I stopped and looked at Brigit and Grace. I could see they were equally repelled and attracted by my tale and possibly me too. I was in complete control and it felt rather good.

"I said I didn't know what to do. Beverly said it was okay because she had played Mom and Dad with her friend Jane all the time. One of us had to be the mom, and one of us had to be the dad. We were supposed to kiss. The mom was supposed to say she had a headache, and the dad was supposed to force the mom to give him a kiss."

"My Lord," Brigit said, her face flushed. "What on earth did you do?"

"I said I didn't want to play."

"What did Beverly say?" Grace asked timidly.

"Well she tried to force me to kiss her. But I punched her in the face, and she started to cry."

"Did you leave then?" Grace asked.

"Yes I did. But let me tell you I really used to wonder when I saw Beverly and Jane walking down the hall at school holding hands. I hated her."

"Well I should hope so," Brigit sniffed.

"Oh not for that. She told me Anne of Green Gables used to play Mom and Dad with Diana all the time. It sort of wrecked the story for me. Even if she did eventually marry Gilbert Blythe."

We sat silent for a minute or two. Finally Brigit spoke.

"Grace and I will do the coffee. We'll each make two kinds of squares and serve them on disposable napkins. Sound all right to you?"

Grace and I agreed. I gathered up my coat and slung my purse strap over my shoulder and walked out of the room. I looked back as I shut the door. Brigit and Grace were staring at each other, shell shocked.

I kept a straight face until I was in the car and turning the key in the ignition. Only then did I allow myself to smile and then to laugh.

The station wagon engine coughed and sprung to life. Was this what I was really like?

I looked in the rear view mirror for traffic and saw my mascara had smudged. Once I was dead I wouldn't have to worry about stretching the delicate skin under my eyes, I thought. In my dotage no sacs of crepey derma would sit, puffy, on top of my cheekbones. My eyeballs would be rolled up balls of rot, surrounded by papery skin that stretched over jutting sockets.

Was this the real me? Someone who took advantage of silly, narrow-minded women? I sat in the car in the parking lot at the back of the church and looked at the lush clematis vines climbing up the ash-grey corrugated cement finish on the church wall, noting how green the leaves of the vines still were despite it being mid-October, and became conscious of myself.

At the centre of the personal space that I was always vigilant to protect, in the middle of the negative energy field that I used to repel all positive atoms, the person who had stepped outside of her usual self and reacted, was me. Me. I was stunned. I never thought of life in terms of myself. What I thought. What

I wanted to do. I always tried to think of how I could adapt myself to other people, their needs, and their wants.

"No one is interested in you. No one wants to know what you think," Marie would say. "People are selfish. They want to talk about themselves. To speak of yourself is selfish. Are you selfish? Is that what your real mother taught you to be?"

"No," I would answer.

"You are not important. The other person is important. Everyone else but you is important. Remember that."

It was confusing to a child. What if someone asked me about myself? What if they were trying to do the same thing I was? It could, in a science fiction story, lead to self-effacement, erasure. Or was I the only one who didn't matter, who wasn't important enough to have anything to say about myself that people wanted to hear?

I learned to gauge the situation, adapt myself to the mood of whomever I was with, be the person they wanted me to be. I had to constantly be on the alert, watching, remembering that I personally had nothing to offer.

I had given Grace Peabody and Brigit Olsen a taste of the real me. Would they tell Gord? What would he say? Laughter bubbled from my gut. I tried to stop them, but the giggles blew past my uneven bite and I laughed aloud. I had given the old harridans a dose of their own medicine and I didn't care because I knew I wouldn't be around long enough to face the consequences of my actions.

My encounter with the church ladies left me feeling uncertain. Once the bubbles of laughter had subsided after my impulsive morning prank my head began to ache. My stomach churned ominously. I didn't regret my actions. But I was confused. Instead of feeling happy I found that I was severely angry.

I wanted to shake Grace and Brigit until they realized that every human being deserves at least one chance in their lives to show who they really are. I wanted to shake Marie and ask her why she had treated me with such contempt.

I didn't feel like going home. Stevie and Clare needed socks and underwear. I would go to the mall and after I was done shopping I would go to the Food Court and treat myself to an order of Texas Fries. I had wanted to try the fries for several months but they were definitely not an item on my diet list. However, with my suicide pending, all diets were off and I was free to indulge. Thick, greasy fries, heavily salted, with half a cup of spicy chili, sour cream and grated mozzarella cheese, would set me back $3.79.

I watched as the whistling teen at Fries Alive! ladled chili on top of my fries. A company cap designed to look like an upside down fry container perched on his shaved head and the bright yellow short-sleeved shirt hung loosely on his gaunt frame. Heavy rings adorned his fingers and earrings pierced his left ear from the bottom lobe all the way to the curve at the top. Had each successive perforation been less painful? Or had they all hurt equally? I pushed back an unlikely image of Marie stolidly punching holes in little girls' ears at a kiosk in the middle of the mall.

It was still early when I arrived for my date with the fries. Slow-moving seniors were dawdling over second cups of coffee and the remains of thick gooey cinnamon buns. Mothers were dragging tired toddlers to their strollers. I carried my tray to the farthest corner of the non-smoking section. I sat down, took the container and Coke off the tray, pushed the tray aside, opened the tab on the can of Coke, waited for the fizzy sigh of escape from the carbonated water, and took a sip.

I grabbed a fry that was sticking out the side of the container and piled chili, sour cream and cheese on it. I popped it into my mouth and chewed. Mmmm. I could feel my arteries hardening already. It was delicious.

Marie. I had always felt I owed Marie an overwhelming debt that could never be repaid. There was nothing in the entire universe that I could do that would be stupendous enough to expunge the ultimate sacrifice Marie had made by adopting me.

"I've given up everything for you," Marie would say, tight-lipped. "You've ruined my life."

How was it possible to make amends for that? I tried to do everything as exactly as requested. I defended Marie against other family members. I agreed with Marie no matter what the issue was. I came home right after school and cleaned the house so that when Marie came home from work she could sit down, relax and have a beer. I would tell Marie jokes and make up funny incidents that never happened to amuse her when she came home, raging. Marie would either listen and gradually be soothed and coaxed into a reluctant civility or she would glower and lash out, making me stand, silently, shifting from one foot to another, waiting to escape.

I felt responsible for these rages, this intense unhappiness; Marie sullenly sulking in her chair by the big picture window for entire evenings, everyone on edge.

I had ruined Marie's life. If only they hadn't felt the need to adopt me. If only Marie could be happy. If only I could vanish, fade away in a wisp of light, Marie's house could once again be transformed into the sunny happy home it had been before my arrival.

Once, after a public scolding in a fairground, or a circus, I couldn't remember which, a happy event nevertheless, with sunshine and brightly coloured balloons swinging back and forth in the heat, I had been left behind, alone, isolated. Kindness and affection had been withdrawn as a punishment for whatever infraction I had committed. For a moment or two I had imagined myself to be quite alone in a wide expanse of concrete, standing very still. A peculiar but not unpleasant feeling began infusing my body. Slowly, from my toes up to the tips of my hair that seemed to be blowing straight upward, reaching for the white clouds that sailed merrily by in a friendly wind, I began to feel incredibly light. I looked down to see that my body was transparent. It was shiny, clear, acrylic glass. Bits of rock and dirt whirled against it in a sudden dust storm and bounced away, clattering on the cement slab nearby. It didn't hurt at all. I blinked, and the world, suspended in silence for that moment, clicked on again. I took the peach jawbreaker that I was sucking at the time out of my mouth, dropped it on the ground and crushed it beneath my diamond Achilles heel.

Marie. She taught me well. I did as she bid. I sucked up all the emotion I felt in my life and I buried it deep within me. What else could I do? And what was the result of her 'kind' counselling? I was about to commit suicide. A life well-led in self effacement, often ends in self-erasure, I thought glumly.

I felt a lump in my throat. It was swelling and growing, making it difficult to breathe. An unbidden rush of tears flooded my eyes. Tears plopped on the table and the top of the pop can. My nose began to run and I sniffed to stop it. I grabbed a tissue from my purse, and as I blew my nose I checked to see if anyone had seen me crying. I relaxed when I saw that my distressed life had no impact on anyone.

The lump in my throat rose and heaved again, serving notice that a vomit was imminent. Saliva issued forth from under my tongue as the grease in my stomach roiled and coagulated rhythmically, preparing to erupt. I grabbed my purse and dashed to the ladies washroom. It was large and light and the clinical cleaning smell provided the final impetus to barf. I knew by the rising tides in my stomach that I would not make it to a cubicle and so I ripped the lid from a garbage can and hurled into it. When I was done, I looked into the mirror beside the can.

My eyes were bloodshot and my face ashen. I breathed deeply to settle myself. I tried to remember the rules to meditation breathing. As I concentrated on the breath that I was inhaling and exhaling I appreciated that I really didn't know how to meditate. I could never maintain a neutral attitude to the infinite number of visuals whipping past my mind's eye, to refrain from letting them affect me. Why couldn't I just let the feelings arise and simply observe the stream of consciousness in the detached manner the author so favoured? I couldn't, I thought as I wiped my eyes, which is why my mind was such a mess. No one can tell, though. I look and act normal for the most part. Thank God I have a permanent solution in the works.

I planned to kill myself at home so strangers wouldn't find me lying on the sidewalk, a pool of blood spreading around my head and sticking to my hair; my doll-like eyes disconnected from the world; or by a group of half-cut weekend fly fishermen, wading out into the stream in the misty blue morning before daybreak, seeing a sodden lump washed up on a rock in the middle of the rapids and turning it over to find me with my face nibbled away by the steelhead they were trying to catch;

or worst of all, a procession of cars slowing down to gawk at the spectacular single car smash up on the freeway, the critically injured female being cut out of the smouldering wreck, ironically, by the Jaws of Life. Suicide is a private matter. I wanted something quick with no margin for error.

Gord had several guns he stored in the rafters in the garage. I know he owned two kinds of guns, a .22 rifle and a .33 shotgun. They had been passed on to him by his father, a United Church minister, when his father had upgraded to heavier artillery. His father was also enamoured of dynamite, but had not yet passed any on to Gord. Gord was not a serious hunter. He enjoyed sitting in a swampy marsh now and again in the calm of a fall evening, smoking cigars while he waited for the migrating ducks to come and roost for the night. I had gone duck hunting with him in the early years of our marriage. I learned to shoot the .22 and was quite an accurate shot. The shotgun was too heavy for me, and I had a tiny scar on my left buttock where I landed hard on a sharp root after being catapulted into the air by the kickback.

I went out to the garage to look for the guns after I got back from my disastrous lunch. The garage was a mess. We didn't use it for the car, but to store skates, skis, bikes, barbecues, Christmas decorations, a coffee table and small outdoor glass patio table with four chairs that a neighbour, who was moving, had forced upon us. The garage was dusty, and I started to sneeze. I looked up at the rafters. Between slats of wood I could see suitcases, storm windows, old baseboards, old cardboard boxes of junk, magazines and a car top carrier. I would have to climb up somehow, and, holding on to the slanted ceiling, pick my way through the mess to find the canvas-wrapped guns.

I pulled the table over from beside the door and placed

it beneath the widest opening between the planks of wood. I emptied a heavy blue milk carton of its collection of pine cones and set it on the table. I needed one more object to place on the milk carton. A paint can proved to be too small, a chair too big. Through the grimy garage window, I spied a tiny stool of Clare's sitting dusty and forgotten under the back steps. The stool was the perfect height. I hoisted myself into the dim attic of the garage.

It was smaller than it looked from below. The only way I could get around was by semi-squatting and shuffling forward in little hops. The planks bent perilously under my weight and several boxes shifted in my direction. I righted them only to set off a chain reaction that sent wood scraps and metal rods clattering to the floor. I paused, squinting in the gloom. I thought I saw a canvas package in the corner by the garage door. I inched toward it, but the end of the plank I was walking on suddenly ended. No other plank was close enough to allow me a quick step forward.

I didn't want to jump and chance having a loose board come up and hit me in the face so I looked about for an alternative. A narrow plank rested to the side of my right foot. I stepped on to it, dislodging a rack of metal rods that lay touching it. I steadied the rods with my foot and then slid one out of the ropes that loosely held them. I jabbed at the package, satisfied that they were the guns. The rod was quite bendable and after a few futile attempts at trying to dislodge the canvas bag, I retracted the rod and bent it at the end like a hook. I slid it out toward the bag again and just caught the end of it. I pulled on it slowly, trying to roll the bag to the edge of the plank it was sitting on. My plan was to climb down from the rafters, set the card table, milk carton and stool, under the guns, climb back, and ease the guns off the planks into my waiting arms.

It seemed like a good idea. I just hadn't counted on the plank I was standing on to split and crack. My feet fell through the opening and I had to let go of the rod so I wouldn't fall. I fell anyway. I heard the left sleeve of my coat rip and I felt a sharp cut sear my skin from elbow to wrist. I closed my eyes as I fell, only to have them jerked open again by a sharp pain in both of my armpits. The metal rods had come undone and caught me as I dropped. They lowered me slowly as they bent under my weight.

By this time, the rods had bent to the extent that they fell through the planks, and I landed with a thunk on the cold floor. My heart was beating frantically and my arm hurt. But I was also strangely exhilarated. I looked up to see the gun case. It had rolled to the edge of the planks and was midway to the floor. I hoped they would survive the smack on the cement. It would be pretty hard to shoot myself with a bunch of gun parts. I needn't have worried. The guns weathered the drop beautifully. They hit the floor, bouncing off the lawn mower first, the rifle discharging a forgotten bullet that pinged off a cast iron griddle hanging on the wall and then through the garage window that had just been replaced the previous weekend. The glass shattered outward with a crystal *pow*!

The single mindedness of the bullet as it searched its mark, ricocheting off the griddle and breaking the glass, made me feel faint. That's what the bullet would do to me if I shot myself in the mouth; it would explode the back of my head with a soft *kerpow*! I sat on the garage floor. Would I shoot myself in the garage? In bed? Perhaps in the bathroom so there wouldn't be so much mess to clean up? Tile surrounded our tub upstairs and would be easy to clean off; that is if the bullet didn't go through the tile as well. I would lock the bathroom door and shoot myself.

That would be no good. Stevie and Clare had learned to pick locks when they were in a church production of *Oliver*! One of the older boys who helped out with the production had taught everyone in the cast how to pick pockets, and as an added bonus, how to pick locks as well. Evening rehearsals turned out to be in violation of his youth parole, however, and he had to drop out of the production halfway through. It was disconcerting as well, that, months after the school had performed the musical, I would lock the door of the bathroom and settle down in a hot and steamy bath for a soak, only to hear a clicking at the door, and Clare enter seconds later, asking what I was doing.

I would hate for Clare to discover my body. She had had terrible nightmares for several nights after finding a dead bird in the road, squashed by a car. I would have to kill myself away from home after all. Better to be stared at by a bunch of curious strangers than by your own children.

I sighed and heaved myself off the floor. My arm was burning where I cut it and I pulled back the sleeve of my coat to have a look. An eight-inch tear on the back of my forearm had already clotted. It had bled quite a bit in one place where the slash was the deepest. I wondered if I would need a tetanus shot. I walked over to the broken window and looked out. The glass had sprayed over the patio in tiny bits. It glinted from Clare's little red wagon and the bottom steps of the deck. I would have to make sure to sweep up every speck, right after I doctored my arm.

Bandaging supplies were low in the bathroom closet. That was not really a surprise considering Barbie™ and Ken's® car accident in the backyard over the weekend. It had taken almost the whole box of Band-Aids as well as gauze and medical tape to patch them up. Clare and her friend Erin had spent a happy afternoon on a blanket in the backyard, crashing Barbie™ and Ken™ in the Barbie™ corvette and then wheeling Barbie™ and Ken™ to the hospital on the blanket in the red wagon, and bandaging them up beyond recognition. Gord had been upset by the waste of bandages and money. Feeling groggy and down, I had hissed maniacally at him not to spoil the girls, good time. Gord had raised his eyebrows and retreated to the basement to fix a tap.

A narrow rectangular cabinet built into the wall across from the toilet held shampoo, conditioner, bubble bath, soap, sun tan lotion, bug spray and medical supplies. I rummaged around on the shelf with the empty Band-Aid box, sticky Chinese liniment and saw, stuck at the back of the middle shelf, two small cardboard boxes.

I pushed aside the liniment and pulled out the boxes. They looked like elastic band boxes. I put the lid down on the toilet, sat down, put one of the boxes on the bathtub ledge, and opened up the other one. This box held the remnants of a Cub camp Stevie had attended where first aid was the weekend theme, the *pièce de résistance* being a personal first aid kit compiled from teachings at the camp. Stevie's box included the wrapper from an Oh Henry bar, used gauze in the shape of a headband, and hockey tape.

The other box, taped shut, held an assortment of petrified condoms and a small aerosol can of spermicide. A bundle of toilet paper sat at the bottom of the box, wrapped around a flat rectangular object. I picked it up and slowly unwound it. An envelope, one inch by two, was at the centre of the wad. I recognized it immediately. Several months ago I had been searching daily for the contents after a particularly nerve wracking day.

I opened the flap and shook the contents into my hand. A white granular powder poured into my palm. It was the six Demerol tablets I had hidden from Gord when I had broken my wrist eight years ago. The doctor had originally given me twelve tablets, six of which I had consumed furtively because Gord thought I should eschew any prescriptive medicines except Aspirin. I was of a different mind, being the one in intense pain, so I had lied when he asked me if I had flushed away the wonderful pain relieving pills down the toilet. I had hidden the pills in my bra first, not wanting them to be out of reach, but the envelope was itchy, and I had had to find a new hiding place. I had used six in all and was saving the remaining six for something special.

Would they still be good after all this time? Could you kill yourself with six Demerol tablets? I doubted it, but you never knew. I was glad to have found them. I vaguely remembered their effect. One tablet provided almost instant insulation from the world. The thickness of movement and thought that resulted was such a relief. It was a warm and fuzzy blanket for the mind.

I called the Medi-Centre. The nurse on duty told me in a stern voice to dispose of the pills at once. The potency could no longer be confirmed. The powder would be unstable. Just like me, I thought.

When she asked me how I came to be in possession of a prescriptive drug for so long, I hung up.

I found I couldn't sleep that night. I was consumed with thoughts of my suicide. I couldn't kill myself with a gun. I couldn't kill myself with pills either. After talking to the nurse at the Medi-Centre I had checked the cabinet behind the mirror in the bathroom to see if there were any pills, that, if taken in excess, might possibly be life threatening. There were three Tetracycline tablets, some Librax that Gord had used for a bad back, eczema ointment and about eight ounces of anti-itch syrup left over from when Stevie had chicken pox.

But I couldn't bear the thought of getting up in the morning and facing another depressing day. It was pointless. Irrelevant. I couldn't carry on the charade any longer. I needed relief; relief from living each day within a skull whose brain, that organ of intelligence, was not refined enough to excise unwanted thoughts and memories. Instead, it retained every thought, conscious and subconscious, every reminiscence, dream, vision, and fantasy, and stored them for future emotional ambush. I needed relief from the constant inner battle between repression and the need for expression, of past skeletons hiding in the closets of my mind. Should we not have the right to eliminate that which we can not face? Why must it be allowed to remain in the recesses, tormenting us until we become so weak fighting against it that the only way to stop the incessant misery is to destroy ourselves?

CHAPTER 4

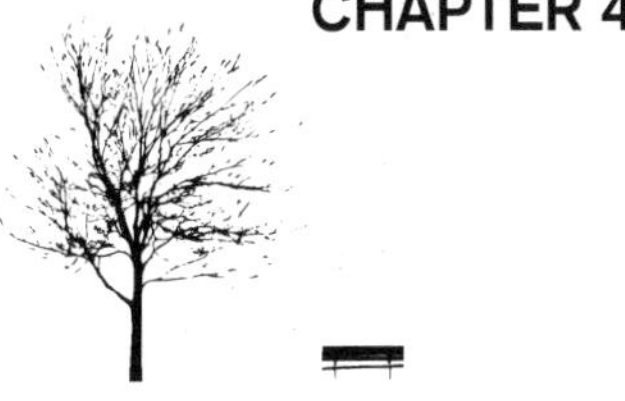

I lay in bed with my eyes closed. It was hot in the room, and I kicked the covers off my feet. Gord was snoring lightly. I jabbed him in the back, and he stopped, grunting. I opened my eyes. I was wide awake. I knew any sleep would be fitful dozing, so I got up and tiptoed downstairs to the kitchen. I got a glass from the dishwasher and poured some water into it from the tap. I drank slowly as I leaned on the kitchen sink edge with my elbows and looked out the window.

It was a clear night. I could tell the moon was full because the trees in the backyard were fully illuminated with a cold, silvery, blue light. The grass shone grey and the shadows cast by tree limbs splashed an abstract black zigzag across the lawn. I needed to be outside the confines of the walls of the house. I needed to feel the cold air and sense the dark night hitting me with a slap as I stepped into it. I got the car keys from my purse, slipped on my moccasins, put on an old red cotton car coat over my pajamas, and went for a drive.

It was a beautiful night. All was quiet. The street lamps shining on the vacant intersections were overshadowed by the moon, which was extraordinarily bright in a cloudless sky. I needed to drive to the outskirts of the city, to be rid of the phosphorescent glow that signalled, in the absence of light, a human metropolis.

I didn't know where to go at first, which road to take. I drove randomly, stopping at lonely intersections, waiting for the light to change, gliding by neighbourhood strip malls with too little parking during business hours and too much in the middle of the night; passing the neon signs of sleeping businesses, and row upon row of houses in row upon row of silent neighbourhoods. And then I knew. I headed south.

It was because of my mother, my real mother that I headed south. Just fragments of memory: her changing sheets on a line; Wynn and I playing, giving rides to each other in a big wooden wagon; my brother Ben calling to my mother and asking if she wanted a ride; her laughing refusal. Thrilled at the image of our mother perched in the wagon bumping down our gravel drive, we all began chanting for her to ride. She acquiesced and sat in the wagon, her skirt tucked under her bent knees. Ben asked her where she wanted to go and after a moment of thought, she pointed and yelled, "South!"

Tonight I headed south on the highway out of the city. I drove for several minutes before turning off the highway. I liked night driving, pulsing along, seeing only as far as the headlights reached, knowing they would eat up the road for as long as I wanted and let me decide how far I needed to sneak away, to escape. In the dark, life, to me, was comfortable, undemanding. In the dark, the interminable battle with my subconscious and powerful emotional hurts born out of tragic childhood events, remained undefined, secret, and unresolved. During the conscious light of day, they chafed, vexed, and demanded equal intellectual and conscious inspection by my mind. In the night, they called a temporary truce, so I could drive south until I felt clean and empty. As I drove, the imagined dirt and grime was slowly sucked from my body, dissipating into the black air behind the car.

I might drive straight down the highway, turn around, and drive straight home again. Or, I might turn off on to a side road and drive along it until I was in total darkness. I would turn the car off, roll down the window and breathe in the night air, fill my lungs with oxygen, that colourless, tasteless, odourless element that existed in a free state in the atmosphere, something to which I also aspired. I would listen to the silence and let it fill me up.

Tonight, after turning off on to a side road, I drove carefully on the heavy gravel. I could smell the damp, thick dust from the road coming through the air vents. The dust tickled the inside of my nose but not enough to make me sneeze. I came to a four-way-stop intersection. I stopped, turned off the car and the lights.

I got out of the car and walked down the road. It was very still. The cold early morning air stole up the sleeves of my wide-armed coat and sharply nipped my bare ankles. I didn't usually get out of the car when I stopped on my nightly sojourns. Rolling down the windows was usually enough. I shivered and wondered fleetingly if any wild animals might be on the prowl for a meaty breakfast.

I breathed in the silence and the slightly acrid scent of decomposing plant life and earth. Fall. Autumn. Death. I walked, stones poking into my feet through the moccasins I wore. I liked autumn. In the world of seasons, fall is death. Winter is dormant sleep. Spring is rebirth. What is summer then? Living.

Summer was my least favourite season. I never knew what to do in summer. I was out of sorts. The heat was suffocating and the days long. There was constant pressure to go out and sweat in the heat at the beach, the park, or at the Dominion Day parade where claustrophobic numbers of people jostled for a better view of bored clowns. I liked fall and winter. Winter especially: frozen nose hairs and earlobes so stiff they felt like they had been stapled; feet like frosted blocks of wood, painful to stand on; body shivers unable to erase the cold felt through and through. And yet, still alive. Still breathing.

I stopped on the road and shivered. I turned and saw that I had walked a fair distance from the car. Skitterings in the underbrush and rustlings in the upper boughs of nearby birch punctuated the calm. The branches of a tightly knit patch of poplars stirred, their dry leaves clicking and crackling softly. A trill of fear seized me, sweeping across my body in a nervous flutter. I started to walk back to the car, quickening my step as I felt unseen long arthritic fingers reach out for me from behind. Why had I strolled so far from the car? I felt in my coat pocket for the car keys. They weren't there. I tried to recall if I had left them in the ignition and fervently hoped I hadn't dropped them in the gravel.

The moon shone brightly on the road and the field to my right. A large windbreak of fir and birch stood across the road from the field to my left. In the dim light the trees looked like a large forbidding wall behind which untold medieval horrors such as public disembowellings occurred. Forlorn castles on craggy windblown cliffs looked great behind walls like this. Imagined walls like this. I stared at the windbreak. The trees seemed to have merged into a gigantic clot that was moving toward the road in jerky oscillations. I felt another waver of fear. I began to run, trying to ignore the clot, trying to push it back off the road.

I knew I was being irrational. There was nothing seeping toward the road. The trees were just trees, rooted in the ground. My imagination was running wild, and I was scaring myself needlessly. I tried to shake off my terror and berated myself for my silly cowardice. I tripped on a sharp jutting stone in the road that made my knee buckle and I fell. The snap of twigs and an ominous crackle of fallen leaves in the dense foliage caused me to gasp. At that instant there was a great swoosh from the top of the windbreak, and a huge black bird shot toward the road, squawking three times as it swooped down in front of me and then off into the indigo night. As the bird passed, the moon glinted off its eye, a lifeless, purple glass bead inside a silver pupil surrounded by an iris snaked in red.

I shrieked, clambered up and ran to the car. The key was in the ignition. I turned it with a shaky hand. I gunned the motor, drove forward about fifteen feet, jammed on the brakes, threw the car into reverse, gunned the motor again, backed up fifteen feet, jammed on the brakes, threw the car into drive and peeled back the way I had come. I raced along the side road to the highway, screeched to a stop inches away from the faded stop sign, and pulled into the right lane of the highway with a sigh of relief. I sped along, checking in the rear-view mirror for police and over my shoulder for the bogeyman.

The highway was deserted. I tried to relax in the safety of the car. My fear was foolish and fickle, not to mention illogical. It was the same fear I felt after traipsing to the outhouse late at night at the cottage: unseen hands reaching out, hairs prickling the back of my neck, me running the last ten feet to the cottage door in dire certainty that I would not make it before being consumed.

One thunderous rainy night, picking my way rapidly back to the cottage through the long, wet grasses along the path, a jagged bolt of lightning lit the trail before me. I looked down, and there, in the middle of the only way back to the cottage, was a snake. It had caught a frog and had choked it halfway down, feet first. As the snake stolidly and emotionlessly engulfed the frog, the frog stared up at me, terrified. Thunder crashed, drowning out my banshee squeal and plunging me into darkness. I was horrified, and for the rest of the holiday often speculated what that scene meant in the grand scheme of things and if it had anything to do with me.

It was fear. I knew that, I thought, as I drove back to the city. Fear so palpable that I had actually seen it once. Was it years ago? Or was it last month? There was no difference in the past, the present, or the future. They were all the same if one lived in fear.

Suffering from insomnia, I was lying on the sofa in the living room late one night. A small movement at the foot of the sofa caught my eye. A wall of black shapes, writhing sluggishly, advanced upon me. Alarmed, I tried to rise but could not. Paralysed, I struggled against my frozen limbs as the forms crowded around me, pushing in. I screamed, but no sound came out. I willed the wall of fear away, but it advanced smoothly, inch by inch. A picture of the frog, being pelted with rain on the soggy path at the cottage, beyond fear, in catatonic acceptance of its fate as it was eaten alive, mocked me. I watched the moving mass, seeing it wavering, merging into a thick rubbery wall with appendages straining to break through. With a bright clarity, I realized that they could not devour me unless I let them. I would not let them, and they had vanished.

Two cars whizzed by me. One driver beeped as he passed. I looked in the rear-view mirror to see if any other cars were approaching and then checked the speedometer. The gauge said I was rolling down the road at a speedy twenty-five miles an hour. I signalled and pulled to the side of the road and on to a gravel turnout. I drove the ten feet to the chicken wire fence at the end of the turnout and stopped. The headlights shone through the fence into a field that had been dug out here and there by a small grader. Rocks of varying sizes had been piled up near the chicken wire fence in a rough pyramid.

Fear had been with me forever, as it had every other human being on earth. But was it as out of control with them as it was with me, had been with me, since as long as I could remember? Was the bird with the purple eye that swept past me, squawking three times, an omen, Biblical in nature, showing me that I had betrayed myself by denying my past? Could I find absolution only by examining the internal conflict that was stranding every aspect of my life in a hellish no-man's-land?

The paralysed man was released from his crippled state when Christ told him to look within and acknowledge his self. What part of his internal reality had he targeted to expose? Had he been afraid all of his life too?

Fear exhibits itself in strange ways in a child, I reflected, as I rolled down the window and took a deep breath of the crisp air deep into my lungs. When I couldn't find escape in tracing the silhouette of the branches of the tree outside my bedroom window reflected on the ceiling, I would creep out of bed and lay on the floor. Or I would crawl into the closet and sit on top of the shoes and boots. The hard edges, the laces and heels jabbing my hip and poking into the skin on my ankle provided relief.

A sharp heat against my ankle bone had me guessing what it was. Was it the point of a heel? Or was it the heel of a shoe turned upside down? I was occasionally startled by the belt of a dress hanging down and touching my shoulder, or a scarf slipping off a hangar and covering my foot. But mostly I concentrated on the objects jutting into me. I wanted to feel the pain.

I wasn't always at home when fear or terror stalked me, when I felt weak and the bile rose in my throat. On these occasions I found that washing my hands gave temporary relief, and there was usually a nearby bathroom, and I would make my excuses and slip out of class, birthday parties, shopping, and go to wash my hands.

I liked soap better than the liquid dispensers normally found in public washrooms. There was a routine that could be devised with soap that was not possible with the pink, slimy glob that squirted from the scratched plastic machine bolted to the wall above the sink. First I turned the water on and let it run while I picked up the soap. I smelled the soap. I always smelled the soap. It was all for naught if the scent of the soap was stinky. It was natural and expected that my nose would run, and that I sometimes would sneeze after the initial inquisitive whiff, but if it smelled clean, if it smelled pure, if it smelled like it could wash the ingrained stench on my hands, then it must be okay.

I held the soap between my hands and put my hands under the running water. Then, holding the soap in my left hand, I would rub my right hand over the soap, first the palm of my hand and then the back. I would clench the soap with my nails, making sure the soap got under each nail. I would repeat this procedure with my left hand and then put the soap back in the soap dish. With the water still running, but not with my hands under it, I would rub the soap into each hand

and each nail and repeat this until my hands began to burn. Then I would rinse my hands off in cold water, rubbing them roughly to rid my hands of soap. I would dry my hands, one by one, on the towel, paper or cotton, until they chafed. I would leave the bathroom, wherever it was; calm and relief in my red and blistered hands.

Sometimes the anxiety and panic would strike when there was no avenue of escape, when I could not excuse myself and slip away. One time I was placed in the front row of the children's choir at church. There I was, exercising my lungs in glorified praise and happily shaking a rainbow-coloured cardboard tambourine I had made in Sunday school. Tiny bells, which the Sunday school teacher had bought at a garage sale, decorated the rim of the tambourine.

I was enjoying myself when I saw, in my peripheral vision, a smoking, viscous mass lapping at me from behind, sending tendrils of curling slime in a pressing wave. I was helpless as wave after wave washed over me, elevating me to dizzying heights until I was adrift atop a tiny bit of slime. If I moved I would fall into the pit and be lost. In self-defence, I held my breath. I held my breath until I saw the wave become disoriented, confused, and in bewilderment, slowly recede and fade. The last thing I saw before I fainted was my Sunday school teacher's mouth open in a gasp. I was taken to the doctor who found nothing wrong with me.

Fainting gave way to what I dubbed my "black attacks." I would begin to shake uncontrollably, my hands, my shoulders, the cold chills scampering down the middle of my back, spreading to my hips and down my legs. I learned to disguise this by pretending I was cold. I wore long-sleeved shirts and heavy sweaters to conceal my tremors.

I rolled the window up, put the car in reverse, checked over my right shoulder for traffic on the highway, and backed out onto the road. I drove home quickly. As desperately as I had needed to escape the confines of my house, I now needed to feel those four walls securely around me. Home, in the driveway, I turned the car off, opened the driver side door, locked it, got out of the car, slammed the door shut and ran into the house. I locked the door and leaned against it as I slipped off my moccasins. I walked into the living room, opened the blinds and went to sit in the middle of the sofa. A blanket that Clare used to wrap her dolls in lay on the sofa, and I caught the end of it and pulled it around my feet and legs.

Fear. Was I afraid to dredge up my past because of the pain that was involved? Or was I afraid because I didn't know what would surface?

"The past is gone. Live in the here and now." That's what Gord would say about the night's events. He was always so sensitive. Typical male.

"What a bunch of crap," he would say. "What cliché are you living now?"

He said words to that effect when I had gone to a First Nations healing workshop. After the workshop, I'd echoed the words of the course leader. I told Gord that I lived with "a pain in my heart." I was about to tell him that my pain was constant, that it never abated, that I thought I was going crazy, that I wanted to smash every dish in the kitchen cupboard.

"That's the oldest cliché in the book," he had said in amazement. "Just take a look at every movie that's ever been made about Indians. 'White man speak with forked tongue. Speak from the heart. I have a pain in my heart.'

I had disliked Gord at that moment. He had reminded me of Marie.

The healing workshop was advertised in the personal interest column of a small south side newspaper. Fifteen dollars for two, three-hour evening sessions. I read the column just by chance, got a babysitter and went.

The workshop was held in a rundown community league hall in the inner city. An uneven broken sidewalk with straggly grass growing out of the cracks led to the entrance. Two rusted garbage cans with no lids overflowed with crumpled takeout bags and empty pop containers. Swinging the heavy doors open, I was surprised to find the place packed.

It was a mixed crowd. I stood by the door, trying to look like I fit in and didn't mind being there alone. Shortly after eight o'clock three women dressed in traditional dress entered the hall and stood at the bottom of the stage area.

"We will be on the same level as you," the leader said. Her hair was pulled back into a high bun, out of which a long fountain of hair sprouted and hung loosely down her back, "To position ourselves on a higher level, such as the stage, would indicate we are of a higher status and that is not true. Everyone is equal in all things." I thought of Gord's United Church and its pulpit set high and apart from the congregation.

A tall, thin woman performed a sweetgrass ceremony to open the workshop. She held up a braid of sweetgrass for all to see, lowered it, and lit the ragged end with a match. The grass flared briefly. She blew out the flame and began to fan the smoking sweetgrass braid into the air, sending the smoky incense out to the crowd. She demonstrated how to cleanse oneself with the smoke by gently waving the healing smudge over all parts of the body. She told us to close our eyes and pray.

I closed my eyes, took a deep breath and drew the fragrant smoke into my lungs. I could see my mother and her shapeless old aunts in their flowered housedresses and moccasins, sitting and talking around a smouldering fire late in the summer evening. Wynn and I lay on the grass beside her, drowsy, calm, accepting her involuntary pats and rubs as we shifted and bumped against her, listening to a language we didn't understand being spoken softly, its hard edges blunted by the hour and the sun, still high in the sky in the land of the midnight sun; the ever present sun, pale, pastel, warm and kind.

After the sweetgrass ceremony was over, a third woman stepped forward and spoke of her internment in a residential school run by Catholic nuns. She spoke of how she had been taken away from her parents at an early age. Of how she had had to make porridge for the other girls, serve them and help clean up before she went to school. She began to sample the communion wine as a way to ease the pain of separation and spent twenty years as a skid row alcoholic bum until one day she awakened in an alley beside a garbage can and realized her life was garbage. She conquered her fear and confronted her past.

After she finished, she sat down. There was silence in the room.

"Does anyone have any comments?" the leader asked.

After several seconds, a white man at the back of the hall put his hand up. He stood up hesitantly.

"Do you want me to be honest?" he asked.

"What do you think?" she asked him, smiling.

"Because I know everyone will want to boo and hiss at me

after I have said my piece."

"I can assure you they will not," the leader replied.

"Does every Indian, Native, whatever, have the same life story? I came to this workshop to dispel my negative feelings to what I consider a universal view of Indians. They are drunks. They are a drain on the welfare system. They do not contribute in any positive way to our society. And what do I hear? Woman becomes alcoholic because of sordid past and lives as skid row bum. It's such a cliché. Has this happened to every native everywhere?" He sat down abruptly.

The leader looked at her companions and smiled.

"I was searching for a way to open this workshop tonight that might describe the First Nations people of today. And with one word you have provided it. Thank you."

The thin woman walked over to the man and solemnly shook his hand and gave him a hug. The man looked uncomfortable and not too sure of what was coming next.

The leader now began to walk back and forth in front of the stage. As she walked she started laughing.

"You all thought I was going to give him hell, didn't you?" she asked.

We all laughed along with her, in relief.

"He's right, though, so I couldn't give him a hard time." She looked around the room. "What's the first thing you think of when you hear the word Indian?" She waited. She walked into the middle of the room and put her chin in her hand. "Tell me the truth," she said. "I'll bet ninety-eight percent of you are thinking 'drunk.' The other two percent are thinking 'good-looking.' Am I right?"

Several people in the audience tittered.

She walked back to her place at the front of the hall.

"Drunk? Am I right? The image in today's society is so stereotypical that he has become a cliché.

"You know, you don't become a cliché overnight. It has taken my people many years to reach the level of degradation we now enjoy. Many years of adverse conditions have contributed to our present plight. We are beginning to realize the depths to which we have sunk. And we want to do something about it."

She went on to talk about the return to the old ways, about how a return to a past culture and healing would eventually prove to be the things that would save her people.

"A lot of people are living with pain these days," she said. Not just our people. All people. You can let the pain remain inside of you and let it eat you alive. Or you can let it go. That is what this workshop is all about. How to take your pain and let it go. You are standing still if you live with pain. Get rid of it and move forward to the rest of your life.

I pulled the doll's blanket up around my shoulders. It smelled like baby powder. Clare loved to change her dolls' diapers several times a day, using copious numbers of baby powder–scented wipes. I sniffed the blanket. I wanted to let it go. I wanted to tell someone. The man who stood up at the workshop was right. All the horrifying physical and emotional disasters that so many First Nations people had suffered came out sounding trite, and then to offer simplistic platitudes of resolution only cheapened the reality of it. But it didn't mean that it wasn't true. And it didn't mean that the suffering wasn't real. I wanted to tell Gord. He was a level-headed man. And that was the problem. To him, my life sounded like a badly written soap opera, and if he thought that, what would other people think?

I picked up my meditation book. I persisted in trying to understand the concepts acclaimed within its covers. It harped on the virtues of getting rid of the adherence to the ego, the "I," otherwise known as self-grasping ignorance. It could be compared to an agitating elf who endlessly ran around in one's head spreading malicious gossip to one's other interdependent self, creating much misapprehension regarding one's mental and emotional self. The plan was to kick this troublemaker "I" out of our heads, freeing us up to concentrate on the first rule of Buddhist teaching which was to gradually drag ourselves to the realization of nothingness in all things. And that was my number one problem: I didn't know who "I" was.

In the meditation on suffering, however, in the all pervading suffering section, we are counselled gleefully to think of experiences that cause us pain and spend a few minutes wallowing in the agony and to note that we are stuck in the cycle of knowing that the very moment of existence, living and breathing, was both the effect of past suffering and the cause of suffering in the future. So. If nothing exists as we think it exists, and the cause of our present suffering is a result of past suffering and the cause of suffering in the future, how did we get to the point where we could tell the elfin "I" to back off so we could exist in a time period where there was no past, present or future suffering?

Well that was the five-dollar question, and, apparently, when one reached that state one would achieve the ultimate transformation or enlightenment.

As usual, I was stumped. But I refused to give up. I liked the idea of being able to wipe my emotional state clean.

I turned to the chapter on visualization in the hopes that

I could reap some insight there. I dreamed a lot, and visualization, it seemed to me, was similar to dreams. I followed the directions and focused very exactly, creating every aspect and nuance of a dream that repeatedly caused me to sit up in bed and scream. What did it mean and what future suffering would be vanquished by comprehension of it?

I closed my eyes, slid down on the sofa and brought to mind the familiar first sound that always led me into recreating the dream. Footsteps. Footsteps softly tapping on a corridor floor, sounding like the footsteps my flat-heeled black boots with the leather soles made. I was walking assuredly down a wide, echoing hall. It was black. I sighed as I gave myself up to the remembrance of it.

My eyes were stuck shut in the dream and I looked at the blackness through transparent lids fringed with lashes. I strained to unstick my eyelids but I could not. I wasn't alarmed because, intuitively, I knew they would open when there was something for me to see.

I felt my heart beat faster as the corridor began to move. Unsteady, I braced my feet and put my arms out to the sides for support. I felt weak and helpless. My eyelids slowly clouded over with the skins of my lids. I was relieved to have my eyelids back and took a deep breath. The air smelled like grape Popsicle and old widowed men.

I thought I must look funny, my eyes stuck shut, my black boots on, and me, precariously balanced, surfer mode, taking deep breaths and going. But going where?

I forced myself to take deep regular breaths. Part of the floor to my left continued to move and I was thrown slightly off balance. I became aware of an antiseptic smell. An intense pumpkin-coloured light flashed across the lids of my eyes, and

I was then able, with fluid ease, to open my eyes to the scene before me.

I was indeed in a corridor: a long, brilliantly white corridor, wide with a low ceiling. I blinked at the whiteness, the light. There was no evidence of light fixtures, hanging or recessed, and yet the light was very much part of the corridor. It hung, brilliant, yet invisible. Warm. Comforting.

People began passing me in the moving corridor. Nurses, operating room attendants, patients, visitors. People. They rode silently and impassively on the moving floor. Everyone was going in the same direction as everyone else. I tried to speak to people passing me but no one would look at me.

I reached up to touch a tall, dark man wearing a green coat, but he pulled his arm away and tilted his head down, so that I only caught a glimpse of his long nose and cleanly shaven cheek before he passed me by.

I turned to face the now oncoming crowd walking down the corridor, but they gave me a wide berth. Why was I here? I tried to scream, to get some attention, to have someone look at me. I tried speaking to a woman passing near the moving sidewalk. She looked like a businesswoman, and she seemed to have clearer features than anyone who had passed me so far. I tried to speak but could not. My mouth could form the words but no sound came out.

I ran up to her, grabbing her sleeve. The woman immediately stepped on to the moving sidewalk in front of me and was carried away. She looked back as she rounded a bend and her forehead glowed neon blue. The energy from the cold blue light shot from the woman's forehead to my own. I saw a beam of blue above my eyebrows for a split second before it disappeared painlessly.

Why was I here? Where was I going? I plodded along. I began searching the faces of the people in the corridor, casually at first and then more urgently. I was looking for someone! That was it! Someone was supposed to meet me here. But I had forgotten who it was.

I became anxious, fearing I would miss whoever it was. I hurried now, looked backward and accidentally trod on the heels of someone ahead of me. I caught the faint whiff of musty perfume and old wood. I stopped. The woman stopped too. Long, coarse black hair, peppered with white, hung down her back. Several crinkly strands stood out on the pale blue floor length dressing gown she had on. The hair looked like a wig. The woman swung her coarse mop around as she turned to face me.

She looked at me through deep purple rings of kohl around sunken eyes that locked onto mine. Luminescent brown irises centred pupils as deep and black as the universe and sat, shimmering, on unending circles of white. Her eyes pierced mine and her knowledge of me was complete. Her ashen face was tinged with a fluorescent blue, and her lips, unmoving, were grey.

"Who are you?" I asked.

The woman's lips twitched in a flicker of a smile. "Who are you?" she asked in return. Then she turned and melted away. I ran through the crowd looking for her. I could still smell the mouldy sweet essence of her in the air, the odour of a dead person that really isn't there. It makes you hold your breath just in case an acrid fume puffs up from the coffin-encased body and sends a little bit of death into your vibrant, living lungs.

I wanted the woman to return. I stood still. People passed,

bumping into me, pressing into me, curving around me to get by. I turned and there stood the woman, transformed. Her hair was brown this time, shorter and curly. She looked familiar. She had a dress on, and underneath it, a body. Her skin was flesh toned and the heavy make-up was gone. The woman smiled at me.

Marie? No.

I tried to smile back but felt tears well up in my throat and fill my eyes. A pain in my chest was overwhelming and I looked at my body to see what was wrong. I could see through my shirt that my heart was physically broken. I had a broken heart. The pain was almost unbearable. I tried to force the two parts of my heart together with my hands. I looked for help from the woman but she had curved away into the crowd. I was alone. I had always known I was alone. Was that why my heart had broken? Because I could not stand the pain of being alone?

I crossed my arms over my heart to hold it together and moved along the corridor. The lids of my eyes were heavy. I felt weak and began slowing down. Why was I following the crowd? Where were they going? I heard my boots tapping on the corridor floor.

I turned around, sensing the woman behind me. She was shorter this time, with white hair buzzed on the sides and spiked up on top. Her face was very white, accentuating the vivid pink lipstick she wore. Jeans and a black jacket, a black T-shirt with a star stamped on the front in white, completed the outfit. The woman was wearing my T-shirt, my black boots. But the woman was not me. A feeling of such profound loss enveloped me that I usually woke up screaming at this point, just as the moving corridor whirred on, sending an unending strip of dark green plastic forever forward, ending the dream.

I shifted on the sofa, yawned, and looked at the tips of my toes. My foot was numb again. If it got any worse, I would have to go to the doctor. My back was sore. My hope for sleep was waning. Exhausted, I closed my eyes and fielded images of the dream reeling through my mind, incessantly, like Chinese water torture. I heard the paperboy drop the newspaper in the slot. It must be around six, I thought drowsily.

Seconds later Gord's alarm went off, and I fell asleep

CHAPTER 5

The day dawned bright and calm with all signs pointing to another sizzling late fall heat wave. No new breeze had sailed through overnight from foreign lands leaving fresh scented air in its wake. A tepid morning gave every sign of becoming rank by mid-afternoon and downright noxious by the end of the day. As I stood looking out of the kitchen window after having shipped my chatty children off to school, I heard the weatherman say there would be one more week of Indian summer before the wind and rain would begin. I looked in the refrigerator and saw three covered dishes containing remnants of tofu lasagne, curried rice and Hungarian goulash, our leftover supper for that night. The night and all nocturnal proceedings therein had been marked in the appropriate history books and had no place in the hopeful light of the new day. I decided to drive to a park on the North Saskatchewan River and take in some healing sun.

A bridge, high above a narrow, semi-rapid patch of water, connected the north side of the river to the south side. The bridge was old and restricted to pedestrians and slow moving bicycles. The river was surprisingly high. A birch tree, dislodged from its riverbed home by some careless earth grader, bent out over the rushing water, the tips of golden and red leaves bouncing in the sparkling current.

I looked down over the edge of the railings of the bridge at the coursing stream. Thick rivulets, like well-toned strips of muscles, braided together forcefully over huge liquid covered rocks before being sucked into whirling eddies that sent them shooting over a slight rise into a frenzy of white water. It was a favoured spot for suicides to leap to their bumpy deaths, I remembered, as I stood in the middle of the bridge. Only one woman had ever survived the jump.

According to the papers, a distraught seventeen-year-old girl had pitched herself over the edge after the break up of a romance. She broke both legs, fractured her pelvis and nearly drowned before being fished out of the water by two eleven-year-olds who were dirt biking by the side of the river and heard her yelling for help as she clung to a rotten log. There was a picture of her in the paper, a contrite boyfriend handing her an enormous bouquet of flowers.

"I don't know how he is going to pay for these, but I don't care," she had said.

I wondered if they were still together.

"Thinking of jumping?" a voice asked.

I turned my head and saw an old man wearing a grey windbreaker, tan pants, a baseball cap, and large wire-rimmed aviator sunglasses. He was walking a miniature black poodle wearing a red and green knitted collar. The poodle walked stiffly up to me and sniffed my foot.

"Well, you never know," I said, smiling.

The old man wheezed out a laugh and looked down at the water.

"Long way down. Lots of rocks too. Bet it would hurt."

We both stared at the water.

"You aren't really thinking of jumping, are you?" he asked

again, in an offhand manner that the searching look in his eyes belied.

"Not me," I said. "I'm afraid of heights."

He laughed. "Good, because I don't know if Pooch here would jump in after you. Take care," he called over his shoulder.

I walked over to an old, rickety picnic table and sat down, feeling the wood in the dilapidated bench creak and shift under my weight. Ragweed, ironweed, chickweed and Russian thistle all vied for growing space underneath the table. I bent the weeds down with my foot to keep them from grazing my legs and feet. Two medium-sized clear plastic containers sat in the middle of the table. A lettuce leaf and a broken black plastic fork lay in the bottom of one of the containers. The second container had been placed upside down on the table, crumpled up napkins imprisoned within. Fast food gourmets with no time to dispose of the evidence. Give me a hammock, I mused, strung between two trees, overlooking a wide, silent valley, carpeted with green, where one could peacefully doze away the afternoon, in quiet surrender. There I could be happy. A lethargy brought on by the warmth of the sun stole soothingly over me and I basked in it.

A pricking sensation on my arm roused me from my stupor. It pinched tenaciously. It was a mosquito, sitting on my arm, the large stinger embedded, drawing blood. Her body grew round and fat as she sucked. Her wings fluttered as she worked. They looked like glass. Wings of glass.

I had never seen a mosquito at work before. Usually when I felt the prick, I immediately brushed it off or slapped it to death. It was fascinating in a way. Oblivious of me, she took what she needed to survive. She left her poison behind, stuck in me to fester, contaminating the tissues, zapping the life out of them, surely, methodically. Then the mosquito, replete, lifted itself heavily and flew lazily in the air, sluggish from its overdose of blood. I watched as it lighted on the picnic table.

I sat up, wanting to know where it was going, carrying my blood.

I became very angry that this minute creature could so heedlessly wound me. How many times over the years had I been stabbed and injected with venom, which had never quite worked its way to the surface? It was killing me now, I thought fuzzily. My eyes trailed the mosquito. It zigzagged its way across the table, drugged by its recent fresh kill and landed on the top of the upside down container.

I leaned over the container and examined it. I half expected it to dart away, but it sat on the container, pulsing. I drew my face as close as possible to it. Its head was black, as if covered by an executioner's hood. What did the face look like, I wondered, unmasked? How could it just sit there? Was I so invisible, so insignificant that even the lowly mosquito could trample over me, trifle with my physical, emotional, and psychological needs with no fear of reprisal?

I took my hand and slapped it against the top of the container. I let my hand linger on the container for a second or two and then I slowly peeled it away. I looked at my palm. The mosquito lay crumpled up in the centre of it, surrounded by a splash of red. It was wingless. I glanced at the top of the container and the wings, for some reason, had stuck to the plastic. I inspected them. Long, veined, a dull grey, they had none of the iridescent rainbow sheen within the scales and margins, as I had thought at first glance. They were delicate nonetheless, and I marvelled at the screen of gauze stretched tautly between the elongated oval shape of the wings. Transparent and strong, they still had to be bound to the body cavity to enable it to live and fly away.

I flicked the dead mosquito off my hand and scraped the blood off my palm on the edge of the table. I moved the container closer, leaned my elbow on the table and my cheek on my hand and gazed at the wings. I looked at the wings of the mosquito through heavy lashes. Once again, I slipped into a sluggish open-eyed daze, the vacant stare a predecessor of sleep. I felt my body sweep up into the air as I closed my eyes. There was a jolt as the wings clasped on to my back, but once they had connected, I melted up off the table and streaked toward the open sky.

Faltering at first and afraid, I beat my newly acquired appendages furiously as I dove toward the ground. The flapping lifted me up just in the nick of time and soon I was gliding through dense molecules of air, smoothly and serenely. I noticed I was getting lighter and lighter. Scales were falling away. No. The barbs. They were being sucked out of my skin by a soothing tropical wind, laden with healing balm. I sailed through cotton batten clouds and teal blue skies. I was free. No. I was free falling, hurtling toward earth.

I opened my eyes just before my head hit the picnic table. I sat up, dazed. The sun had gone behind a tree. The picnic table was in shade. I took a moment to acclimatize myself. I had been daydreaming. Or dozing. Or a bit of both. The day hadn't cooled down at all. Quite the reverse. I knew I should go home but felt disinclined to move. A jogger ran past, giving me a salute and a smile. I ran my hands over the top of the rough and paint blistered picnic table. It was old and many people with varied talents had carved on its surface. A heart encased the letters D. M. and P. H. The name "Cory" had been scratched lightly into the wood in several places. In the middle plank, in neat square letters that had been coloured in with ballpoint pen, it simply said, "Fuck!"

Exactly, I thought, and got up to go home.

Stevie was already home when I pulled into the drive. He was hanging out the door with the phone in his hand.

"Mom! For you!" he shouted.

It was Gord. "Don't forget we have the criminal trial lawyer's party to go to tonight," he said. "It starts at 7:30. I'll meet you there."

"What? It's not on the calendar."

"I told you weeks ago. Remember? At the hockey tryouts?" He sounded impatient and threatening, as if he expected an argument.

"Did I tell you to put it on the calendar?" I asked.

"I thought you said you would," he countered.

"I don't remember."

"Well, anyway, it's tonight, and you said you would go."

I didn't usually attend functions with Gord. They were boring, and I didn't have the patience to converse with some self-absorbed lawyer in a three piece suit. Once in a while, though, Gord would ask me to accompany him to a cocktail party. I vaguely remembered promising to go to this one.

"Is this the one in the hotel?" I asked.

"Yes," he replied. "The Coolidge Inn."

"What do I wear and do we get anything to eat?"

"Wear the usual and I'm sure there are appetizers."

"Okay," I sighed. "I'll get a babysitter. Are you coming home first?"

"It's kind of a hassle to drive all the way home when I can just walk over from the office."

"Okay. Will there be anyone there I can talk to or do I spend the night talking to the philodendron?"

"Look for me. I'll watch for you. Okay?"

"Well," I said, but he had already hung up.

"Was that Dad?" Clare asked, coming into the kitchen and throwing down her backpack.

"Yes. He and I are going out to a party tonight. Do you want to come upstairs with me and help me pick out a dress?"

"Yah!" she replied, as if it were the most exciting thing in the world.

I stood before the mirror in my good black dress. I had bought it at a designer sale at Army and Navy when I had gone there for pajamas for Stevie. I turned sideways and sucked in my stomach. I sighed.

Clare peeked at me from within the folds of the quilt at the foot of our bed, the rest of her hidden by the bunched up, tangled mess of cloth.

Stevie wandered in from the hall singing.

"Baby belug-a-a-" he warbled, off key as he flung himself down on the bed and landed on Clare, who began kicking at him.

"Are you referring to me?" I asked as I unzipped the dress.

It wouldn't do. Too dressy. And obviously too small. I stepped out of it and hung it on a hanger. I stood before an array of out-of-date, frumpy clothes.

"What do you mean?" Stevie asked, puzzled.

"I mean, am I fat? My legs look like two blood sausages without the casing and my stomach is hanging down to my knees," I said, sifting through the clothes.

"Ewwwww!" they both screamed as they rolled around

on the bed.

"No mom. We sang Baby Beluga today in music. It's by these singers called Sharon, Lois and Bram."

"Oh," I said. "That's right. I remember that song. What's the other one they sing that I like?" I pulled out an old blue cotton print dress with ribbing down the front and an elasticized waistband. It was mid-calf length. I could get away without having to wear stockings. There was enough colour in the print so I wouldn't have to wear earrings.

"Skinamarinkydinkydink?" Stevie asked.

"Yes. That's the one," I replied.

"I love you," Clare sang.

"And I love you too, dear," I said, distractedly. "If I wear this dress and put a coat over it, I should be okay."

Stevie and Clare burst out laughing.

"Nooo!" they said in unison. "'I love you' is part of the song."

"Oh. I forgot." I sat down on the bed.

"Mom. If you put a coat on no one will see it," Clare said.

"Why don't you want to take your coat off?" Stevie asked

"I guess I don't feel good about myself today and I need insulation," I replied.

"Low self-esteem!" Stevie and Clare crowed in unison.

"Possibly," I said. Maybe I could discuss my suicidal thoughts with Stevie and Clare. Brutal honesty was a trait that all children specialized in.

"Do you need a hug?" Clare asked.

"I would love a hug," I said, throwing myself back on the bed. Stevie and Clare shrieked and scrambled to claim a spot next to me. I put my arms around their warm wiggly bodies.

They snuggled up to me.

"Feel better?" Stevie asked.

"I do feel better," I said as I held my children close.

Wearing the coat had been a mistake. I was hot. The Empire Room at the Coolidge Inn was packed like cheap sardines, and the low ceiling and the wall-to-wall body factor generated a lot of heat. My face was covered with a fine film of uncomfortable sweat. My dress felt damp on my back and clung to my knees. I felt like I was encased in a zip-lock bag, with airtight holes for the head and arms.

It was dark and noisy in the room. I stepped inside the doors and stood a little to one side to let my eyes get used to the dark surroundings. The Empire Room was packed. It was difficult to pick out any one person. Conservative suits with indistinguishable heads mingled with more dark suits. There was a steady hum of voices chattering, broken occasionally by a whinny of laughter, or a pompous guffaw.

In the gloom it looked like I was attending a convention of harbour seals, bobbing and arfing sociably while suntanning, co-existing amiably on a piece of sea rock jutting out into the ocean, not too far from shore.

The bar was situated in the centre of the room, ringed with heavily padded red leather stools. A canopy sunshine ceiling over the bar provided the only lighting for the room. The bartender stood behind the bar shining a glass, holding it up to the light, wiping off an invisible smudge before sliding it in the brandy glass holders just under the canopy. Dozens of glasses in different sizes hung, sparkling under the canopy, each glass mirroring the light with one bright shining spot. Trays of appetizers had been placed every few feet along the oak bar top and young, lone-wolf type lawyers lounged every other few feet in between, vying with the canapés for delectability.

I peered through the smoke-infested room, looking without success, for Gord. I knew I would have to leave the safe shore of the wall and leap into the fray to find him. Hoping that I would not sustain any form of cancer in my short journey to the bar from the second-hand smoke, I began to push my way through the crowd.

The first party I ever attended with Gord had been a lot like this one. I'd stood in a clump of people, holding a glass that kept getting bumped by other people threading their way back and forth across the room. It was noisy, smoky and dull. I had taken my drink, made my way to the nearest rhododendron, poured the drink in it and gone to see *Extreme Prejudice* starring Nick Nolte.

After that I only accompanied Gord when it was absolutely necessary. If it was a party held at a lawyer's home or backyard, I would filch a six-pack of Molson Canadian out of the ice-filled garbage pail by the patio doors, load a plate with salad, cold cuts and store-bought brownies, find the rumpus room and watch *Columbo* on TV.

I wasn't a very good lawyer's wife. I had no interest in how a particular judge came to his final ruling in a case. Torts and applications for discovery left me cold. I found details of child abuse or bestiality trials distasteful, to say the least. To me, pretentious wives, phoney smiles, and disinterested inquiries about my life, while standing around a bowl of rancid dip and soggy chips, was a waste of time.

A final push through the crowd brought me to the bar, right in front of an appetizer tray. I took a slice of cucumber decorated with a wavy spritz of devilled egg and a dot of red pepper and ate it as I scoured the room for Gord.

"Take off your coat and stay a while," leered a short, chubby red-faced man, who looked like Roseanne Barr in drag.

"Do not address me," I said, and scanned the room.

"Hoo. Hoo. Hostile," he grumped, and stared at me. He stuffed several beef rumakis into his mouth, whipped the toothpicks out of his mouth and debonairly threw them over his shoulder. They stuck precariously in the beehive of a tall, thin woman dressed in a tight black leather suit. All signs pointed to her being a prosecutor.

"Pretty hostile," I cautioned, as I turned my back on him only to find myself face to face with two sloppy drunks embracing. "Sorry," I said and turned back to the red-faced rumaki eater, who had moved on to a plate of artichokes topped with pale, congealed cheese.

He stared at me for a second and then said, "You know, you're not very friendly."

"I'm not trying to be."

"That could be it." He belched softly.

"Beer?" he asked, sliding one of his four toward me.

"Thanks," I said. I took a sip and watched the bartender expertly polish a glass and hang it up carefully on a rung above the bar with the rest of its sisters and brothers. "Why aren't you in a group of other lawyers discussing *voir dire* or something?"

"Boring," he said. "I only come for the food. Have my supper here. A few drinks. Go home. Watch *Columbo*."

"Are you even a lawyer?" I asked.

"Ha. Ha," he said as he popped another artichoke into his mouth.

Another woman pushed her way to the bar between the man and me.

As I headed out across the floor again to scout for Gord, I heard the man ask the woman to take a load off her feet and stay a while.

I felt a bit like a tankard, breaking ice, nosing my way through the floes. It was slow going and I soon found myself pushed up against the bar again, although at the end this time.

A tray of drinks sat unattended on the bar. I looked at it, looked around for the bartender or a waitress, and then picked it up. I had noticed earlier that waves of people parted magically for tray-carrying waiters striding through the crowd yelling, "Coming through!" I launched myself and yelled the same. The Red Sea had not parted faster for Moses. The human wall miraculously melted an avenue of escape. I fled into it. Finally something lawyers respected more than their own opinions. Booze. I walked straight toward a wall with a little alcove, framed by two huge plants, one tiny recessed light glowing dimly. It appeared to be empty, but as soon as I stopped yelling "Coming through" the crowd began to close around me and I couldn't see. Buffeted and jammed sideways, I backed my way to the wall, curving my arm around the drink tray to protect it.

I could see the plants in my peripheral vision and knew I was almost home. I stepped between the two plants and breathed a sigh of relief. To celebrate my safe passage across the floor, and to quench the thirst that had worked itself up, I picked up a Singapore Sling from the tray and sucked it down through the pink plastic straw until I heard the final death rattle slurp among the ice cubes. The sweetness of the drink caught in the back of my throat and I gagged.

Coughing, I dropped the glass into the soil of one of the plants and turned to look at my party refuge.

It had once been a coat check closet. Rails for hangers had been built into the wall. Several plastic trees stood at attention in one corner. I figured I would hole up in it, drink a few drinks and then continue my search for Gord. I picked up a highball and threw it down my throat. It tasted like scotch, or rye or whiskey. I could never tell them apart. I felt calm. Tranquilized. I debated whether or not to try another drink when something gripped my left leg right above the ankle. Startled, I looked down and saw a pair of man's legs sticking out from under the leaves of one of the plants. His hand began to move slowly up my leg, and when it reached my knee, I took what looked like a gin and tonic and poured it over where I judged his head might be.

"Thanks. I needed that," he said. "It's too hot in here, don't you think?"

I parted the fronds of the fake plant and saw a man sitting on the floor, his back against the wall. He had crumpled black curly hair with flecks of grey at the sides and he wore a rumpled raincoat over an equally rumpled suit. A half-empty bottle of vodka sat in between his legs.

"Was that out of line?" he asked, staring straight ahead. "I was just affirming to myself that it was indeed a leg that had positioned itself next to my arm and I sent out a feeler, so to speak."

"Sorry about the drink," I said.

"Pull up a wall, and we'll have an enlightened discussion on whatever you like."

"What if you're a pervert?"

"A pervert. Ha." He took a long drink from the bottle and continued to stare ahead of him. "Please. Tell friends. It might spice up my love life."

I looked out at the buzzing crowd and then at this semi-drunk possible pervert and slid down the wall next to him. It was a careful and precarious slide, what with trying to be ladylike about it and holding a tray of drinks at the same time. I placed the tray on my lap once my bottom had settled on the floor and poured a beer for myself from an open bottle on the tray.

"I thought at first I was having a kind of multi-layered illusion," he said. "Seeing all those legs walking by and then suddenly to actually have a leg right beside me. I had to separate reality from illusion. I reached out and touched what I thought was an illusion. And of course the reality of it was reinforced by the drink you poured on my head."

"I said I was sorry."

"No. That's okay. I might have done the same thing to you had our roles been reversed."

"Fortunately for me they weren't."

"Women. They've always got an answer."

"So it's a woman who has you brooding on the floor behind the plants?"

"I didn't say that."

"You didn't have to. I could tell by your whole demeanour, not to mention the sad sack tone of your voice."

"Go away," he said. "I'm sorry I asked you to share this spot."

Should I really go away? It was hard to interpret glib offhand remarks, especially from a person you have known for five minutes. Where was Gord, anyway? I resented having to hunt him down at this party or to wait for him to find me. I was always waiting for him. I waited for him to finish law school before we could start having a life. Then I waited another few years while he established himself. Then I waited for him to become more established. I waited for him to come home for supper, for birthdays, to fix a toilet, to deal with an irate serviceman. He was always too busy for me. Was I going to have to wait for him forever? I was tired of pushing my way through smoky rooms hoping to catch up to him.

"Depressed?" my floor buddy asked. Although his hair was grey, his face was quite youthful. Erase the dull, glassy stare and he would be quite attractive.

"Naturally. Isn't everyone?"

"Well, fuck," he said.

"I don't really care for that kind of language," I said.

"Not many women do. You got a cold?" he asked.

"No."

"Because after you said you didn't care for that kind of language, you sniffed."

"I did not."

"Did."

"Didn't."

"Did."

"Look."

"You look," he said. "You can tell by the tone of my voice that I am huffy, and I can tell by the long snotty sniffs and the shrug of the shoulders and the pursing of the lips, what you and all women mean. Getting back at me."

"Why was it necessary to swear?"

"Because I wish to God they'd bring my wheelchair back so I could get the hell off this floor. I've been sitting here for the last half hour. People walking by, thinking I am some sort of drunk. You. You thought I was a pervert. Believe me it was out of sheer boredom that I touched your leg. I thought it was someone coming to get me." He took another drink and shook his head.

For a moment I was stunned. I felt like an idiot. To my horror I began to laugh. Giggles turned into guffaws, which in turn grew to a roar.

"I'm sorry," I gasped. "I don't know what's come over me."

"It's okay," he said, looking at me queerly. "It's nice to see someone able to take a light-hearted look at paralysis."

This remark prompted another paroxysm of laughter.

"You crossed your legs a while back," I said. Tears had begun to roll down my cheeks and I put the tray down on the floor and searched in my pocket for a Kleenex.

"Oh go ahead. Don't hold back. So often it's gloom and doom with people around me. Once I tell them about the accident, or they see me in my wheelchair, they start acting weird. I'd rather people be straight with me than false. Like you."

I wiped my eyes with my fingers and blew my nose with a drink napkin from the tray. "You also bent your knee."

"Does that mean I'm not paralysed anymore?"

"Could be."

"Hallelujah, I'm saved. I'm saved. I'll bet if I got up, I could walk again. Let's go for Chinese food to celebrate."

"I'm a married woman."

"I don't see a husband trailing you."

"We arranged to meet here but I can't find him."

"So why are you sitting on the floor talking to a paralytic."

"You've had a miraculous recovery, remember?"

"Oh yeah. Well. Leave a message for him at the front desk and let's go for dim sum. Late night dim sum."

"I don't even know your name." My serviceable pink cotton underwear that rose high enough to cover my bellybutton and then some, leaped to mind.

"It's Bart."

"Bad Bart."

"Tsk. Tsk. I would have expected something more original from a woman who will sit on the rug in the Empire Room drinking booze from a stolen tray."

"It's late. I've had a hard day."

"So, let's go. The Duck Egg. It's close. I'm starving."

I looked at him. He was putting various things back into his pockets and retying his shoe. He lifted the vodka bottle to eye view and then drained the contents. He smiled at me. "Waste not, want not."

A cliché. Sort of. A man after my own heart. He held out his hand for me and I took it. It was very thin and cold, and his fingers curled around my own hot ones and pulled me up with surprising strength. I looked at him surreptitiously as I brushed off my coat. He was slightly taller than me and very thin. He had large brown eyes, piercing eyes that raised my previous assessment of him from attractive to handsome. Certainly not the eyes of an axe murderer. Of course it was always the kind-looking, sensitive types who murdered their entire families and propped them up in the living room so they could watch Rescue 911 as the murderer, oblivious to the incongruent nature of the scene, sat at a TV tray and ate takeout.

I cast a quick glance around the room for Gord. The room seemed to be moving faster than before, people eddying here and there at a much faster pace, in twisting pools. I was safe in my little inlet. Did I really want to leap back into that stagnant slough that was the party and search through the dreck for Gord?

"Okay," I decided. I could always refuse to walk down dark alleys. And I could scream and run if he attacked me. My high heels would be a liability, but I could kick them off and run. I winced as I envisioned an impatient intern savagely tweezing bits of rock and dirt from the bottom of my raw and bloody feet while I sat on an examining table in the emergency department of the Grey Nuns Hospital.

"Great. Let's go."

CHAPTER 6

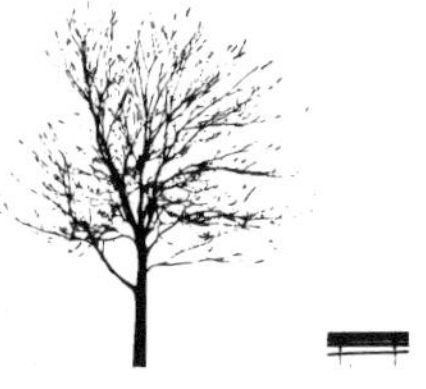

It was a short push to the door. We walked quickly through the hall to the main foyer, arm in arm, to counteract the unsteadiness it was obvious we both felt. Coming out of the soft, diffused lighting of the hall, which was supplemented by a glowing yellow and blue neon sign advertising a local car rental agency, to the brilliance of the gigantic incandescent chandelier dominating the entrance to the hotel, we were momentarily blinded by the light, but, resolutely, pushed our way to the automatic doors which released us into the dark.

"This way," he said and guided me to the right. We reached the end of the parking lot when he said, "No, I think it's the other way." He steered me around abruptly, and we walked back the way we came, smiling crookedly at the doorman, who tipped his hat in reply.

I halted at the black expanse between the hotel and the bank, the usual shortcut to The Duck Egg.

"Don't worry, I'm not going to mug you," Bart said, sensing my hesitation.

"What a silly thought," I replied nonchalantly. "I was merely pausing to breathe in this wonderful night air."

"Yeah. We've been granted a reprieve from winter it seems."

Our footsteps echoed in the quiet alley, marching in sync and then out of step. A heptagonal square of sky, formed by tops of buildings, showed it was a clear night and that the sky was a deep luminous blue, made so by the full yellow moon off to the right. And the air, perhaps because of the heavily treed park in the plaza by City Hall, smelled earthy and full of the ripe summer past. I breathed deeply.

Before children were an anchoring reality that precluded impromptu weekend getaways, Gord and I had hopped a plane to Las Vegas one wintry night. We flew out of Edmonton in a blizzard and landed, three hours later, in warm desert air. We drove our rental car straight from the airport into the desert, and when the lights of the city had faded we parked the car at the side of a sandy road, slid down an embankment and walked hand in hand through the hot sand, past cacti and giant yucca plants. We sat on the sand and looked at the same deep luminous sky framed by the spiky leaves of the desert Cactaceae.

"I like a nice sky," I said.

"Humph. Looks like a line up," Bart said.

The Duck Egg had been a fixture in Edmonton's Chinatown since the Second World War. The red bricks of the building were cracked and crumbling and, in fact, the outside of the restaurant resembled an edifice that had recently been bombed. The neon sign was only partially lit, spelling, the "uck E."

By the time we got to the door, we were able to walk right in. The restaurant was crowded, and we waited by the door to be seated. A harried but friendly Chinese man with meticulously combed hair, a lurid green and yellow-striped short sleeved golf shirt and menus in hand, walked up to us, smiling.

"I have some good news and some bad news for you," he said. "First the bad news. I have a table for you but it is right beside the kitchen. You will be looking into the crab and lobster tank all night."

"And the good news?" I asked.

"The good news is that the bathroom is right down the hall from the kitchen. Sounds great to you?" he enquired, already leading the way.

The waiter seated us, deposited menus into our hands and left. I looked at my menu, thinking it might have been a mistake coming to a restaurant with a possibly perverted, definitely more-than-a-little-drunk man, whom I only knew as Bart. I lowered my menu and looked at my late night dim sum companion. Bart's brow was furrowed, and he rubbed his chin with his left hand as he concentrated on reading the menu. Did we order a dish and share, our chopsticks tangling as we each reached for a pork and cabbage pot sticker at the same time? Or did we order our own food and consume it ourselves, a protective arm encircling the plate, so as not to have any foreign tropical or sexual diseases show up at the next yearly medical? The genial waiter returned and flipped his ordering pad open.

"One large order of hot and sour soup, two green onion cakes, and two glasses of water." Bart slammed down the menu and looked at me. "Okay with you?"

"Fine," I said. New medicines were being developed daily to thwart and to better treat illnesses that hapless individuals contracted by chance, or on purpose, I reasoned.

"Geez, you're easy to please. No feminist hackle raised over my chauvinist disregard for your right to order."

"I happen to agree with your choice," I returned.

Bart took his napkin and showed it to me. He twisted one end while fluffing out the corners of all the other ends to make a flower. He carefully tore off the pointed ends of the napkin, throwing them on the floor, and presented the flower to me. "Voilà," he said, "entertainment while you wait."

I took the flower and twirled it in my hand.

"Why were you sitting on the floor?" I asked.

"Me?" he asked. He reached out and plucked a napkin from the dispenser on the table and started fashioning another flower, a different shape this time. "Well. A person is born. They live. Someone wrecks their life. They die. I am just post life, right now. I'm allowing myself to wallow in pity. Forgive me." He scrapped the flower and threw the napkin on the floor. He looked over at the other diners and hummed a tuneless melody. "I've given up. Melodramatic, huh?"

"Maybe you should see someone," I suggested

"I told you she dumped me."

"I mean a counsellor. Talk it out."

"That's not my style."

"Sitting on the floor pretending you are disabled doesn't do anything."

"You aren't going to start analyzing me, are you?" he asked huffily.

"No."

"Good. Because I hate moralizing women. They get this gleam in their eyes and you know they're going to try to fix you." He grabbed a salt shaker with both hands. Then he hunched over in his seat, put his elbows on the table and studied the salt shaker. Abruptly he slid the shaker back to its place by the napkin holder and stood up.

"Gotta go to the can," he announced.

"Okay."

"I'll be right back." He grinned at me falsely, showing all his teeth, stood up, took a breath like he was going to say something, thought better of it, tapped the table with his knuckles, and set off for the bathroom.

I leaned back and closed my eyes. The clatter of forks and chopsticks hitting plates formed the background music to the fast-paced chatter in the room. It rose in a shriek here, only to subside and meld into the general conversational hum there, only to break out again behind me. The three or four drinks I had gulped down at the Empire Room, combined with cocooning myself in my coat, were making me dozy. I yawned and opened my eyes.

A group of Chinese students sat at a large table by the front window. A young man with round wire-rimmed glasses and hair that fell over his forehead into his eyes, forcing him to fling it aside every now and again, was relating some hilarious anecdote to his fellow diners. He would tell part of the story, pause, fling his hair back, and wait, at which point everyone at the table would roar. One of the women at the table burst out laughing as she was putting a long noodle into her mouth, causing it to stream over her plate. The table broke out anew, oblivious to the irritated glances they were getting from diners nearby, angry that their plans for a quiet dinner were being ruined.

Water burbled in the grimy-edged water tank, the upper moulding frosted with feathery slime that swayed back and forth in fast jerky waves. The lobsters, piled high in the tank, clawed in vain against the glass as they rose and sank, helplessly, buffeted by the strong current from the oversized filters.

I looked toward the kitchen and saw the waiter who had

seated us, standing to one side of the swinging doors, staring at me. I put my chin in my hands and closed my eyes again, letting the myriad of sounds wash over me. I yawned again, wondering where Bart was and wishing I was home in bed. I felt a pressure on my shoulder, and opening my eyes, saw it was the waiter.

"Yes?" I asked.

The waiter looked at me strangely, no trace of a smile. "Would you still like to order?"

"I beg your pardon?" I said. "I thought we had already ordered."

"Well yes," the waiter said. "But your friend. He has gone."

"What?" I looked behind the waiter to see a young girl at the serving window accept steaming plates from two hands in the kitchen while she looked sympathetically at me and reported, in Chinese, the happenings at my table.

"Yes. I go to the kitchen. Get order for someone else. I see him talking to salad boy. The boy point to the back door. And the man goes." The waiter looked at me expectantly, unsure of the response he would receive to the disturbing news it was his fate to bring me.

"He's gone?" Great, I thought. Stood up by someone I didn't even know.

"Do you still want to order?"

"No. I don't think so," I said uncomfortably.

"How about I bring you a cup of tea? Free. On the house." The waiter smiled and whisked away before I could refuse his kind offer. The young waitress walked by, her tray empty, and gave me a mournful smile.

I crumpled the flower napkin Bart had made for me. What had I been thinking?

"Here you are. Tea. Very good tea. And a fortune cookie." The waiter set a mug of hot tea in front of me with a flourish. "I hope you get a good fortune," he said, bowing curtly, and turning on his heel, marched back to the kitchen.

I held the mug of tea in my two hands, put my elbows on the table and took a sip. The tea was hot, black, and extremely strong. I looked at the rest of the diners through the steam wafting up in front of my eyes. The woman who was so annoyed with the loud students was watching me as she chewed on a dry rib. She looked away as her eyes met mine. Seconds later, after my eyes had completed a visual sweep of the room, I glanced at her again and she stared at me as she sucked coke from a wine glass with a straw. She spoke to her husband and he, affecting nonchalance, turned around and flicked a look at me.

The fortune cookie lay on the table in its cellophane wrapper. I used to save the Chinese fortunes I got, keeping them in the zippered side of my purse. I'd take them out occasionally and reread them, needing to be reminded of the good luck that was soon to come my way. But when my purse was stolen out of my locker at the YWCA, and all the future predictions on the tiny pieces of dry white paper that named my destiny were gone as well, I took it personally for quite a long time, angry at the unseen forces that had stripped me of the concrete guides to my own personal fate. I picked up the cookie and tore the edge of the cellophane with my teeth and broke open the cookie. No fortune fell out. There was none. I felt cheated. I'd always gotten a fortune. Is this good or bad, I pondered, as I picked a piece of broken cookie and crunched the sweet, dry gluten.

The woman was still staring, hoping to witness some sort of dramatic reaction to my being dumped by Bart. I yawned.

I gathered up my purse and made a detour to walk past the woman's table. She blanched and studiously began examining her chopsticks. The waiter, a stack of menus in his arms came up to me and smiled.

"Did you get a good fortune?" he asked.

"Would you believe there wasn't a fortune in the cookie?" I said. "I ate the cookie anyway. Thank you so much for the tea. That was very nice of you."

"No fortune? You are lucky then," he said. "You get to make your own fortune."

I stood outside The Duck Egg. I debated whether to take a cab or the bus. A taxi stand with several cabs waiting, their drivers leaning up against front fenders, smoking and chatting with fellow hacks, stood outside a Chinese convenience store across the street. I was about to cross the street and hail a cab when I saw a #17 bus turn the corner and pull up half a block down from the restaurant. As I ran to catch it, the bus barely paused at the stop before pulling away from the curb. Black smoke belched out by a quivering tailpipe partially obscured an advertisement for the upcoming season of the city's largest theatre, The Mainstage. *Metamorphoses*, by the Roman poet Ovid, in modern translation by playwright Mary Zimmerman, was listed as the season opener and promised a deeply moving personal experience, something I could benefit from. I yelled for the bus to stop and to my amazement it did, right in the middle of the street. I clambered aboard, puffing from my sprint.

"Thanks," I said as I hauled myself up the stairs and collapsed on the sideways seat across the aisle from the driver.

"This is my first shift as a bona fide bus driver," the young man behind the wheel said. "And you are my first customer."

I looked back and saw that I was indeed the only passenger on the bus. "Neat," I said. "Do I get to ride free?"

"I think you do," he said. "But don't tell anyone, okay?"

"Okay. Fine. And thanks."

"Hey no problem. Oh yeah. I'm supposed to let all riders know that the #17 has changed."

"Really? Does it still go down by the University?"

"Oh yeah. But instead of turning at 114th Street the way it used to, we now go all along Saskatchewan Drive. It catches more people that way."

"Great."

"Is that better or worse for you?" he asked.

"About the same, I think. I haven't taken a bus in a while."

"Good. We aim to please at City Transit," he said and screeched to a stop at a red light. "Darn. I've got to get those stops a bit smoother."

We rode the rest of the way in silence, swerving and lurching through traffic, screeching to a stop at red lights, stopping with a jolt at bus shelters, and then careening back into traffic until the little mom-and-pop neighbourhood corner store that signalled the entrance to the Drive swam into view. The driver swung on to the Drive. On an impulse I rang the bell as the lookout point came into view. On one side the Drive was lined with lavish homes, mostly well-kept older bungalows sitting a discreet distance from the road, lush green lawns surrounded by bland generic bushes, precisely clipped by the hired gardener once a week.

On the other side of the road the untrimmed mountain ash trees and corresponding generic bushes, as property of the city and thus less frequently maintained, grew wild and free, and led, after covering a small field of grass in need of a mowing, to a lookout point where the river valley and parts of the freeway could be viewed. A wooden bench screwed into a cement pad sat in a clearing at the edge of the lookout. I got up and held on to the rail as the bus skidded to a stop.

"Thanks," I said as I stepped off the bus.

The doors closed behind me with a whoosh. The bus hissed as the driver pulled away from the curb and tooted at me, but as I turned to wave, he was already wrestling with the big round wheel, manoeuvring his craft back on to the sea of concrete.

I stood on the sidewalk. It had been hot on the bus, and I welcomed the cool night air. I looked at the line of opaque yellow street lights curving away from me along the bend in the road, suspended like rhinestone droplet earrings against the sky. I turned around and looked out over the river valley, dark except for a zigzag of lights coming from cars speeding along the freeway, and twinkling lights from houses on the bluff across the valley. I stepped off the sidewalk on to the cold blankety grass. It brushed my ankles in feathery pats as I walked toward the lookout point, dipping down into miniature valleys that still held the warm air from the day, closing around me like kind loving arms, and then rising out of that warmth to meet solid whiffs of cool air that had me breathing in sharply and shivering slightly.

I sat down at the bench, my hands in my pockets. It was silent except for what? I contemplated. Except for the heartbeat of the earth, I thought. Trite. Cliché. Again. Maybe I was just being sentimental. That night, I didn't care. I could feel the heartbeat of the living earth, hear ever so slightly its living breath vibrating the boughs of the nearby pine trees, the rustling of the leaves of the willow and birch and the stiff sway of the stalks of the tall grasses by the path that led along the hillside. I listened. What was the Earth calling out to me? I felt an electricity envelope me. I had felt this sensation before. But when? Where?

I got up and began to follow the path along the hill. It was flanked on one side by a thick underbrush of willow trees, wild raspberry bushes, and tiny spruce trees, all fighting for the same growing space along the slanted hill. On the other side, rose bushes grew intermittently, thistles and thick patches of wild grass forcing uneven spacing, some of the bushes growing solidly on the cusp of the hill. As I walked along I thought it would not be such a terrible thing to suddenly transmute into a rose bush in this tiny wood, spending the rest of my days with my roots dug firmly and deeply into the soil, weathering rain, snow, sun and wind, and knowing that this was the one spot I had been created to inhabit, looking out into the world through my pink petal eyes each spring, knowing I belonged; looked upon by passers by as a thing of beauty and worth.

A vague sense of something familiar about this portion of the path made me slow down. I bent over, searching. My feet crunched unseen leaves and snapped a small stick. And then I saw it. It was hidden by bushes, but instinctively I knew where to look for the sign of the entrance. I pushed through the brush, separating branches that strained to keep me out, scratching my coat and catching my hair. I stepped up a little incline, my feet sinking into the damp leaf-strewn ground. And there it was: Clare and Stevie's secret fort. A natural indentation in the hill, caused by erosion or a collapse of earth had caused a cave-like hole in the hill, over which various roots and plant life had grown, obscuring it from view. I had been to the fort several times, once to make sure it was safe and other times as an invited guest.

Clare and Stevie had discovered it on one of their treasure hunts. They tirelessly explored the lookout, on foot and on their bikes. The windowsill in their shared bedroom was lined with huge pine cones, the sunlight fading them and the dust accumulating between each curling brown lip of cone, forgotten as they trudged on in search of more loot. Stevie had found an old jawbone once, half sticking out of the thick mossy dirt beneath a birch tree. It was yellow and discoloured, and dirt was embedded in eroded cracks in the bone. But it had all its teeth, which is more than you could say for the guy at the corner store who had examined it closely while Stevie picked out licorice and sour soother candies as a reward to himself on the day of the find.

I had been washing potatoes at the kitchen sink when they burst in to show me what they had. They theorized enthusiastically as to the origin of the jawbone. They had hoped it was some kind of dinosaur bone, one that had never been discovered before. Scientists would come and cordon off the area and begin a dig. Because they had been the ones to find the bone, they would be allowed to wander over the sectioned-off area and chat with the archaeologists uncovering the rest of it. Eating cookies at the kitchen table and drinking orange juice, Stevie had theorized that maybe it was a caribou jawbone, which would prove that caribou travelled through our very neighbourhood on their yearly trek to the Arctic.

That theory had been blown out of the water when Stevie found out that caribou only lived in the Arctic. It turned out to be the jawbone of a large dog, but Stevie and Clare kept it anyway, and their aunt Grace, a weekend potter and sculptor took it to her workshop one Saturday afternoon and with her drill, transformed it into a rather neat cribbage board, with comic likenesses of Clare and Stevie tattooed on the sides.

I crouched down, pushed aside the vegetation and peered inside. Although it was very dark I could still make out the edges of objects heaped in a near corner of the hideout. The whole area could not have been more than seven feet long, four feet high and three feet wide. I swung the trailing vines, which had drooped over the entrance again, up over the embankment, securing them behind an exposed root.

The light from the moon, brighter it seemed, out here in this bit of nature than in the ordered linear buildings of downtown, shone into the musty enclosed space, and I could see that much had been done to make a fort a home. A small ratty cardboard box with a pile of dead leaves in it sat to the left and rolls and rolls of birch bark stood on end next to the box. A section of linoleum that I recognized from the time Gord re-did the kitchen floor covered the ground, and an old car blanket, which had been banished to a shelf in the garage, lay in the middle of the linoleum in a hump. A rotted two-by-four had been set at the entrance as a sort of ledge, with rocks of varying sizes placed on top, equal distances apart.

I walked duck like on my haunches and crawled into the mini-cave, inched my way around so that I faced out, and sat with my legs to the sides, my head bent. While I was adjusting my coat, my elbow knocked something over. It fell with a soft click on the flooring. I squinted at it and seeing it was a jar of some kind, picked it up. It was cold and made me shiver as I held it up to the entrance where a shaft of moonlight shone in. It was a mayonnaise jar, smudged and smeared with dirt, full of something very light. Shaking the jar I saw that they were feathers, all kinds and sizes of feathers, from small, soft, downy snowbird feathers to larger blue and black magpie and blue jay plumes to still larger grey and white seagull feathers, placed in the jar point down.

I opened the jar. The lid was loose and made a scraping sound of rust against glass as I unscrewed it. I shook the jar and blew into it gently. The seagull feathers shifted but did not rise. The downy feathers of the snowbird swirled against the insides of the jar, and drawn by the force of my breath, rose up out of the rim of the glass to float in the air before me. I blew on the delicate insulating puffs of some long gone bird and watched the miniature plumes float lazily in the air. One, caught by a night draft creeping into the enclosure, was whisked briskly up and out of my sight.

I shivered in the sudden current of air. I held the jar close and shivered again, feeling the tingle. My feet were cold. I reached over and tucked the car blanket around my feet and legs. I leaned back and found a natural slope to the hill that accommodated my back and head nicely. I laughed, envisioning how I must look, with a dress, raincoat, good shoes and freshly washed hair, crouched in a hole in the side of a hill, an old car blanket slung around my feet. I did feel secure, though, in my nest in the soil, my womb. Here I was, I mused, rooted in reality. The husk of the seed that confined me here in the earth could now be shucked off. It was a joyous birth; no struggle for growth in the arid climate that was my life. I saw tender shoots straining through to the light above, challenging the unknown future. I was the seed to be enlightened. I smiled at my whimsy.

I tried to see beyond the thicket. Faint lights from houses on the hill across the freeway pinpointed signs of life. I yawned. But did I have the right to assume that the tender shoot had any kind of a future? In my meditation book a prayer and a request to Tara, the Liberator, a manifestation of love, compassion, wisdom and the accomplished activity of enlightened beings, would, supposedly, see the request as a done deal. Not so, not for me anyway. There was a catch. In order to meet with fortune and fame, one must have, in the past, created or requested the causes or circumstances of one's future success. Obviously I had made no such request of Tara and I was suffering big time now. I had no hope of attaining Nirvana, the state of complete personal freedom from suffering and its causes. I could only hope that an appeal to Tara's compassionate nature would yield some merit points for me. Tara's ethereal nature, floating in a cloud of light, rays emanating from her body, streaming down like nectar, flowing continuously like rain running down a wire, impressed me and gave me hope.

I yawned again. I was tired, so tired. I would have a little rest before I went home, I thought and closed my eyes. I tried to call to my mind's eye a picture of Tara, dressed in an emerald green gown and seated on a lotus and a moon, hovering above the ground. An image of her sprang up with little effort. I saw that she was pointing down. And as I drifted off to sleep I looked and saw my feet, floating in a cloud of light.

And then I became conscious of my feet, my bare feet. I was standing on cold, white marble, with the merest of grey fingers running through it like smoke wisps seen rising fleetingly over a dying campfire at night. The marble was smooth and oddly soft, like the bottom of well-worn white leather moccasins. I saw that I was on a wide step that curved away to nothingness in the white that surrounded me. I felt giddy, as if I was going to fall, and just as I began to be afraid, another step materialized in front of me. I ascended slowly. I began to cry.

Had I died? Tears blurred my vision. I wiped the tears from my eyes. The lustreless haze that surrounded me melted, and I found myself sitting beside a large colourfully embossed white pillar that stood as the extended entrance to a shining gold door, far away. Spiralling scrollwork wrapped itself around and around the pillar up to an archway of clear glass that made the foyer incandescent from some translucent source overhead. The foyer led to the gold door. I knew I must gain entry.

As this thought flicked through my mind, I found myself standing in front of the door, my hands pressed against the smooth metal. An engraved border of gold framed the door. I ran my finger along the groove between the border and the door and pressed my cheek against it. My cheekbone jutted into the door, and I watched as my hot breath sent out undulating waves across the shining gold. I rolled my head back and held my ear taut against the door, listening. I looked at the door. It was impenetrable. I felt its magnitude, and my imagined vision of the inherent cosmic power that lay behind it both scared me, and, strangely comforted me.

A wind sprang up, blowing rice paper–thin leaves, tinted red and orange, around me in a whirlwind, and up against the door. They plinked when they hit and fell to the marble with a *chik*. My hair blew in my face, and as I raised an arm to brush it away, a leaf pricked the palm of my hand. An electrified bolt of pain shot through my hand, jerking it forward and clapping it to the door. I screamed, pulling away, closing my eyes. I felt the piercing pinpoints of blood spurt and cleave to the golden door, melting it, erasing it, reducing its power with my pain.

And just as suddenly as the leaf had pricked me, causing pain, it stopped. I opened my eyes. I had gained entry. I was beyond the door.

I looked at the layers of black that surrounded me. I stood alone in the infinite blackness, each beat of my heart echoing back to me in crashing crescendos. I slowly became aware that the dark was tempered by a soft yellow light that began filtering down around me in delicate rays from above. I looked up through the lacy haze and saw the source of light. It was an opaque orb, slowly descending, flicking away the black in gentle pinwheel motions, each spin erasing the black raven wall and relieving the existence beyond.

I was in a long, narrow room. I saw a door in the room on the far wall. I grew cold as I peered at the door. It was black but that was not frightening to me. It was the knob, razor sharp cut glass, each point of the deeply etched diamond pattern jutting up to slice the hand that grasped it, square cut prisms anchoring the brass handle to the door. I felt giddy, anxious. I knew I must make my way to the door, firmly grasp the delicate crystals of the knob, crush them into my hand, and open the door. I knew the fine, barbed splinters would twist into my flesh, piercing the skin. Tears sprang to my eyes as I knew the depth of pain that was to come. I clasped my hands and wrung them tightly, feeling the supple skin-covered flesh and bone.

Why must I always bleed? Why must it always be the fine-edged lance that caught me, spinning through the air, catching me, searing me, neatly slicing through the woven, living cells of muscle and fat and tissue, split apart; spurts of blood leaping from the wound in surprise, spattering the cement in irregular wet slaps? I would look at the bloody gash, throbbing, pulsing, growing larger with every beat. And I would skim the pain from the surface of the wound and suck it deep within me. I would breathe it in and diffuse it to dark corners of little cells throughout my body, anaesthetizing them bit by bit until I could take quite deep breaths and hardly feel that sharp stab in the area surrounding my heart at all.

Sometimes I would close my eyes and imagine that I could step outside of myself, flying to the ceiling of whatever room I happened to be in, hovering, making sure I was still alive. I always was, but lately I seemed to be moving slower, as if I was becoming saturated, waterlogged, and it was dragging me down. I was beginning to move in slow motion as if I was solidifying. I had a vision of one day flying up to the ceiling to see how I was doing and find I was locked in a stationary pose, unable to move. Perhaps it would happen at the kitchen sink, or reaching out to give Clare a hug. And it nagged at me. I tried so hard to keep free of any emotional claptrap that might interfere with the blank film I continuously ran on the grey celluloid in my head that I could not turn off.

A bright picture on the wall of the strange room I found myself in flashed at me. I walked toward it. I concentrated on the picture, trying to separate the splotches of colour into forms or objects but they refused to be still in their frames. They squirted languorously on the canvas, bright green bumping into canary yellow bumping into red, each contact changing their shapes and sending them rolling languidly into another direction, like a multi-coloured lava lamp, stuck to the wall. I reached out to touch the picture but the frame, shuddering, shot straight up where a slot in the ceiling swallowed it with a clank.

I felt the wall where the painting had disappeared. It reached out, oozing, to massage me, separating the fingers and filling the space around them as cosily as a thick flannel glove. The force of the field near the wall spread to my wrist, and I felt a tug on my arm. I pulled back instinctively and found my arm caught. An acrid vapour sprang up and gauzy grey talons formed out of the cotton batten fog, clamping down on my arm.

I screamed and tried to wrench my arm free. The talons, twisting and stretching, grasped on to my legs, anchoring me to the floor, pulling me very slowly into the cocoon. I looked around me and that was what the room had become. A cocoon, an impenetrable prison of white wire screen, wound tightly around and around, packed with glue-laden batting and hermetically sealed with a thick papier mâché paste.

Cold. Airless. Dead.

I grew angry and fought against the hold. I clenched my hand around the holes in a futile attempt to crush them. The cocoon, thrown out of alignment by my grip on the holes began to bump and grind in its revolutions, bouncing my hard-packed body in jarring thumps against something solid, weakening the plaster so that I could wriggle out of parts of it and kick away others. My body went limp and I began to cry. A cry of relief, a cry of thanks, a cry this time from my lips as I freed my fingers from the holes, so full of rage that I thought I might pop, explode, my body expiring in a snap, like that of a fire cracker at the instant of ignition. My voice lost its strength and yet I still released my anger, rasping my protest until every life-giving breath had been forced out of my body. I swooned and fell against the steps. I turned my head and saw the black door.

Flashes of my hand, shards embedded deep in my palm, made me pause. They would heal, in time, I thought. I got up and walked to the door. Before I could think about it anymore, I grasped the knob, gritting my teeth, and wrenched on it. It was cold, and sharp. I gripped the knob tighter and felt the first slice bite into the skin. Tears formed in my eyes and ran down my cheeks. But that was okay. They would dry, in time. And I remembered the crystal knob from the closet of my room so long ago, where all my life had been suppressed and sealed, and I realized that now was the time to set it free. The woman with the long coarse black hair from my dreams swam into view. In slow motion, she turned to look at me, the strands of her hair shooting neon darts into the night like fireworks.

I opened my eyes to see a shooting star exploding in the sky. For the briefest of seconds, I didn't know where I was. I had fallen asleep in the fort. It was dark and cold and I shivered. My neck was stiff from the unnatural position it had been in, leaning against the dirt wall. I sat up, feeling the throb in my head. There was too much information in my head. Was that possible?

Mr. Beeman, my grade seven social studies teacher, came to mind. One day, he strode into the classroom, slammed his books down on the desk and shouted, "No one can steal your thoughts. You can be imprisoned physically, shackled, roped, and chained so that all you can do is breathe. But that is all. You will still be free. No one can force you to think the way they do. Choose the prison. Choose the shackles on your ankles but keep your thoughts and you will always be free."

But what if the prison is in your head? What if the chains and shackles *are* your thoughts? What do you do then?

CHAPTER 7

I was playing a game at school called Seven Up with a friend. I bounced a ball against the gym wall, and before it came back to me, I had to clap my hands under my right knee and behind my back. I loved this game and practised constantly after school and on weekends with Wynn. She had her own ball, and between counting and breathing and clapping her hands, she would pant out tips on how to improve my game. It was harder to play at home because I had to bounce the ball against the side of the house. The house had wooden siding, and the ball bounced askew if it hit the part that jutted out at the bottom. I practiced against the back door but after the door had unexpectedly opened, first by my mother, whom I hit on the shoulder, and then by my auntie Marilyn, whom I caught with an out-of-control fast pitch to the forehead, I was banished back to the side of the house.

When it was my turn, I bounced the soft red ball against the wall, concentrating hard. I watched the ball hit the wall. I raised my knee simultaneously with letting the ball go and quickly clapped my hands under my knee and then readied them to catch the returning ball. I began again, conscious in my peripheral vision of my friend and a dozen others playing the same game along the wall.

There. I was done. I looked around. Everyone in the gym was standing still, looking in the same direction. A basketball bounced several times on the floor past me from the boy's corner of the gym. I looked to see what everyone was looking at. It was my oldest brother Ben. Father Borden and he were standing in the gym doorway.

"Go!" My friend said, pushing me.

I went, still holding the ball. I felt the manufacturer's label sticking out of the ball against the fingers of my left hand and I traced them with my fingers as I walked to the door. It was quiet in the gym. I could hear my hard shoes clicking on the floor. I had forgotten my running shoes, but the gym monitor had let me go, just this once.

I saw Ben crying. As I approached and raised my face for some explanation, he knelt down and grasped me to him, burying his face in my neck. He had on his winter jacket and the fur got into my mouth.

"It's okay," he whispered.

What? What was okay? I looked at Father Borden's serious face.

I let the ball drop. I wished I could finish the game but I knew I could not. I had to go. But where?

Church? And why?

My mother usually picked a pew toward the back of the church, but that day Father Borden led us right up to the chancel, right up to the communion rail, and motioned for us to kneel down. I would have preferred to sit farther back, in one of the pews where the windows would bathe me in coloured light. There were no windows at the front of the church, and the communion rail and altar area seemed dim after the brilliance of the aisle. I knelt. The communion pew was padded and covered with dark red leather that sighed as I knelt down.

Ben, his head in his hands was crying. Wynn and I huddled together. Father Borden, one hand on his forehead, prayed, his lips moving slightly. Vaguely uneasy, I was unaware of what had happened and no words had been spoken to tell me what was wrong. Everyone was just very sad. I knew it was important or I wouldn't have been taken out of school. We hadn't gone to church for a while, and the last time Father Borden had visited our house my mother had argued with him and slammed the door in his face.

Pray.

I clasped my hands and looked at the red carpet that led to the altar. I had come to church with my auntie Marilyn one Saturday afternoon and had seen a woman with a white scarf tied around her head vacuuming the rug around the altar. I was surprised. I never imagined that a church would have to have maid service. I took it for granted that the cleanliness of the church was seen to by a pair of divine cleaning hands piously waving over the chancel once in a while causing the dust to vanish in a puff.

I checked the floor, looking for fluff. I looked at Christ, hanging by some wires from the ceiling on his cross. I wondered who cleaned Him. I wondered if they got a feather duster, tied it to the end of a really long stick, stood on a step ladder and gently flicked the dust off the top of the crown of thorns and those outstretched arms and bloodied toes. Did they dust off the loincloth too, or just let it go?

Father Borden sighed and got up. We all took this as a sign to do the same. Father Borden put his arm around Wynn and led her to the back of the church. The sun had gone behind a cloud. He took us to the rectory behind the church. We sat in the living room, which smelled like church with food smells added. Two sofas sat in the middle of the room facing each other. A plain brown wood coffee table bridged the gap between them. A serviceable taupe rug covered the floor and matched the short, lined drapes scrunched to the sides of the living room window. A picture of Christ, some official looking documents and a diagram on how to give mouth to mouth resuscitation adorned the walls.

A small plate of cookies sat in the middle of the coffee table. They were flat, irregular and very dark brown. Home-baked no doubt by the plump whispering nun who had admitted us to the rectory and whose skirts swished when she walked, clacking the big rosary beads and huge ring of keys that hung from her waist. We all took a cookie at her silent urging. Ben looked at his. Wynn got up and looked out the living room window, leaving hers on the sill. The nun looked at me benignly, smiling vacantly at no one in particular, and tiptoed away. I bit into the cookie. It was hard and tasted a bit like an old willow stick I had once picked up from the side of the lake and chewed while I waited for my dad to be done separating nets. Old.

I ran my hand along the cushion I was sitting on. It was a dark brown brocade with yellow highlights and I could feel the outline of the flowers and curling stems of the pattern with my fingers. I came to the edge of the cushion and pressed my hand down between the two sections. The bottom edge of the cushion pushed against my closed fist. I opened my hand and deposited the cookie between the two sections and withdrew it just as Father Borden entered with a pitcher of orange juice.

"What are we doing here?" I asked as he bent down and set the pitcher beside the cookies.

He looked surprised at my question, and then he came and sat down on the sofa beside me. It squeaked its protest. He took my hand between his two, paused while he reflected on what to say, and said, "Your mother has gone away."

"Where?"

Again, he looked at me in surprise.

"To heaven."

To heaven? To heaven? Going to heaven was ultimately good, I knew that. But it was not good if that was where my mother had gone. "Why?" I asked.

"Why did she go to heaven?" he asked, looking pained.

"Yes."

"Well, she was sick, and she died."

"And then she went to heaven?"

"Yes. Your mother has gone to heaven," he confirmed.

"How do you know she went to heaven?" I asked, wanting to scream at the horror of what I was being told.

"Well," Father Borden began, "Your mother was a very . . . "

But I didn't hear the rest of what he had to say. There was a roar in my ears. it was deafening, filling my skull. I watched Father Borden's mouth work as he spoke to me about my mother, his dry whitish lips pursing as he sought the right comforting words, and then parting as he spoke, his tongue darting about behind his yellowed teeth. I ran to the door, opened it and began running, running as fast as I could, away from there. I ran until someone caught me and held me and would not let me run anymore.

I don't remember ever going back to our house. My brother and sister and I were farmed out to relatives and friends. I was put up by a friend of my mother's named Denise who had a daughter, Joan, the same age as me. They lived in the old town by the water. I liked visiting Denise's house. She would give Joan and me a big bowl of dried bread crusts, and we would stand on a piece of rock that jutted out into the lake and feed the sea gulls, each trying to toss a crust high enough in the air at the exact moment a gull was flying overhead, to see if it could snatch the bread out of the air as it swooped by. When we finished feeding the birds we would play hide and seek on the rocks behind Denise's house and wade in the water to try to catch minnows or start a fire in the fire pit.

We were fire bugs. Joan and I gathered dried leaves and twigs, scampering over the rocks like ants, culling the underbrush for starter kindling. Denise would come out of the house and set our bonfire ablaze with a flare of her cigarette lighter and caution us not to start a forest fire. The three of us would squat around the fire, blowing it lightly to make sure it caught. Then we would toss on wood from the woodpile until the blaze hit dizzying heights and the heat burned our cheeks. A big spark spat out of the fire flew onto my favourite dress one time and burned a hole right in the middle of a flower on the skirt. After that, I could stick my finger through it and scratch my thigh without having to hike up the dress.

A suitcase had been packed for me to take to Denise's. It had a pair of Wynn's pajamas stuffed away at the bottom, three pairs of socks, two pairs of jeans I didn't wear anymore, two white blouses, a green pullover sweater and two pairs of boy's underwear. I put the pajamas on and crawled into the bed across from Joan's. Denise came in and sat on Joan's bed. Joan climbed into her lap and Denise stroked Joan's hair out of her face and kissed her cheek. Joan laid her head on her mother's chest.

"You are very welcome in our house," Denise said to me.

I didn't answer. Denise got up, Joan clinging to her. She tucked the covers around Joan and gave her a kiss on the cheek. She then turned to me and came over to my bed. She bent down and gave me a kiss on the cheek and squeezed my shoulder. Then she said goodnight to us both and softly closed the door.

"Your mom died, eh?" Joan said in the dark.

"Yeah."

"I liked it when she came over and would chase us and pinch our bums."

"Yeah."

Not long after, a fat woman in a tight green jacket and mannish green hat came to Denise's. The next morning I was on an airplane with my brother and sister and going to live with grandparents we had never seen. I had never been on an airplane before. It was loud but the noise helped take my mind off the nauseous feeling in my stomach. I hadn't seen Ben and Wynn for a while and they looked different. I watched them, excited, look out the window, adjust the seat belts and peek into the pocket on the back of the seats in front of them. There was a distance between us that I didn't understand. I felt shy around them. I felt them slipping away.

They were my father's parents. I remember him having a big argument with them on a pay phone in the Post Office that had something to do with my mother. He never mentioned them and all I knew about them was that they lived in a big city. My grandmother was short and fat, with thighs that bulged ominously out the sides of her thin, blue flowered housedress. She wore stockings rolled down, like unglazed donuts, around her ankles. During the day she wore them just above the hem of her skirt and if she bent over from the hips, you could see the elastic just above her knees cutting into her vein-roped legs. Filling the sink after supper with hot soapy water, she would lift her skirt, give the tops of the stockings a quick snap, and sigh as they shot down her ham calves to her cracked white nurse's shoes, tied with grey laces.

My grandmother was a woman of few words. She communicated by pointing or nodding or shaking her head. She grunted occasionally and knitted her brows to look threatening. She, her house and everything in it, reeked of cabbage and old dishrags. I thought at first that she rarely spoke because she was holding her breath to ward off the smell, but when I ventured this theory to Ben, he hit me on the back and told me our grandmother was Polish and didn't speak English well at all. My grandmother was not unkind, but she was gruff and stern. It was only when she tended the gigantic vegetable garden that filled the entire backyard that her brow cleared and she looked content.

The three of us were enlisted immediately for weeding, repotting, raking, planting potatoes, zucchini, peas, carrots, lettuce, beans, cabbage, onions and staking the huge tomato plants that grew sturdily against sticks. We anchored them with pieces of garden hose spliced together and taped with black electrical tape.

Enormous bunches of peonies grew in the sun by the back door. They were big feathery pink and white balls of blossoms that, upon closer perusal, startled one with their characteristic infestation of peony ants.

One fall day, I sat on the back porch steps and watched the wind blow the yellow and orange leaves from the mountain ash and poplar trees in the yard next door. I heard my grandmother and grandfather arguing in Polish in the kitchen. My Grandmother came to the back door and closed it, muting the argument.

That night we were allowed to watch television while we ate, something that was not usually allowed. The next morning we saw our suitcases had been packed. My grandmother motioned to my grandfather. He picked up the suitcases and led us out to the front sidewalk. He gave a piece of paper to the waiting cab driver and hurried back to the house. Ben and Wynn climbed into the cab. The driver opened the cab door for me. He drove us to the address on the paper, the Kiwanis Home for Orphaned children.

When we arrived at the orphanage we were herded into the matron's office and welcomed. Ben wanted to know why our grandparents had sent us there. He wanted to call them and ask them to take us back. The matron listened without commenting and said she hoped we would be happy at the home and if we had any problems we should come and see her. Ben was taken away by a uniformed young man. But when a uniformed young woman took Wynn by the hand and led her out the door, I rebelled so utterly and completely at this final violation that Wynn and I were allowed to be together.

Wynn and I were taken down a hallway, up some dark stairs and into a long dormitory where we were deposited into a small room with two sets of bunk beds. Wynn climbed into the top of one of the bunks and slipped under the covers. I climbed up to and slipped under the covers beside her.

"I'm scared," she said.

"Me too."

"Are we going to be here forever?" she asked.

"I don't know," I replied.

"Will you sleep with me tomorrow night too?" she asked.

"Yes," I replied.

The matron had said that we could keep our socks and our shoes. She said that when they wore out we could pick some new shoes from the community box in the hallway in our dorm. As I listened to the sounds of whispering and muted thumps in the room next to ours, sounds of settling down for the night, sounds of getting comfortable and cozy in familiar beds, sounds of saying a final goodbye to the events of the day that, for us, would be indelibly stamped in our memories. I wondered how long it would take for my shoes to wear out.

I hated the orphanage for two reasons. One reason was the ward helper. The ward helper oversaw the girls in our ward. She supervised our getting up in the morning and our going to bed at night. She was supposed to help the younger children with their hair and their clothes, but she did not. She schlepped down the ward halls, pigeon-toed, in ill-fitting, dirty, pink mules, the bulk of her soft stomach straining against the tan shirt and brown jumper uniform of the orphanage. When she raised her arms to scrape her greasy bangs behind her ears, we, the inmates, were afforded a glance at the big damp sweat stains under her arms.

She slapped us on the heads, rummaged through our possessions, lied to the matron about infractions and caused us to lose privileges. She would be sixteen in six months, would be freed from the orphanage, and so really didn't have anything to lose. I hated the power she had over my life. She tried to take a scarf of Wynn's once and I grabbed it back and called her a thief. She gave the scarf back, but I earned her eternal hatred and she picked on me every chance she got.

The Sunday night movie was a favourite activity at the orphanage. After supper each Sunday we would all get into pajamas and troop down to the basement hall where one of the male helpers operated an old movie projector and ran child-oriented comedies and simplistic dramas that ended with the requisite moral lesson. Everyone could go except for those who had accumulated five or more infractions during the week.

I loved movies. Auntie Marilyn had often treated Wynn and me to movies at Yellowknife's one and only movie theatre, the Vista Vue. She would come to our door, knock and shout that she needed two escorts to go to town to see a very important movie. These invites seemed to come out of the blue but looking back I saw that they often came just as my mother was combing our hair and wiping the remnants of supper from our faces.

The Vista Vue's double doors were glass from top to bottom, and I marvelled that I could see right up the thick red-carpeted stairs to the dark brown wooden pay booth at the top of the stairs without even opening the door. Auntie Marilyn said it was against the law to watch a movie without eating, and so would pile a bag of deliciously greasy smelling popcorn, licorice, toffee and lemon lime pops into our arms before grabbing us each by the shoulder and herding us down the slanted aisles and into a row of seats in the middle of the theatre. I liked the cartoons, whispering to Wynn during the boring parts of the main feature, and sitting beside my auntie Marilyn, watching her laugh or cry or boo or clap, intent on the moving images on the screen, absorbed in the slice of fictional life unreeling before her, becoming, for an hour or two, part of it.

Fatso, as I had secretly named our ward helper, manufactured the requisite number of infractions each week so that I never did get to see one Sunday night movie at the orphanage. And after the first night when she informed I would not be joining the rest of the children in the basement and laughed and slammed the door to the ward in my face, I affected an exaggerated nonchalance toward the Sunday night treat, lying in bed as everyone trooped down the hall, my hands behind my head, my feet crossed at the ankles. After the movie, Wynn would crawl into bed with me and carefully relate every detail of the story. Years later, when I finally saw *The Three Lives of Thomasina* and the scene about the cat in the rain on the tree branch, it was like I was seeing it for the second time.

The second reason I hated the orphanage was because of the first Saturday of the month. Right after lunch on that Saturday, instead of going out to play, or staying inside to play, we were sent back to our individual wards to straighten our uniforms, comb our hair, wash our faces, and go to the bathroom. When we were ready, we had to line up in the front hall, a long, wide hallway that led from the double front doors to the matron's office, a washroom and a small gym. The front hall floor was dark brown linoleum with tiny yellow and green flecks. It was polished to a hard gleaming shine, and I had many chances to examine it as I stared hard and unrelentingly at it for an hour the first Saturday of every month.

During that hour, various people came, in groups, in couples or alone, and looked at us. Some asked questions; some just looked. The matron told us to be friendly and so I was friendly, at first. When I learned from the other children that the people who came to look at us might adopt us and take us to live in their homes for the rest of our lives, I was horrified and resolved not to be one of the chosen children. Why would anyone, I thought, want to go and live with complete strangers.

On one occasion I was placed beside a thin girl named Emma, from another ward. She had two thick braids hanging down the front of her dress. She had freckles and a turned up nose. A woman stopped in front of her and asked her what her name was. Emma replied and the woman asked her if she would mind if someone changed her name. Emma said no. I learned later that Emma had gone to live with a family who wanted a girl to go with their two boys.

Fatso taunted me, saying that with my scraggly hair and toothpick limbs, it was a wonder that anybody gave me a first glance, let alone a second. Her taunts worked in reverse. I was glad to be compared to a baby eagle, just out of the shell. It lessened my chances of being chosen. I instructed Wynn, who was much prettier than I, to glower and snarl if anyone looked her way. It must have worked. No one ever stopped to size us up and once the hour on the first Saturday of every month had passed, we were free to go back to our dorm, change into our play clothes and play.

Wynn and I spent the winter at the orphanage. I know this because one day I ran outside to play and a warm breeze prickled the hair on my arms and legs, making me stop and look around. It was spring. The sun was shining and the sky was blue. I ran to find Wynn. We were going to play hide-and-seek. I wanted to find a really good hiding place. The girl who was "it," who counted to one hundred and then set out to find all the hiding children, had her head resting on her arm, hiding her face so she would have no idea where all and sundry were scattering.

I was a bit slow to start because I had Wynn with me. She liked to be near me and although she slowed me down, especially in games like this, I didn't mind. I grabbed her hand and pulled her after me. I led her quickly to the back gate by the side of the old double garage that housed the orphanage van and company car.

Wynn balked as I unlatched the gate. "We aren't supposed to go out of the yard," she said.

"It's okay," I replied. "We're just going to go around the back of the garage, through the garden, to that place behind the rose bushes. No one will ever find us there. We can sneak up the back stairs, go through the building, and out the front. No one will see us and we'll probably be the only ones to get home free.

Getting home free was the ultimate desire of all who played hide and seek. Pitting oneself against the individual who was "it," who was the master of all they surveyed and sought, was a formidable challenge. To hide, and be actively sought, and to have the possibility of one's life light extinguished with the merest touch of the seeker, spurred the hider on to untold heights of physical and emotional evasion.

"But what if someone catches us in the building?" she asked, still worried.

"We'll say you had to go pee and I was taking you," I said.

Wynn thought about it slowly. "Okay," she said. "We'll say it was an emergency pee."

I made sure the gate was latched properly and we snuck furtively around the back of the garage. We had to go out of the yard to get to the rose bushes because a chicken wire fence had been erected, partitioning off a section of the backyard that was to be renovated into a larger garden area. Trees had been uprooted and bushes cleared from the fenced-off area. It lay barren, loosely turned black dirt waiting for the seed.

There was no way through the yard except to go around the garage, re-enter the yard on the other side and walk through the new garden area to the rose bushes. Once we were in the back alley, though, we forgot about the hide-and-go seek game almost immediately. Rose bushes covered the fence across the alley from the garage, and their light delicate fragrance, released by the warmth of the sun, filled the air. I picked a rose for Wynn and stuck it through the top button of her uniform.

Rose bushes had a special meaning for us. In Yellowknife, before our mother had died, Wynn and I would visit the town dump every Friday afternoon. The dump was situated up over a hill behind our house and we would climb the hill, survey the dump from the summit and then wend our way down a crooked trail flanked by multitudes of rose bushes. Their scent was the first to assail our noses as we walked along the trail. Sweet, flowery. No match for the unrelenting stench of rot that followed.

"Remember when we used to go to the dump?" I asked Wynn.

"Yeah," she said. "Do you think we should look into some of the garbage cans?"

"No. We don't have time."

The orphanage bell rang, signalling that play time was over. Without hesitation we ran. Instead of going back into the yard the way we had come, we opened the gate on the opposite side of the garage and ran into the yard. The second bell rang. That meant trouble. It was Sunday, and although I knew I had no chance to attend the Sunday night movie, I didn't want Wynn to miss it because of me. It was the second part of *The Shaggy Dog*, and I wanted Wynn to see it so she could tell me what happened.

I entered the yard first and started to run through the tilled dirt in the new garden area. I stopped midway through, turned around, and beckoned Wynn to follow me. Wynn stood where she was, her mouth open in horror. She was staring at my feet. I looked down. Slowly but surely I was sinking into the wet muck, the cold dirt seeped up around my legs like glue. I tried to lift one of my legs but it was cemented to the spot. I tried to lift my other leg but lost my balance and fell forward into the muck.

Wynn was crying. She had taken several steps into the garden and stood ankle deep in mud. She started to wail as she lifted her arm and pointed. From the corner of my eye I could see the matron and her helper running toward us. I tried to tell them that the whole mess was my fault but my mouth was full of mud. They stopped, looked at me, and inexplicably fell into each other's arms and howled in laughter.

No punishment was meted out to either Wynn or me for our flagrant disregard of the rules. Wynn went to the movies. I stayed in the dorm. I knew it was only a matter of time before I had to pay for my sins and I was racked with guilt for months afterward thinking we had been kicked out of the orphanage because of me. The orphanage van took us to the airport the next day and we were all shipped back to Yellowknife. I thought it was so we could be together, but, instead, we ended up separated. Forever.

Several families in Yellowknife wanted to adopt us, but separately. Final details were being worked out, and until everything was settled, we lived with a woman named Mrs. Quesnel. Mrs. Quesnel was an admirable woman, we were told, who "took in" children in need. Looking back on her in my adult life, I wondered what extreme punishment would be delivered to her by her God, or conversely, what rewards would be heaped on her by Satan, for her treatment of each child that passed through her care.

One by one we went to the people who claimed us. I was the last to pack my little brown suitcase and go to my new home. Several weeks after unpacking my suitcase and putting it in the closet in a room I shared with a new teenaged sister named Janice, I wished I could pack it back up and carry it out again. One night I was awakened by a blast of light as the bedroom door was thrown open. The door banged against the wall. Yelling from the kitchen, which the bedroom opened onto, assaulted my ears, and through my sleep-hazed eyes I saw a huge figure framed in the doorway. I saw Marie, in a frenzy, pacing the kitchen. Her hair was wild and she clutched her housecoat tightly around her throat with both hands.

"Grab her. Get her. Grab the whore! The slut! Get her, get her!"

I thought I was the one about to be attacked. I screamed and scrambled to the corner of the bed, trying to hide under the blanket. I stuffed the blanket into my mouth and screamed through it. I shrank against the wall, trying to make myself as invisible as possible, desperate for an avenue of escape. There was none. I closed my eyes to shut out what was to come. But the figure strode past my bed. I saw the figure heave Janice out of her bed and throw her on to the kitchen floor.

I remember Janice's gasp and the whack of her wrist against the door frame as she tried to get hold of something. I heard the scratch of her nails on the door as she was pulled out of the room. I saw her holding onto a kitchen chair. Seconds later the belt came thwacking down again and again and again on her head and shoulders and legs. Marie, in a seething, feverish rage, pranced and screamed, egging the figure on.

After the beating, Janice crept into bed. I listened to her sobs from across the room, at first wrenching, gulping, and then slowly subsiding into a fitful sleep. I lay against the wall, and was awake when the black of night lifted to grey and then faded into the first streams of pale yellow from the rising sun coming in through the tiny window above Janice's head.

Being careful not to wake Janice, who slept on top of her covers, I went to the closet, took out my suitcase and carried it to my bed. I quickly shed my flannel pajamas on the floor and took out my clothes from the orphanage. I dressed quickly and looked for my shoes. I noted with some surprise that they were my own shoes, the ones I had worn to the orphanage. Although battered they still had a lot of wear in them. My mother had bought them for me, half a size too big, so I could grow into them.

I planned to pack my suitcase and sneak out of the house before anyone awoke. I would go to Auntie Marilyn's, or Denise's in the old town. I was sure one of them would hide me. My hand was on the door when Marie stopped me. What could I do? She pleaded. With tears. With promises. Emotional blackmail. And I fell for it. I stayed. And I lived with the coward who couldn't walk out the door. So, it was my fault. Wasn't it?

I stayed in my room, alone, for most of that day, staring at my shoes. They were all I had left from my former life. What had happened to everything else?

I had no memory of things being packed up, divided, sold; things from the first six years of my life, things that connected me to a time, a place, and a home. I remembered the house and the yard. I committed them to memory. But when, in my adopted life, my mind's eye needed a refreshed visual of the actual residence and property, I would contrive to pass it by, and I could never understand why it looked so small, grubby and unkempt. The tar paper on the front of the house flapped in the wind. Weeds overran the drive where my father used to park his truck. I would walk up the back alley and search for the place where I would play ball against the house. The siding was faded and broken. There was no fence, and skinny, cowering dogs paced slowly back and forth, watching me as I walked by.

I would remember the long narrow kitchen with a wood box near the door. The stove, kitchen counter and cupboards and a window above the sink lined the wall on the left. A long wall on the right featured openings at each end that led to bedrooms. A kitchen table at the end of the room sat under a window that overlooked the old town. If I stood on a kitchen chair, I could see a bit of the Yellowknife bay, down past the old car junkyard and a mile or two of dwarf spruce that was interspersed with small wooden huts dotting the way to the water.

My father fished the bay for plentiful herring. Galvanized washtub after galvanized washtub filled with wiggling fish often crowded the kitchen, slopping fishy water on the floor during the herring run. I remember walking into the kitchen once and being grabbed from behind by my father. He turned me upside down and threatened to plunge me head first into one of the tubs. I shrieked and clawed frantically at the empty air. And then he picked me up and threw me into the air. The warm solid jolt as I landed in his bristly arms was immensely satisfying.

I had things that I packed away in a small worn cardboard box that said Eddy Matches™ in faded red and blue letters on the side, which I packed with me as my family and I moved through our lives together. And when cleaning the basement or attic many years later, married and with children of my own, I would open the box and marvel, at first, why I had hauled these trivial and slowly disintegrating objects to this place and time. But upon closer perusal, when I should have been crumpling and tossing, and dusting and sweeping, I would be pulled back to the baggy box of so long ago, and at first quickly, and then more slowly, and then perhaps even lovingly, I would sit down and sort through the box and smile and gently fold everything up again, and tape the box shut again, with a new strip of tuck tape, and place it on the shelf, until it needed to be looked at again. And I would remember that these were the memories I was saving to pass on to my own beloved children.

There was no living room in our home. It had been given up to beds for kids. My parents had their own bedroom. In one corner there was a bench built into the wall with sides that went right up to the ceiling. The seat of the bench could be lifted up, and several feet above the bench was a bar where my mother had hung clothes. If one of us was sick and needed special attention, we were put to bed on the bench where my mother could keep an eye on us.

During one of my illnesses, sweating through the intense discomfort of a high fever, I was vaguely aware of my mother getting out of bed and going to the kitchen. When she came back she pressed a crinkly package into my hand. I lay on the bench in the dark, the fever pulsing through me and brought the package up to my face and squeezed. Air trapped in the small cellophane package gave way with a pop and I smelled chicken bones, my favourite candy. I listened to my mother breathing peacefully, my father snoring slightly, as I lay in the dark crunching, and wondering if my feet had ever been so itchy.

I had nothing left from my childhood: no christening gowns or hand knitted baby socks with different coloured heel and toes; no favourite pair of red corduroy pants, reversible, worn so thin they are smooth and the cord can only be felt along the double-sided seams; no first card to Mother on Mother's Day, a squashed crepe paper flower on the green construction paper stem; no things to show who I had been.

I knew now that was my problem. I never felt I belonged anywhere. I didn't fit in with anyone else. I was different from anyone else who had a history, a heritage. Perhaps that was why I liked old things. Antiques. Victrolas with whittled down matchsticks for needles, matchsticks that created that far away wavering sound that can only come from thick 78s turning on the turntable. I loved cranking the handle on the side and hearing the whir and click before the record began to play.

I sought out wooden hand-carved silent butlers with velvet padded sweeps and inkwells with delicately etched silver plated covers, stained glass baby bottles with nursery rhymes, a picture of Jack and Jill, tumbling down the hill, in clear glass, cut glass cruets with sharp, pointed, solid glass stoppers that scraped as they slid into place. It was history. These things had belonged somewhere and meant something, in someone else's past. Not mine. But when I picked up an object like a worn brass plant pot with roaring lion mouths anchoring the handle to the pot, when I ran my hands over the smooth surface and felt its dips and scars, I could imagine that I knew the journey it had taken to come to be in my hand, and I could set whatever it was that I had bought on the windowsill in the kitchen or on the tea trolley in the hall, where I could look at it often and imagine that I knew where it came from.

When I received a cheque in the mail on my nineteenth birthday for nine hundred dollars from my mother's estate, I saved it. I wanted to buy something I could keep as a sort of remembrance of my mother. Gord wanted me to spend the money on rent, or food or tuition. But I refused, and the nine hundred dollars sat in our savings account for several years until one day at a country auction sale, I saw an antique hallstand that I bid on and got for nine hundred dollars. It was light oak with a small bevelled glass mirror in the middle of the back. There was a glove box with a lid that opened halfway down the stand, and on either of that were openings for umbrellas or canes. Two black metal trays at each were designed to catch the rain from the umbrellas. Panels of wood on the sides of the mirror had been cut out in several S-shaped designs, giving the hallstand oriental overtones. Rooting around in a box of old lace at an antique show at a mall, I found an old lace butterfly, which I framed on green velvet and hung next to the stand. These two things, the hallstand and the lace, I told myself, had been given to me by my mother.

CHAPTER 8

I was fiddling with Spiderman's crotch, trying to get the Velcro strips to line up so I could sew them in place, when the doorbell rang. It was nine in the morning, on Tuesday, October 26th. I had just sat down at the kitchen table sewing machine to try and finish Halloween costumes for the upcoming school parties on Friday. Stevie needed his Spiderman costume ready for Wednesday's Cub Scouts party. Clare varied between wanting to masquerade as a cowgirl, a princess or a bat. Gord had told her that a princess cowgirl bat sounded like just the ticket, and I think she was seriously considering it.

The doorbell rang again and I got up to answer it. I peeked through one of the frosted panes of glass at the top of the door and saw Doris, a neighbour from down the street, Doris was lonely, a retired widow with time to kill.

"Dear, are you there?" she called and knocked crisply three times.

"Hi. How's it going?" I asked as I opened the door.

"Here," she said and handed me a brown paper bag.

I took the bag and looked inside.

"Peanut brittle. Heavy on the brittle," Doris said. "Can I come in?"

"Sure." I held open the screen door and Doris heaved herself up the first big step with a laboured "oomph."

"What are you doing? Costumes?" she asked, pointing at the sewing machine.

"I'm trying to figure out how to take the bulge out of Spiderman's crotch."

"What?"

"Stevie's costume," I said as I opened the bag, gently broke a piece of candy and took a small piece to nibble on. I held the bag out to Doris and was refused with the shake of her head. "It bulges out in that certain area. Stevie refuses to wear it like that. He says it makes him look like he's hiding a baseball in his pants. Hardly. But I've got to fix it or he won't wear it. Tea?"

"Of course."

"Red Zinger™?"

"That's fine, dear," Doris answered.

"Good. Because that's all I have," I said, popping two tea bags into the small teapot I kept at the ready on the counter by the stove. "I want to go to that new tea shop on 99th Street. A store full of loose teas, apparently. Mix and match your own personal blends."

"Let me know when you're going and I'll tag along. I noticed you hadn't been out of the house for a few days, so I thought I'd better come over and see how things are. I thought maybe someone was deathly ill, unable to move, and I'd have to move in and nurse him or her back to health. That would be fun," Doris said. "At least I wouldn't have to sit at home all day making peanut brittle."

"No one is sick. Sorry. Stevie might be mental, as they call it these days, but other than that, we're about the same as usual."

"Stevie is so cute. I had a pair of leopard skin tights on the other day. I got them on sale at The Bay. Anyway, I thought I looked right spiffy. And I meet Stevie coming down the sidewalk. I model them for him and ask him what he thinks. He takes a look and then he says, "You look great, sort of like a lizard."

"Very complimentary. Let's go into the living room and have our tea. I've put everything we'll need on this tray."

"Well, it gave me a laugh. So much for my new image."

"Stevie is a real charmer. Gets it from his dad.

"So," Doris said, stirring some sugar into her tea and looking meaningfully at me. "Everything okay?"

"Of course. Why do you ask?"

"Hand me some peanut brittle."

I handed her the bag. She selected a piece with lots of peanuts. Three silver bracelets jingled on her right arm and against the coffee table as she set the dish down again. The bracelets were a standard fixture on Doris's arm. She never took them off, even in the shower, she had confided. They were a present from her husband in the first heady days of a passionate courtship. Sex, sex, sex, she had said, and then, more importantly, love. Doris said she considered the bracelets similar to a ring, and the jingling reminded her of him and she liked to think he was always near her.

"Is this peanut brittle any good?" she asked.

"It's very edible."

"Okay. Good. I'll bring over the other fourteen sheets I have at home."

"You don't have to do that, Doris."

"I know I don't have to. I want to."

Doris said the same words two years earlier when, shortly after Marie's funeral, she had knocked on the door with a paper plate wrapped in plastic wrap, and said, when I opened the door, "I heard about your mother from the old ladies across the street and I brought you some peanut brittle. Can I come in?" She had asked that same question the same way, and inched her way into the front hall. "Sorry about your mother. Here." And she'd handed me the plate.

I said what one says when one doesn't really know what to say. I had said thank you and that she shouldn't have gone to the trouble. Doris had replied that she knew she didn't have to and that she wanted to do something. For the next two hours, she managed to consume one third of the peanut brittle along with several cups of tea.

Doris moved to the neighbourhood and into a house her late husband had bought. He owned six houses scattered around the city that Doris had sold off one by one after his death. The one in which she now lived was a two bedroom bungalow with a small yard.

She sat at the end of the sofa now, her hands crossed on her lap. Her short round body was encased in a designer sweat suit and her short grey hair was tucked neatly behind her ears. Some of her outfits overstepped the boundary of good taste, but, like all eccentrics, she neither knew nor cared. The kids thought she was weird, and Gord was overly friendly to her, a sure sign she intimidated him. To me she was just Doris.

"Now don't think I'm a nut," she said.

"Too late," I replied as I took a piece of brittle from the bag.

"No really," she said. "I've got two favours to ask of you."

"No you can't come live with us, Doris."

"No, really dear. I have to ask you a favour. One for now and one for in about a month." She paused. "But I don't want you to think I'm loony."

"What would you be afraid of asking me?"

"You'll think I'm silly."

"I think you're silly that you think I'll think you're silly, if you know what I mean. What is it?"

"Well, the first favour . . . "

"Yes?"

"Can I come over on Halloween and help you give out candy? Maybe go out with you or Gord and the kids? I love Halloween, but it's boring all by myself."

"Sure. It will be a madhouse but you're welcome to join in. Come for supper. Help clean up after. Wash my floors. Swiffer my blinds."

"Great. Are you sure Gord won't mind?"

"No. He'll love it."

"He always looks at me like he thinks I'm crazy."

"He's afraid of you."

"Really? I wonder why?"

"I'm just kidding. Come over. It will be fun. Okay, now that that's settled. What is your second favour? I know, you have two tickets to something or other and you want me to go. Who is it? Julio Iglesias?"

"Good lord no."

"Billy Ray Cyrus?"

"Who's he? No. No. It's a seminar. A New Age seminar. You know. Getting in touch with our higher selves, that sort of thing."

"Hmm. Do we have to sit on the floor with our legs crossed and say 'om'?"

"I'm not sure. They say to wear something comfortable."

"Doris, wear something comfortable means writhing around on the floor pretending we're in a parallel universe."

"Come with me, please," Doris pleaded. "Because if it's absolutely awful I won't have the nerve to get off the floor and crawl out. If you're with me, I know you'll just get up and go. Please?"

"When is it?"

"November 10th."

"Well. If I can get a babysitter, I'll go with you."

"Great. Now. What are you going to be for Halloween?"

"Oh, probably a harried mother, traipsing around after her children as they go from house to house taking candy from strangers. If this happened on any other night of the year, we'd be calling the police."

"You have to dress up. I am. I always do."

"What are you going to be?" I asked her.

"That's my secret. What are *you* going to be?"

Halloween was a great success. Doris arrived promptly at five o'clock bearing special treat bags for the kids and a six-pack of Kokanee beer.

"The treats are for the kids and the beer is for us," she said, huffing into the kitchen with her load. "Two beers each and they are already ice cold. I think I'll have my two right now, one for each hand."

"Hey, no sneaking candy," I said to Clare who was already chewing something which required a lot of masticating.

"Brafraw wawa ter," Clare mumbled through the goo in her mouth.

"Cherry blasters!" Stevie yelled, digging into his treat bag.

"Hi Doris. Let me take your coat," Gord said, coming into the kitchen.

"For the unveiling?" she asked, giving Gord a seductive

smile.

"Huh?" Gord looked puzzled.

I told him Doris had dressed up.

"What did you dress up as?" Gord asked her.

In answer, Doris unbuttoned her coat, took it off and tossed it to him. She threw her arms out and posed. Bolts of lightening did a double zigzag down her chest on a vivid red long-sleeved T-shirt, and the stars and stripes on the short shorts she wore arched out over plump legs in black stockings. A white cape with silver stars on it hung down her back.

"Wonder Woman!" Stevie shouted. "That's awesome, Doris."

"I know I look like a bee in drag," she said. "But I've always wanted to be Wonder Woman™. Believe me this costume's not as comfortable as it looks."

"It doesn't look comfortable at all, Doris," I said, laughing.

"And it's only for a couple of hours. Thank God," Doris laughed. "And where is your costume?"

"You're going to dress up, Mom?" Stevie asked.

"I was thinking about it," I said.

I had gone so far as to try on a black form-fitting bodysuit that I had bought on sale some time back and had never worn. The elastic in the material was obviously the same stuff used to make bungee cords because it cinched me in so tight and accented the natural curves of my body so artfully that, after several turns surveying myself in the mirror, I came to the conclusion that I really didn't look that bad. I put a thick, fake diamond studded wristband around my neck as a choker. I don't know where it came from but it complemented my costume well. I decided to be a black cat. I made a tail and ears from an old bathrobe belt. I pinned the ears on to a black headband of Clare's. I caught a glimpse of myself in the mirror in our bedroom, wondered why I was wasting the time and quit.

The doorbell rang.

"Pizza!" Stevie yelled.

"Go. Get dressed," Gord said, as he headed for the front door.

"Yah, Mom!" Clare shouted. "Go get dressed!"

"I'll help Gord," Doris said. "You promised."

"I did not promise, Doris, but since everyone will not be appeased until I do, I might as well."

I plodded upstairs, paused at the top, and then sighed and went into the bedroom to transform myself into a cat. When I came back down, I stood at the bottom of the stairs, sucked my stomach in, arched my back, took a breath and breathed out a throaty growl. As if on cue, everyone stopped mid-action, turned, and looked at me. A stunned silence followed.

"Dear God!" Gord said, his jaw slack. His eyes roved down my body, bulging out at each contrived curve. They made their way back to my face where he, catching himself in mid-ogle, closed his mouth, swallowed, grinned and said, "Mom's a cat."

"Grrooowwwll," I said, in what I hoped was a seductive meow.

"Mommmm! Ewwwww! Grooosss!" was the united reaction of the kids.

Doris laughed. "See what I mean about the costume? And just think, we only have to hold our stomachs in for another two hours."

Gord stayed home to hand out candy while Doris and I trailed behind the energetic two that kept exhorting us to hurry up. Later, after Doris had limped home, Gord and I sorted candy at the kitchen table. I caught him looking at me strangely.

"What?" I asked, tossing an open roll of pink and blue rockets, one hundred percent sugar, into a garbage bag on the floor.

"You look quite fetching tonight," he said, opening his mouth and popping a caramel in.

"Oh." I was surprised. It had been a long time since Gord had flirted with me, casually, the frank sexual banter that couples engage in, effortlessly, during daily life together, creating a loosely woven plait of continued intimacy that was realized physically during spontaneous night-time passions. I had been too involved with what had been coursing through my head. It always seemed to be that way. My past wrapped around me like armour. It shielded me from the present. Prevented me from living in the present. That's where I lived my life, and it was a shock to be jerked into what was happening in the present.

I cracked a peanut and ate it. "I felt a little silly, but I didn't want Doris to feel bad, you know? She went to all that trouble."

"I'd like to see you arch your back in that thing," he said as he popped another caramel into his mouth.

I laughed. "I think you've been eating too much sugar."

"I could attach a chain to your collar and lead you around the bedroom." He fluttered his eyebrows at me, Groucho Marx style.

"You are being rude, young man," I said, smiling in spite of myself.

"You think that's rude?" he asked, getting up from the table. Not knowing what he had planned, I got up and started backing out of the room. He caught me by my waist and pushed me up against the wall. He flicked out the kitchen light and kissed me long and slow and deep.

I wasn't much of a kisser. I never knew if what I was doing was correct. But this was nice. It was a promising appetizer to some yet unplanned full course dinner. And I found I was feeling quite peckish.

"I could help you out of your costume," he whispered in my ear.

"I thought you wanted to watch Sport Line at eleven," I whispered back.

"Oh yeah," he said, coming back to reality and the things in life that really mattered. The centre of his palms lightly massaged my breasts, causing my nipples to harden and stand erect. "I could tape it, and watch it after."

"After what?" I asked, running my hands down his back, around his hips and up his chest.

"After I do unmentionable things to several parts of your body that would never be conversationally correct for the Sunday dinner table."

"Oh," I said.

It was with uninhibited eagerness that we explored each other that night. I welcomed the caress that ran from my thigh to the softest and most intimate of spots between tender folds that swelled in anticipation of delights to come. I responded unabashedly, seeking to give the same sensual pleasure that I was able to receive so fully. Our bodies rose and fell in heightened excitement, responding to the urgent need we both felt.

Later, I lay on my back in bed. Gord had quickly kissed me, thrown on his pajamas, and tiptoed downstairs to catch the last half of Sport Line, which he had forgotten to tape. I lay between the cozy folds of the messed-up quilt. I imagined the bed was a canvas and the quilt was thick, deliberate strokes of colourful paint that had been swathed by a robust Welshman, long fingers clutching an oversized brush, and immortalizing a satiated woman, me, within the curves.

"Who was that tonight?" Gord asked, as he crawled back into bed and snuggled up to my side, rearranging the lines of my imaginary painting to now include two nude figures, straining, but unable to reach each other, separated forever by parallel lines of paint.

"What do you mean?"

"Well, you were quite enthusiastic, for one thing."

"Halloween."

"What?"

"Halloween releases the inner you striving to get out. One day a year we, for some reason, give ourselves permission to be who we want to be. That's why you see so many vampires and Freddy Krueger's around."

"Oh really, miss pop psychology," Gord said, his voice muffled in the quilt. "Why can't you just be like that all the time?"

"Good question."

I was glad Gord hadn't said he loved me. I would have had a hard time responding to that. "I love you too" was the automatic response, and I had said it more times than I could remember. I didn't know how Gord could love me. I was always so aloof. I always held back any emotion. I had reasoned that, if I found out later that what Gord was telling me were lies, it wouldn't matter so much because I hadn't laid all of my emotions on the line.

"Gord?"

The room was silent. Gord was asleep. He was breathing rhythmically, his arm a dead weight on my waist. I heard a fly buzz suddenly in the light fixture. It had gotten caught between the glass and the ceiling and was whipping itself up and down, flagellating frenziedly in the confines of its little cell. With a *bzzzipp* it shot free and zoomed into a wall. I heard it drop with a *plip* on the floor.

"There's a bug in here," I said.

His body twitched a bit as he fell into a deep sleep, and there was no response to the nudge I gave his shoulder or the poke in the leg with my toe.

I, on the other hand, could lay awake for hours. I felt lucky if I got five good nights of sleep a month. I read, tossed, turned, tried creating erotic fantasies about Eric Clapton, but nothing worked. I lay awake at night for weeks on end, the dark circles under my eyes rivalling the moon dog orbs of Billy Joel.

And when I was able to fall asleep, dreams of my past slipped through the cracks in the armour plating around my breastbone, like smoke from a burning building. Furtive. Deadly. Dreams were keeping me awake. Dreams of women with searching blue eyes and marble steps and glass doorknobs.

A thought about that glass knob had occurred to me a few days earlier. I was tidying Clare's dresser, and in my dusting, I picked up a small heart-shaped necklace. Seven tiny pink hearts swam lazily in the sparkly solution that was enclosed in a clear plastic heart-shaped container. The sun came out from behind a cloud at the precise moment that I picked it up, and the sparkles within the heart glinted brilliantly for a brief second, dazzling my eyes, making me blink. It came to me that the crystal knob was the key to my heart and that I must open the door so all the pieces that were scattered about could be knit together as they once had been so long ago. I pushed aside cynical thoughts that my musing was trite.

I heard the fly revive. It buzzed drunkenly on the hardwood floor. In the dark I heard it rise tentatively and hover over the bed. It zipped confidently across the room and thudded softly into the dresser.

I didn't want to think about the dreams or Clare's plastic heart necklace. It was just another cliché in a long list. Come out of the closet. Exorcise the past. It was either that or kill myself. And the idea of killing myself had faded. I was still depressed. More so than ever. But at this point I didn't have the energy to arrange my death. I would plan something when I felt more up to it.

My physical state was another matter, though. The numbness in my foot had spread to my knee. I was also numb, upon occasion, on the left side of my face. It felt like dental freezing, refusing to unfreeze. My skin was tender over various parts of my body and quite sensitive to heat and cold. I kept putting off going to the doctor because I was afraid of the diagnosis. I would have to do something about it soon.

In my meditation book, the author, who presumably practiced what she preached, and who, according to the back cover information, desired to pass on her knowledge in a "delightfully" readable book, was very explicit in explaining what true compassion was not. True compassion, according to her, was not the tears we shed at seeing the sad, dirty, fly-ridden faces of children staring bleakly up at a camera on television or a brief sentimental involvement in the lives of friends or neighbours grieving for some personal loss.

True compassion was the ability of a person to understand

why and how a distressful life situation occurred, and, because of further enlightened abilities, eliminate it.

The writer then went on to crush any budding hope that meditation on compassion would be fruitful. In her opinion, the most an ordinary human peon could hope for was an "attitude" of compassion because our own minds teemed with confusion and misconceptions. And yet she provided instructions on how to achieve a meditation on compassion. It seemed like a fairly simple concept. Words from the mouth of the Dalai Lama himself; "If you want others to be happy, practice loving compassion; if you yourself want to be happy, practice loving compassion."

This was easier said than done. It was all so confusing. The only clear cut case of my practicing compassion that I could bring to mind was Marie. I tried to use Marie's illness and subsequent death four years earlier and my attending to her during it as a case study. I didn't wish Marie ill but when I heard her case was terminal I felt no emotion at all. Cancer in her ovaries, which then metastasized through most of her organs and entered her brain rendering her unable to care for herself, and she had been placed in the palliative care ward, terminal unit, at the Grey Nuns Hospital. When I thought back on it I could never envision myself as a figure of compassion. I believed I was there so no one could say I shirked my duty and to ward off future ambushes of guilt.

Despite my aversion to hospitals I visited Marie every day. I hated hospitals and the odorous smell of medicines, the acrid stink of ammonia from floors that were continually being swabbed down by bored men in green uniforms; the unhealthy sweat of old men shuffling along corridors in cloth slippers and faded blue housecoats; the musty aroma of wet coats and boots, worn by friends and visiting loved ones. To me, hospitals felt like incredibly filthy places, the illusion of antiseptic sterility a superficial mask for the infections, the cancers, the tainted blood, the death and the dying that goes on regular as clockwork within its pastel cement walls.

Marie never knew who I was. That bothered me a lot. Here was a woman who had wreaked havoc on my life for thirty years and each time I visited her it was like she had never seen me before in her life. I was a complete stranger to her.

I wanted recognition. I wanted abject desolation from this pitiful human being, who was suffering so greatly the last weeks of her time on earth. Was she paying for the cruelties she had perpetrated upon me? I wanted a bended knee request for forgiveness in one of those few moments of lucidity. I wanted my pound, my ton of retribution. But, daily, she denied me this satisfaction. Why did I continue to visit her? She didn't know who I was, so why did I go?

"Because she was your mother," Gord had said.

"But I hated her. I hated the way she treated me."

"But she was still your mother."

I had screamed at him then that she was not my mother. I was furious and told Gord that we only have one mother. We have one mother who loves us before anyone else and, once she is gone, no one can take her place.

"My real mother would remember me," I had sobbed.

"Maybe not. This isn't the movies. This is real life. It doesn't matter how awful she treated you, Marie was your mother and that's why you keep going back. A lot of kids grow up in horrible situations, with real parents who neglect them, beat them, but you ask any of those kids where they would want to be, and they would say they wanted to be with their mothers."

I hated Gord for saying that Marie was my mother. For saying that I loved her. How did he know how I felt? I didn't love Marie. I just kept going back because she needed someone to be there. How could I just leave her? I could tend to her physical needs but that didn't necessarily mean I loved her.

It was especially irksome to see her pore over an old picture album. She could name every person in the album and recount some little tidbit of information about them except for me. One day she pointed to a picture of a woman on her wedding day, standing under a tree behind a small cloth-covered table on which sat a white, two-tiered wedding cake.

"I know that woman," she said.

"Yes you do," I agreed. I was busy mixing perm solution. The nurses in the palliative care unit had asked me to give Marie a perm to try and tame the scraggy mess that framed her face.

"Why won't she come see me?" she asked.

"Who?"

"Janice, the woman in the wedding photo."

It was a question that many people had asked. Earlier on in her illness, when she was lucid, Marie had called Janice and asked her to come and see her. Janice had promised to come but never did. I called her. She said Marie would be dead by the time she came. When I pressed her, she said she couldn't take time off her job as a night security guard.

Marie had examined the picture. "Don't know what it is I've done to her. I want to see her. I love her, she's my daughter."

Janice never saw Marie before she died. When her will was

read, she hired a lawyer and tried to sue the estate for her fair share, even though there was no opposition.

Janice's vindictive retaliation exacted for real or imagined hurts that happened so many years ago, against a weak and wasted woman who could not fight back or at least explain, was cowardly. What of her hurts against Marie? They could be even more obscene than what she now censured her for. Maybe that was it. Maybe she couldn't stand the thought of being forgiven when she herself refused to do so. She wasn't of that noble ilk. She wanted to hold on to her hurt. It was the only thing that allowed her to keep hating.

I was confused. Janice, by withholding, was doing what I wanted to do. Or was she? Janice wanted revenge. I wanted validation that the things that happened to me were real, that they had caused me pain, that Marie's participation in said things were the result of something beyond her control, her will. But what would that do? Would it make me loathe her as Janice did? Would my life suddenly become an emotional bed of roses after her confession? Would all be forgiven? Dimly, I saw that I could not force disclosure from Marie just as Marie could not force Janice to visit her before her death.

Marie died alone, minutes before my nightly visit. The nurse led me to Marie's room. I had never seen a dead body. The last time I'd seen Marie she was near death. She lay flat on her bed, with no pillow. The pale green hospital blanket was tucked up under her arms, and her hands lay folded on her breast. They were still. Her deep, gravelly breaths seemed to echo as if she were in a large, empty cavern. I stood looking at her inert form, listening to her phlegmy gasps. Her brow was furrowed. She had always said that she was afraid to die.

I didn't feel like crying. I felt nauseous. I wanted to be anywhere but at the foot of this dying woman's bed. I thought of Gord. I remembered envisioning myself standing in the middle of a frozen grain field, my arms stretched out like a scarecrow, flash freezing every inch of my skin, trying to expunge the repugnance of the moment, sealing my pores with ice, a temporary impenetrable barrier against inevitable encroaching death.

Back at home, the razor-edged picture of Marie lying on the hospital bed, seeping life, lost impact as my own nausea continued to sharpen in intensity and pain. My vision blurred. My blood felt as if it were boiling. I lay down on the bed in my cool dark bedroom as my skin was seared from the penetrating pierce of some torrid invisible heat. Water evaporated at the sight of me, shimmering.

I had no outward sign of illness. No fever. No sores. I had the pain, though, the numbing pain in my foot and arms, the left side of my face dead to the touch. It occurred to me that I was dying, emotionally, from the inside out and the pain in my limbs and face was the final degeneration of living tissue. I could no longer skim it from the surface and distribute it throughout my tissues. I was saturated. There was nowhere for the pain to go. Soon the numbness would spread, paralysing me to the point of death.

It was then that I saw the light, a pale yellow light in the corner of the room that grew larger as I gazed at it advancing toward me. Within the wavering circle a delicate fluttering caught my eye. Glowing hands reached for me. I was dying and the angels had come to take me. I reached out for them. I waited to be lifted into the white clouds that framed the circle.

But the hands passed through my physical body, reached, and held, reverently, my bruised and battered soul in soft eternal healing rays. I saw a little girl standing in the light. It was me. Could I ever be her again? I strained forward into the energy of the glow. My forehead pulsed a neon blue as I pleaded to be taken out of my dense, grounded body. Slowly, blinking eyelashes flecked with gold swayed back and forth. No. A hand pointed to a moving sidewalk and I saw myself being carried around an invisible bend.

I didn't need Marie to tell me I had been wronged. I saw that after her death. I don't know if I visited her when she was dying to satisfy proper social etiquette or because of a correct attitude of compassion, as the meditation book counselled. I recognized that I had never looked upon myself with an attitude of compassion. I had never delved into my own mind and dealt with my own misconceptions, thereby creating the possibility of freeing myself from my suffering, which then, supposedly, allowed happiness to be a part of my life. And in order to be happy, the Dalai Lama instructed, I needed to look upon myself with loving compassion. And for someone who had crept through life, travelling incognito, that was going to be tough.

CHAPTER 9

"Mom. Will certain parts of your body fall off if you touch them too much?" asked Stevie.

"What certain parts?" I asked.

"I don't know," he replied. "Oh never mind."

"Never mind, huh? Did something happen at school to make you ask about certain parts of your anatomy?"

"What's anatomy?"

"Your body, sweetie pie. And I ask again, young man, did something happen at school?"

"Well, my pants were tight."

"And?"

"And I was adjusting, you know, in my private area. Megan saw me and said my dink was going to fall off."

"And you believed her?"

"She said she had evidence."

"Megan has a penis in her cubby hole?"

"Mom! Eww. Megan's little brother plays with his penis all the time, and her mother told him if he didn't keep his hands off it, it would fall off."

"That's ridiculous."

"So it's not true?"

"I didn't say that."

"Mom!"

This enlightened repartee took place in a long line at Supersaver Food Mart, grocery cart overflowing, second to the till, five days after my strange transcendental night-time experience. Physically, I was fine. The nausea, the numbness in my face and body, the fever, real or imagined, had disappeared. I was exhausted, though, and drifted dully through the days. My spontaneous crying took an upswing and I still felt shamed at bursting into tears upon opening the door to the utility man, who merely wanted to check the gas meter in the basement.

The line was at a standstill. A loud Englishwoman in a vibrant purple sweatsuit, black leather cap, black stilettos, and a suitcase-sized matching black leather bag, was arguing about her bill. The cap, jammed sideways on her head, bobbed precariously as she vehemently shook her head. Twenty-three cents was the apparent overcharge. I was tempted to toss her a quarter. It was worth it to get the line going.

Crackers and curly noodles in an otherwise empty pantry had led to the excursion to the food store, Stevie in tow.

"Chocolate bar?" Stevie asked, showing me a Crunchie Bar beside his gap-toothed grin.

"That's a chocolate bar, all right," I said, tapping him on the nose with my finger.

"Mom!"

"That's my name. Don't wear it out."

"Please?"

"Are you going to help me put these groceries away when we get home or are you going to pull a disappearing act?"

"Disappear, unless I get the chocolate bar, then I will help," the master negotiator said.

"Deal!"

Happy, Stevie hopped up onto the adjoining counter and began swinging his feet. He examined the back of the Crunchie Bar, oblivious to me watching him. A fine spray of hair stood at attention on the crown of his head. His luminous azure eyes sparkled through long thick lashes. I love you, Stevie boy, I thought, and felt a lump in my throat. Tears welled. I looked down into the grocery cart to hide the impending flow. I saw fifteen cans of peaches, fourteen ounces each. What had spurred me on to such a hoard? Was I going to make something and had forgotten what? And then it came. A memory. A memory regarding peaches. And the tears came. I hated the memory. No. I hated remembering it.

Memories are a voyage into pain, I thought as I got a handkerchief out of my purse and blew my nose. When the memory surfaced unbidden from my memory banks I could no longer pretend it didn't exist or that it was someone else's memory. The only way to get rid of the pain was to remember. It was my memory, and I was responsible for it. Why would the pressing of my five-year-old finger into a nail on the doorframe of a now non-existent house be so indelibly engraved on my mind? Why could I so clearly see the snow, spinning off the roof and encircling our house? I am an unwilling captive to the memories in my mind, but they are there and I must deal with them, acknowledge them, if I am to survive. I surrendered to it and tried my best to recall every detail.

It was a bitterly cold day. It was so cold that Wynn and I were not allowed to go outside. Everyone was at school, and the afternoon stretched boringly into years in our spectacularly quiet home. I was standing at the window. The cool midday sun shone weakly through the glass, igniting the feathers of frost that snaked, leaf like, across the pane. Amber-coloured sparkles glistened softly. I breathed on the lacy edges of ice, instantly extinguishing the golden twinkling, the intricate embroidery, melting it. One small drop of water tried to tear its way down the glass but froze mid thought.

I looked out the window at the fir trees in our front yard. Weighted down with snow, they swayed laboriously in the zealous gusts of wind. Snow blew off the roof in irregular blasts and swept across the yard like a sheet whipping in the wind. Puffs of snow suddenly sprang up off the branches and twirled upward into nothing. As I stood there, the sun disappeared, and clouds rolled in. It began to snow lightly. Soon, though, as the blizzard gathered force, the snow began to pelt down and was worried into frenzy by the domineering wind. The streetlight at the end of the road clicked on. The sky was black, and I shivered as I heard the wind surround our house, seeking a way in.

I could hear my mother talking to herself and pacing in the kitchen and, taking my five-year-old curiosity with me, I tiptoed to the far kitchen door and peeked in. At that precise moment two of my cousins tramped in, the fur of their parkas hung with beads of frozen breath. They came to play after school on those days when their mother worked; unzipping coats, peeling off padded winter pants, kicking boots across the floor and thumping down cold crinkly plastic bags of homework, snaps of static from hair and dresses followed shivering bodies out the other kitchen door to the living room. Still my mother watched through the back door window until at last a crunching up the path signalled that Ben had arrived home.

Ben stamped his feet and shook his arms to warm himself up. His face was red, and the scarf he had wrapped around his head was matted with pellets of snow. My mother spoke to Ben worriedly. He listened and nodded. My mother hurried out of the room. Ben winked at me and smiled. My mother returned, carrying a heavy sweater. It was my dad's fishing sweater. My brother put it on under his coat.

"Hurry," my mother said, "before the office is closed. I just couldn't take the girls out on a day like today."

"It's okay, Mom.

"I really feel terrible about making you do this. Are you sure you're warm enough?"

"Mom!"

"Okay. Go straight there and straight back."

Ben ran out the door and was swallowed up by the black.

My mother shut the door against the glacial wind.

"Where did Ben go?" I asked

"What?" my mother turned and looked at me distractedly. She began pacing the kitchen floor, began to talk, more to herself than to me. "Ben went to pick up the welfare cheque. It was too cold to take you two uptown to get the cheque. My goodness, you would have frozen to death halfway there. I don't know if I could have pulled the sleigh through all that snow. But we have to have that cheque. We have no money. I hope he's okay. Maybe I shouldn't have had him go. I should have had him stay here and I should have gone. That's what I should have done. I didn't think of that."

I stayed in the doorway, not wanting to be under foot, and yet not able to leave her alone with her worry. I stood in the doorway, running my hands up and down the frame, bumping over the rough spots, pressing my fingers into the nails, starting to worry as well.

It seemed like forever before Ben returned. My mother had begun to get supper, banging pots, spilling water and then, in frustration, throwing a rag down onto the floor and mopping up the water savagely with her foot. The door burst open and in one flurry of snow and wind, there he stood.

"Did you get it?" my mother asked. She dropped the pot lid she had just picked up from the top of the stove. It clattered on the Formica counter, revolving around and around in ever shorter circles until it stopped with a clack.

"Yes," Ben said through lips swollen with cold.

My mother rushed over to him. "Here. Let me help you get those things off." She began unwrapping the scarf from his head and unzipping his coat. He stood there, too cold to move.

"Where is it?"

"Inside my jacket."

My mother reached inside to get it.

"Other side," he said.

My mother rummaged around in the inside pockets of Ben's coat. "It isn't here."

"It must be."

"I've checked twice. I can't find it. You check. You know where you put it."

"I put it right here." Ben felt the inside of his meagre jacket and came up empty. "I have it. I know I have it. I had it in my hand and I put it in this pocket."

My mother started to pace frantically, folding and unfolding her arms.

"You're sure you picked it up."

"Yes."

"Third floor of the Bentall Building."

"Yes. I've picked cheques up before, remember?"

"And?"

"And I picked it up and came home. I put it in my inside pocket because it's a deep pocket and I didn't want to lose it. I was worried about it and double checked. It was still in my pocket."

"Where is it then?" she yelled, becoming hysterical. "Where is the cheque? Show me the cheque!"

"I can't find it."

He took off his coat and checked all the pockets. He checked his jeans, his shirt pockets and the floor all around him.

"I don't know what happened. I had it. I swear."

And my mother, my gentle mother, exploded.

"You lost the cheque!" She screamed like a madwoman. "You lost the cheque!"

She grabbed my brother by the front of his shirt with both hands and shook him until he was unsteady on his feet. Then she threw him against the back door. The look of shock on his face was as pure and uncomprehending as my own. "How do you think we're going to live for the next two weeks?" She rasped, her voice an angry, frightened mix. She turned away from Ben. Her foot scraped against the pot lid on the floor. She bent over, picked it up and threw it against the window over the sink, breaking the bottom left pane.

"How am I going to buy food? How are we going to eat?" She whirled around and, finding herself in front of the kitchen table, swept the Melmac plates and cups that she had set for dinner, onto the floor. One plate landed on its rim and it rolled in a large arc to where I was standing, half in and half out of the kitchen, watching my mother's breakdown in horror. I scooped it up and held it tightly against my chest.

"I'll tell you what you are going to do. You are going to go right back out there and look for that cheque."

"But . . . where will I look?" Ben stammered.

"You'll look from here to the welfare office."

"But it's dark. And windy."

"You lost it. You find it. Go. And don't you dare come back until you find it. I don't care if you have to look all night. Don't you dare set foot in this house without that cheque. Go!"

Ben went. My mother slammed the door after him. She burst into tears and opened it almost immediately and yelled at him to come back. She ran out into the snow calling his name. I ran to the door and watched her peering into the night, leaning into the wind, her hair a writhing medusa of curls. When she came back she cursed him for going. She cursed herself for letting him go.

Dinner that night was subdued. Canned peaches that my mother banged down on the table and opened frenetically with a small hook can opener, poured into bowls, and set in front of us was the offering. She made toast, sniffling as she buttered the bread, and served it, uncut, in a heap in the middle of the table. We ate silently, the tapping of the spoons against our plastic bowls an uneasy Morse code.

Banished to bed the instant supper was done, I quickly changed and took up my post at the kitchen door in my pajamas. My mother was sitting at the kitchen table, her head in her hands, when the door flew open, and Ben, robot-like, walked stiffly into the room. He stood there, in the warmth of the kitchen, not moving. Then, very slowly, he pulled off his right mitt with his left hand and threw it on the floor. He flexed the fingers of his right hand several times before reaching over to rip off his left mitt with his right hand and wearily flung it to the floor. He began to unwrap the purple scarf from around his head, shaking off the frost that clung to it like dust. His eyebrows remained white and his beet red cheeks were traced with blue. As he shed clothing, my mother stood up slowly. She rushed over to him and, grabbing the end of the scarf, helped him unwind it the rest of the way.

"Well?" she asked. He unzipped his jacket, not speaking.

"Well?" she asked again, in a shrill voice.

"I couldn't find the cheque," he said, shrugging his shoulders slightly.

"You couldn't find the cheque?" she whispered.

"No."

And with a howl, she shoved him away, first slapping his face. He started to cry.

I wanted to run to him. I wanted to tell him our mother didn't mean it. I wanted to tell him her ruthless anger was borne of fear, of desperation, of isolation, of all the factors present in the life of a woman, widowed young, and left the sole provider for three small children. But what can a five-year-old do but crush the door frame between her fingers and hope for a miracle to break the evil spell that held my mother in its hypnotic grasp.

In the end, I didn't have to do anything because as soon as my mother slapped my brother, she broke down into tears. She grabbed him and hugged him. She apologized for the cruel words she had spoken. She asked for his forgiveness. She clung to him, unable to forgive herself. Ben, weary, wrapped his arms around my mother and they stood, clasped in each other's arms, crying. Unable to remain a bystander any longer, I ran to them and flung myself against their legs. My mother bent down to comfort me.

"Go get your jacket off and I'll get you some supper," she said. She broke away and looked at Ben. Ben stood awkwardly, an odd expression on his face.

"What's wrong?"

"Well," Ben said, smiling ruefully. "I don't know what to say"

"Don't worry. We'll figure something out. I'll call the welfare office on Monday and tell them what happened. They'll probably cancel the cheque and issue another one. I wish I'd thought of that in the first place.

"No. That's not it."

"Then what?"

"Don't get mad."

"I won't get mad. Tell me."

"Well. I did what you told me. I went out and looked for the cheque, even though I knew I probably wouldn't find it. I mean, it's pitch black out there. There's a hundred mile an hour wind and there's a blizzard too. So, how am I ever going to find the cheque, I'm wondering?"

"I am so sorry. I cannot believe I sent you out in this." My mother started to cry.

"It's okay. Don't cry." Ben said. "I went uptown and I looked all over the place. I mean, where do you start to look? I looked on the road, the sidewalks, by trees, in the doorways of the post office, the drugstore, the pool hall. It seemed so useless. And I was frozen. I couldn't believe how frozen I was. My thighs felt like blocks of wood. And I couldn't even open my mouth it was so stiff. It was useless. So on the way home I tried to retrace my steps. You know, think about what I had done every second after I picked up the cheque at the Bentall Building. And before I knew it, I was standing outside looking at the porch. Then it hit me. Just before I came into the house, the first time, I unzipped my jacket and checked to make sure the cheque was still in my pocket. I had it. I had it in my hand. I put it back into my jacket pocket and zipped up. But you know, as I was putting it back into my coat, a great big gust of wind blew some snow off the roof right on top of me and I couldn't see for a second or two. I shook off the snow and came into the house. Then, when I went to get the cheque for you, it wasn't there. I couldn't understand it. I felt awful. How could I be so stupid?" He shook his head.

"You must hate me," my mother said. "I've got to do something. I can't just stand here. I'm going to get you some peaches and toast." She went over to the toaster put in two pieces of bread and popped the handle down. She began gathering the bowls from the table, carrying them to the sink. She got a can of peaches from the cupboard to the right of the sink and then sank down onto a kitchen chair and burst into tears.

"Don't cry, Mom," Ben said. He walked to the table and pulled a chair out and sat down. I crept to the counter where the toaster was set up and put my hand over the top to feel the heat on my hand as I listened.

"It was weird. I had the cheque right up to that very minute. I retraced my steps to our back door. I was afraid to come in the house. While I was standing there, I looked up to the side of the house right by the corner. You know how the snow always blows into that corner and sticks there? Well, a whole clump of snow had blown into the corner and it kind of arched out over the back door. I was trying to think of what I could say to you and looking up into the corner at the same time when I noticed something sharp sticking out of the snow. All the other snow was smooth but there was this one sharp thing sticking out of the snow."

The toast popped up.

"Oh my God," my mother said.

"So I reached up and picked at it. I got hold of the corner and yanked. And it was the cheque."

"You found the cheque?"

"Yes."

"You found the cheque? Why didn't you say so? Why didn't you tell me the instant you stepped through the door?"

"I was going to. But then it hit me as I was taking my scarf off, that I should play a little joke on you."

"What?"

"Yeah, well you seemed so upset that I had lost it in the first place that I thought I'd say I couldn't find it and then surprise you by telling you I'd found it after all. I thought you'd think it was funny."

My mother sat at the table, turning a can of peaches over and over in her hands.

"I guess I should have told you right away, huh?"

Ben got up, went over to his jacket, picked it up, reached into his outside pocket and slid out the cheque. He walked back to the kitchen table, sat down in his chair and handed the cheque to my mother. "I found the cheque."

I don't know what happened after that. I remember the cheque sat on the counter, crumpled and water stained for several days, which I thought was pretty strange considering all the fuss my mother had made about it in the first place.

"Mom!"

Startled, I snapped out of my reverie. Stevie was looking at me, with worry on his face. I looked at the cashier who was staring at me, her mouth open. The Englishwoman was packing bananas and carrots and celery into a roomy, tan-coloured canvas tote bag as she watched me curiously.

"Are you crying, Mom?" Stevie asked.

"Crying? Why would I be crying?" I said, sniffling and patting my cheeks with my hanky. Damn. I looked behind me and saw a woman in the Hawaiian dress unloading my groceries on to the conveyer belt with exaggerated gentleness.

"But what about the tears?" Stevie persisted.

"Tears? These tears are a because of my allergies," I improvised. "I'm having a bad allergy day." I turned to the woman unloading my groceries. "Thank you. I'm sorry I've been holding things up."

"That's okay, honey," the woman said, keeping her distance. "I know all about allergies, how they can affect people in weird ways."

"Thanks again," I said and quickly unloaded the rest of the groceries from the shopping cart.

"Bags?" the cashier asked.

"I've got bags. Thanks," I said trying to look upbeat and normal.

"Why were you crying?" Stevie asked as we drove home.

"I wasn't crying," I said, trying to decide whether or not to shoot the yellow light or lurch to a stop and catapult the groceries out of their carefully packed plastic bags. At the last second I erred on the side of safety and jammed on the brakes. The groceries clunked and rolled out of the bags.

"Think anything broke?" Stevie asked.

"Hope not. Remember when those four bottles of spaghetti broke and Dad grabbed them out of the trunk?" I asked.

"And all the spaghetti sauce ran down his leg. He was pretty mad," Stevie laughed.

Sitting at the light, I glanced at Stevie. He was looking out the window, his hands linked together on his lap, his thumbs tapping out the rhythm of a tune playing in his head.

"Sometimes I feel sad. So I cry," I said. Stevie remained silent, his thumbs stilled by my voice. "You know me," I continued. "I cry at cheese commercials."

Stevie turned his head and looked at me. "Why do you cry at cheese commercials?"

"Hmm," I said. "I've often asked myself the very same question. For one, violin music, which is played during the commercial, tends to bring out the emotion in a person. Every commercial tells a story while it's advertising a product. The announcer in the cheese commercial talks about how the kid is going to grow up and leave home in about twenty years after he's eaten all his cheese, and I think about how you kids are growing up and eating cheese and how, in about twenty years, after you've eaten all your cheese, that you will be leaving home, and it makes me cry."

"I don't even eat cheese," Stevie said.

"It's a ploy, a strategy. The producers want to appeal to our emotions, to hit a nerve that will evoke a favourable response to their product. The commercial is aimed at mothers who naturally want to feed their children the right foods. So they engineer a schmaltzy sound track with a sappy story that they hope will tug at the heart strings of mothers, who will then rush out to buy thousands of dollars of cheese."

"Can I eat my Crunchie Bar™ now?"

"Did you understand what I said about the cheese commercial?"

"Sort of."

"What do you think I meant?" I asked.

"Uhhh. People cry about things that are important to them."

"Good answer," I said, as I slowed down for jaywalkers, two elderly women, waving gloved hands at the bus they wanted to catch, to stop for them. "Good answer."

Gord berated me for my grocery store breakdown later that evening as he sat at the kitchen table rotating the wheels on Stevie's roller blades. I stood by the stove rolling balls of ginger-flavoured cookie dough in cinnamon sugar, placing them on a cookie tray and flattening them with a fork.

"Stevie tells me you were crying today at the supermarket," he said.

Damn, I thought, as I slid the first batch of cookies into the oven. I quickly glanced at him. His lips were pursed and his ears twitched as he ground his teeth. His eyes had begun to widen and flicker a dull orange. This was not a good sign. Gord was "morphing" into lawyer mode, and our conversation from this point on would proceed as if I were a particularly scurrilous witness for the prosecution.

"What happened?" he asked.

"I was thinking about something that happened to me when I was a little girl, and what can I say, it made me cry," I said. How was he going to rip that statement apart?

"That's kind of a heavy thing to lay on a nine-year-old," he said in his opening statement.

"I know. I didn't plan it. It just happened," I said, watching his face for a sign of the direction his interrogation might take.

"He was very upset. He said you just stood there with tears running down your cheeks. God. What is your problem? Couldn't you wait until you got home and put the groceries away and maybe make supper before you took time out of your busy day to run to the bathroom, lock yourself in, and indulge yourself in a mini-breakdown?" Gord carefully put the skate down on the table, sighed heavily, and looked at me.

I looked at the roller blades that Gord had placed on the kitchen table. The screws that held the wheels to the roller on the bottom of the roller blade boot rested gently on the highly polished antique oak trestle table that I had bought with money given to us as a wedding present by Gord's Tuesday night hockey buddies. Any sudden movement in anger or frustration by Gord as a result of our conversation would surely produce deep scratches in the wood. I was tempted to ask him to remove the skate from the table, but not being one hundred per cent sure that he would not drag the blades across the wood in spite as he removed it, I remained silent. I looked at Gord. He was glaring at me. Ah. Direct confrontation.

"Well, as you know, and have pointed out many times, I have a myriad of problems. You never fail to point this fact out, your query most often preceded by a hearty, 'what is your problem?' So. Pick one of my problems. It's your choice today. Tell me. What is my problem? Why did I start crying in the middle of the grocery store today? I would love to know, because then my healing can begin." I picked up a handful of dough and squeezed it through my fingers until no dough remained, only my clenched palm.

"You want me to tell you what your problem is?" Gord laughed bitterly. "There are only so many hours in the day. Where should I begin? Oh. I know. Let's start with you being completely crazy. That's a pretty good start."

"Thank you, counsellor, for your compassion and understanding," I said, scraping up the dough I had squeezed on to the counter and rounding it into another dough ball. I began to pinch off pieces of dough, rolling each piece into a ball and setting it in a line, readying it for dipping into the cereal bowl of cinnamon and sugar.

"Go ahead. Ridicule me."

"And you, complimentary to a fault," I shot back.

"I just want to know what happened today, as cleanly and as simply as you can tell it."

Gord's daily emotional state rivalled that of a piece of romaine lettuce. This was actually a good attribute in a lawyer. Gord could dissect situations with the clinical precision of a doctor with a scalpel, with no messy emotional distractions, file each pertinent fact into its own mentally numbered sub section, and move on to the next item on his list. He was scrupulously fair as well, and this combination was lethally attractive to me when we first met. I always knew where I stood with Gord. His generally stolid nature was a comfort to me.

He was the polar opposite of Marie, whose mood swings kept me perpetually on edge, my pre-ulcer acting up daily. Unfortunately Gord expected the same methodical reasoning from me that he used. Feelings were not allowed to interfere in the serious business of his life. It exasperated him that I used high emotion as freely as he repressed it, to handle the tricky business of my own life.

During arguments where he felt compelled to defend his reserved character he would often comment that even though he did not wear his emotions on his sleeve, it did not mean that he had none. An incident from his childhood established the definite possibility that this was true. Gord's father, a strict disciplinarian whose word within the family was absolute, had taken Gord aside when an altercation in kindergarten with another boy had left Gord in tears. He had sat him down, and, in a way or manner that indelibly branded Gord's psyche, conveyed to Gord that any show of emotion, especially signs of weakness, was not allowed, because he would then set himself up as prey, a vulnerable victim. Never cry, his father had told him, and he had not.

I surveyed Gord. He needed everything to be cut and dried. Life is not like that, I would tell him.

"Why can't we ever discuss anything on a rational plane?" he said now.

"Rational!" I said gleefully, no longer angry. "I believe you made a remark questioning my sanity just a few short minutes ago." I grabbed a dish towel that was hanging on the handle of the oven door, opened the oven door, leaning back to miss the gust of hot air escaping, and slid the cookie sheet full of fragrant sugar-coated ginger snaps off the rack and on to the top of the stove. Selecting a spatula from the copper utensil pot beside the stove, I gently picked off each cookie and set it on the counter to cool.

Gord fumed. He loathed being called irrational more than

anything else. Granted, I had stretched the point, but it was worth it as payback for him calling me a nutter.

"I'm simply saying you should not lay your problems at the door of a nine-year-old. Get help."

"Stevie asked me why I was crying. What did you want me to say? Do you want me to lie? Do you want me to teach him that it's wrong to show emotion? Should we teach him that adults never feel sad? Maybe I should forbid him to cry. Tell him it's weak."

"I will not be drawn into a discussion about what a droid you think I am. Nothing you say will convince me that dissolving into tears like a helpless moron in the middle of some damn store, while your nine-year-old son looks on, is okay. Can't you even get through a trip to the grocery store without breaking down?"

"I'm not so unusual. What about your clients? Do you say the same thing to them? What about that twenty-year-old drug addict who broke down on the stand? Didn't she have to go and have a cigarette before she could take the stand again? What was her problem? Was she so far gone that she couldn't even get through a ten-minute testimony without breaking down?"

"Look. We're not talking about my work. We are talking about you."

"You were very bothered about that girl. Very compassionate to her plight. I've got it. Pretend I'm a client. Pretend I'm that girl who couldn't keep it together on the stand. But then you have something invested in her, don't you? She is a case you must win. She's worth spending time with. I'm just your wife."

"Is it sympathy that you want? Hey, you did a really good

job eliciting sympathy from Stevie. He feels really bad for you. Good work."

"That's not what I mean. I don't want sympathy. I want someone to listen to the words I speak and tell me what they mean and why they are so important to me. Why are you so angry?"

"Who the hell would want to hear what spews forth from your mouth?" Gord yelled, grabbing the roller blades and stomping out the door, banging it hard on purpose.

I sighed and picked up a cookie. I bit into a crisp and chewy morsel of ginger sweetness. The sugar melted in my mouth as I chewed. Why did I ever let myself think life would get better? I take one fun-filled roll in the hay, figuratively speaking, on Halloween eve and immediately transport that into the beginning of a new and improved life, complete with renewed hope. I hope too much, I thought. Things would be fine if only I could dispense with the hope.

CHAPTER 10

Mice. They were the bane of my life, seconded only by my mother-in-law. Actually, mice and my mother-in-law have a lot in common. They both come to stay at my home, uninvited, for indefinite periods of time, and it is only with ruthless persistence that I can get rid of them. At least with mice a stale piece of Gruyère in a hair trigger trap does the trick. Gruyère is not one of Gord's mother's favourite cheeses. The businesslike snap of the trap, my stereotypical feminine screech at the first sight of the irrevocably dead rodent, one or two shrieks while I pick up the trap with barbecue tongs, bag it up in plastic grocery bag, and speedily carry trap to the trash can in the alley is all external anguish. With my mother-in-law, the screaming is all done inside.

It was a bright November Monday morning two weeks after my crying spell at the supermarket. November had begun cold, with raw winds and seasonally low temperatures. The cat-o-nine-tail branches on the mammoth weeping willow tree in the neighbour's front yard whipped back and forth, an unfaltering allegretto in the uncompromising wind. The trend would continue, according to the pert young blonde woman with telltale black roots who forecast the weather on the local TV station.

Wind hustled up the short sleeves of my cotton pajama top and snuck up my yoga-style pajama bottoms when I stepped out the side door to get the morning paper. I shivered as I pulled the paper out of the mailbox and shut the door. A small article on the front page caught my eye. It was about a woman who had received a letter in the mail thirty years after it had been lost in transit, in that endless Bermuda triangle that is the postal system, until someone finally got tired of passing the buck, or the letter, and mailed it to the person to whom it had been sent.

Reading the article reminded me of a clutch of letters I kept in a box packed away under the stairs: letters and small treasures I had saved over the years. I was curious now to see whose names were written, faded, on the top left-hand corners of crumpled envelopes and descended to the basement and rummaged around under the stairs for a ratty cardboard box that had once held my iron.

As I pulled out boxes and rearranged hockey and lacrosse equipment, I heard the familiar scratching and scurrying and knew the mice had returned from their summer sojourn in the fields at the university farm near our neighbourhood.

When the family room had been built, the workers assured me the ceiling would be airtight, as per my request. I had explained that nothing could be worse than having mice clicking on the Styrofoam sound proofing for the rest of our lives, or at least for the duration of their lives, depending on whether or not they went for the stale Gruyère. Two days after the job was completed, and as we crunched popcorn and watched TV, we heard a scrape, a scratch, a plop and skitterings across the ceiling. The mice had arrived.

I first learned of my fear for mice at the "cottage," which was a group of buildings on the shores of a river in Northern Ontario, where Gord's entire family was commanded to vacation yearly and where three weeks of each summer was spent in the company of several hundred mothers-in-law and a mouse. Or was it the other way around? It was unpleasant, nevertheless, waiting for one or the other to leap out from behind a cupboard and squeak. Our cottage, which I christened the Mouse House, was alive with the scrapings and rustlings of warm mouse bodies nestled snugly in the insulation under the wooden shingles of the A-frame roof. Mice ran across the floor, dropped from the rafters, ate through stainless steel containers, and left mouse excrement wherever they roamed.

The first time I actually saw a mouse was the year I opened the trap door in the ceiling of the Mouse House to see how the loft had weathered the winter and came eye to eye with at least a hundred ants carrying away the rotted carcass of a dead mouse, its skin shrunken, fur matted, eyes sunken into the skull, dustballs clinging to its stiff, curling ears. I screamed, fell off the ladder, was laughed at by my husband and children. As I sat nursing sore buttocks, I learned something new about myself: I was petrified of mice.

I stopped digging for letters and listened. I could hear more than one mouse in the ceiling of the family room. There was a noise above me and a tinny sound farther down the wall where they scrambled over a pipe to get into the family room. I shivered at the thought of their cold, slimy paws.

Another noise caught my attention. It was the telephone ringing in the kitchen. I quickly stuffed the lacrosse bag, hockey shoulder pads and gloves, the punch bowl, a flimsy woven basket filled with ninja turtles and their various weapons, magazines and a topless shoebox stuffed to the brim with old AMA tour guidebooks back under the stairs. I sprinted up the stairs in time to hear the answering machine kick in. It was Doris. She sounded quite frantic, asking me to come over to her house as soon as possible.

I didn't phone her back. I was, in fact, surprised to hear her call. Doris had been a little less than thrilled with me after the New Age seminar we had attended the week before. I had forgotten our date and when she'd shown up at my door, in black stirrup pants and a brown and orange Navajo jacket, with flowing turquoise head scarf, ready to be enlightened, I'd scrambled to find a babysitter willing and able to sit for the evening.

I was frazzled, and my mood didn't improve, when I entered a dank community hall with squeaking hardwood floors, to find sitar music blasting out of static speakers, each sustained high-pitched chord piercingly rebounding off one of my front fillings. Naturally, there were no chairs, and Doris and I shared space on the scuffed floor with old hippies sporting scraggly beards, blanched faces, and long hair tied back with leather thongs and the "new" hippies, the grungers expressing their non-conformity with combat boots and plaid shirts. The upshot of the evening, as far as I could tell after two hours, were familiar themes: love is the answer, love conquers all, and, my personal favourite, human being, are instruments of love. We cruise around earth and care for, delight in, hold dear, are passionately attached to our fellow human beings.

It was not what I needed to hear. I listened to the saccharine testimonials of the animated audience and then voiced my own impressions. I tried to explain what life with Marie was like. When I asked the group how I was supposed to lovingly reconcile with my past, I was greeted with silence. The moderator thanked me for my input and announced an intermission. In the car, on the way home, Doris said I had embarrassed her.

I pulled out a chair and sat down at the kitchen table. I picked up a half-eaten slice of toast and took a bite. The toast was cold, and the jam had soaked into the bread. I debated whether or not to call Doris as I chewed through the gummy sweetness. She had been extremely angry at me for stating my opinions so loudly and cynically at the seminar. She didn't know my personal history. She didn't know Marie. And she didn't know how desperately I wanted Marie to be gone from my mind.

"I've heard rumours that you hate me," Marie would say. It was a game she would play. She would call me from my bedroom, and I knew at once from the raised eyebrow and the tapping of the foot that I had done something wrong. It was a pattern she established quite early on in our relationship, and after I was indoctrinated, I would merely wait, my face a blank.

"I've heard rumours that you hate me," she would repeat.

No response was required, and I gave none. I was silent and meditated on Marie's statement. Who would say such a thing? I found it to be true, though, after a while. I never told anyone. I kept it in the back of my mind. I felt guilty because all I wanted to do was escape. I wanted to step over the cement foundation of that house and be free. I could have done it at one time, back at the beginning, but not now. I had to stay because I had chosen to, sort of.

"What do you have to say to that?" she would ask.

What could I say? Yes? She would say I lied. No? I would know I lied.

"You're going to stand there until you tell me who you've been talking to. Who have you told you hate me?"

Relief. The silent treatment. Standing. I would stand in front of Marie, who stared out the window, smoking, glaring contemptibly at me now and again for effect. I would not move. I would not confess, not that I had anything to confess to. We were both silent. Time passed, beat out by the clock in the kitchen. Tick. Tick. Tick. Tick. Tick. One. Two. Three. Four. Five. Time, fluid, stretches deliberately into the present, hangs for one second and then two seconds, and then fades dully into the past. I notice a shaft of sunlight shining on the floor and follow the beam with my eye to the windowpane, on the other side of which, a mere one-eighth inch of glass away, is the entire world. I feel tired, tired of this routine. Standing. Waiting. Something is expected of me. I remember how sick it used to make me feel. Once, after a particularly long period of standing, I walked stiff legged to the bathroom and forcing my knees to bend, had held on to the cold bowl of the toilet and puked.

I would cast glances at Marie and see that she was enjoying herself. I would look at her profile, the lips parting to receive the tip of the filtered cigarette, the deep inhalation of the smoke, the violent exhalation through the nose, the one lifeless eye, the hair drawn back into a severe bun, fake, which she pinned on every Monday morning and combed out every Saturday night while she listened to the hockey game on the radio, Foster Hewitt's voice wavering through the tubes, and know she was in control.

I would compose my face into a study in indifference, my cheeks still, lips together and in a straight line, my eyes downcast so I see the tip of my nose. Round. Too round, I would think and let out a small sigh, controlled, so as not to attract attention.

I had quit trying to figure out what was expected of me. I realized that nothing was expected of me. I had been brought there, immobilized, to witness Marie's suffering. I was the witness she craved to see the horrible injustices she had to bear.

She nagged Curtis about how she was always alone. Not quite. I was there to see the real live martyr in our midst. Marie would have relished the thought of being tossed to the lions. Think of the audience! Unlike the martyrs of old, however, Marie brought on everything herself. Why did she rag on Curtis until she drove him away? Why was I forced into the silent waiting contest? At least Curtis could leave the room. I was stuck. If I tried to slip away she would call me back.

One time I'd stood so long that the beam of light from the window had gone, faded into the night. It made the room seem cooler, dimmer. I imagined millions of exquisitely thin layers of grey gauze hanging suspended between Marie and me, waving imperceptibly. Marie was softened by the gauze; her features blurred. The gauze slowly erased Marie from my vision, little by little with each minute undulating wave of the gauze, until I realized she had disappeared altogether and only the gauze remained, shimmering, silvery, smooth, woven in a distinct diamond pattern weave, an impenetrable barrier, sharp and final, that transformed into an enormous shiny metal fish that swam away into the dark.

It never occurred to me that these sessions had anything to do with me. But they did. They trained me in the fine art of restraint. Like a highly trained seal, I watched for the signal and I obeyed the command. And when my performance was done, I slipped quietly away.

I wondered what the outcome would have been if Marie had stood me before her and said, "They say you love me."

The telephone rang. Without thinking, I picked it up.

"Are you coming or not?" Doris's voice rang through the earpiece.

"I'm on my way," I lied.

"Hurry up," she yelped and hung up.

I didn't like the sound of that yelp. It sounded too much like that of a mouse sighting. Doris was aware of my mouse phobia and that was probably why she hadn't been more specific about why she required my services. I wasn't going to be much help if there was a mouse anywhere on her property.

I couldn't find my black leather boots. I had been searching for them everywhere. I saw my red canvas thong sandals sticking out from the shoe cubbyhole by the side door. I pulled them out and jammed them on my stocking feet and threw on Gord's old jacket, a mouldy, greasy, stained coat he wore for outside winter jobs, locked the door and hurried down the street to Doris's. The wind had died down, giving way to an eerie calm. Faint dustings of icing sugar-like snow fell sparsely here and there as I walked up her drive.

"Get in here," she said, opening the door.

Doris's house was a well-kept fifties bungalow. She had replaced the dull mustard-coloured stucco, pink window trim and dark green roof with off-white siding, black trim and a black roof, when she inherited the house. The overall effect was one of cool elegance, a fitting preface to the interior, where a carefully designed southwestern theme was tied together with a dusty rose, nubbled wallpaper. Pink and mauve Navajo rugs warmed the hardwood floor in the living room and highlighted the magenta stripes running through the rich cinnamon Naugahyde sofa. Round wicker, wrought iron end tables and fake cacti, placed on either side of the terra cotta brick fireplace, screamed less is more.

Doris unzipped Gord's jacket as I stood in the living room. She fluttered her arms agitatedly at me and paced back and forth. Her face was beet red. Little beads of sweat stood out on her forehead and the bridge of her nose. I slipped the jacket off and followed her into the kitchen to the pantry door.

"It's in there," she said, pointing to the pantry.

"Don't tell me it's a mouse, Doris."

"Of course it's a mouse. What else did you think it was? An ant?"

"I don't do mice, Doris. I can't even look at a mouse on TV, let alone in real life. And you honestly think I'm going to kill one for you?"

"Yes."

"Doris. I have one word for you. Exterminator. I can't possibly do it."

"Don't be silly. It's an irrational fear. Silly, really. Here is your chance to overcome it. Now hurry up before it decides to come back here in the kitchen." She grabbed my arm again and tried to pull me toward the pantry.

"I want you to go into that pantry and squash that mouse all by yourself. I will give you my full support from the kitchen."

My heart sank.

"Let me tell you a story," I begged lamely. "Picture this. It's late at night, and I have just returned to a mice-infested cottage. Everyone is asleep."

"Here dear. Take this," Doris said, and handed me a wooden mallet. "Let's start walking toward the pantry as you talk." She patted me on the arm and motioned for me to follow her. I took a step back.

"I have just closed the cottage door, and I hear a noise around the corner of the fridge. I think it might be one of the kids, so I go to where the sound is coming from."

"Try to smash the mouse on the head if you can. Try to do it fast before he runs out of the pantry." Doris advanced, clamped her cold hand on my arm and pulled me forward.

"The moon was full. It was a beautiful night. The moon shone through the screen door."

"That's nice dear."

"It highlighted, to great visual effect, a mouse, his head caught in a trap, dragging himself arduously across the linoleum. One of his front paws was also clamped in the trap along with his head. His free paw and back legs scratched valiantly, but futilely, His free paw and back legs scratched frantically on the floor, as the steel pressed deeper and deeper into his neck."

"What were you doing up so late at the cottage? Everyone was asleep?" Doris asked, just as I was about to open the pantry door. I stopped.

"What?"

"Why weren't you cuddled up to your hubby? Why were you up so late? Midnight skinny dip?"

"No. I was having a chat with my mother-in-law down at the main cottage, an attempt at bonding, which was, as usual, in vain."

"Why do you say that?"

"My mother-in-law has never been interested in anything but wielding the cutlass of consummate control."

"Nice alliteration."

"Thank you. It just popped into my head. At any rate, the heads of those dumb enough to challenge the dowager dragon rolled regularly. I wanted to show her I was harmless, that there was no hidden agenda."

"How did that go?"

"Well. Halfway through the conversation she tells me she believes that I am using her as a substitute mother, something she is not willing to be, that she is sick and tired of people assuming, just because she converses with them, that she is willing to take them under her wing and nurture them. She tells me she has three children and is not willing to take on any others."

"That was kind of a bitchy thing to say."

"Insensitive. Even Gord thought so. And that was why I was out so late. I was having a crash-and-burn conversation with the dowager dragon."

"Did she know you had lost your real mother?"

"Yes."

"Incredible."

"I got her back."

"Oh my. How?"

"I was unrelentingly nice to her. It just about killed her."

"Wait a minute," Doris said. She darted to the kitchen, returning seconds later with an empty ice cream pail and top.

"Are you listening to me?" I asked.

"Yes. Yes. I am. Go on dear," Doris said as she pressed the pail into my hands.

"Well," I said, miffed, "Not to belabour the punch line,

but I screamed and ran to wake Gord up. I couldn't touch that mouse, Doris. I just couldn't."

"And?" Doris asked as we stood outside the pantry door.

"And? And what? I couldn't pick up a mouse if my life depended on it."

"That's why I brought this pail," she said. "Tip it over the mouse and you won't have to touch it at all."

"Gord finished off the mouse, don't ask me how, and picked it up by the tail and pitched it into the river, trap and all," I said, looking at Doris for some sign of sympathy. "I really don't want to do this, Doris."

"Don't be such a chicken," she said.

"If that isn't the pot calling the kettle black, I don't know what is," I said, tartly.

"Get going. I have a life to live," she said, giving me a jab in the kidneys.

"You are a cold woman, you know that?"

"Cold? Me? If someone invited me to go out with them, and I didn't like it, I, at least, possess the manners to be polite, sit through the damn thing, thank them, and go home."

I turned to Doris. "Doris, I am so sorry for the way I acted at the New Age seminar. There was no excuse for my behaviour. I had a bad day and I took it out on those New Age people. I'm sorry. And, oh geez, if I have to get in that pantry and bludgeon that disgusting little mouse to prove how sorry I am, well, Doris, I will."

"I accept your apology and extend one of my own. You did nothing wrong at the seminar. I, on the other hand, was too quick to judge. I'm sorry. I called you today because I consider you a friend. And I never thought of calling the exterminator.

Now let's get at it."

She stopped suddenly, grabbed my arm. "I hear it," she whispered.

I froze.

"Do we want it to come out or do we want to drive it back into the pantry and catch it there?"

I banged on the pantry door to drive it back into a corner. We both listened at the door. Rustlings within the pantry made me feel faint.

"I'll give you a nice cup of tea after you catch it," Doris whispered.

"Some incentive," I said.

I held my breath and pushed the door open. All was quiet. Just the thought of seeing the mouse that now sat so timidly behind a jar of marinated artichokes or a can of peas or a plastic bottle of ranch dressing made me want to shriek like a banshee. My nose started to itch and I rubbed it with the back of my hand. The hair all over my body prickled and I knew at that instant that I could never kill the mouse. The best, the very best I could do was catch it and take it to the pet store.

Doris and I inched into the pantry. Doris pointed to the floor where she had sacks of brown sugar piled high, like sandbags in a flood, beside bottles of spring water in pale blue four-litre water jugs. The mouse's tail stuck out from between the sugar and the water. I took a step forward and the floorboards beneath the linoleum creaked. The mouse bolted out from behind the sugar and hopped blithely over an old peach basket that held onions and an open Tupperware bowl full of potatoes, to scamper up the cornerpost of the shelves.

Doris and I screamed as it galloped over packages of linguine and rotini, toward us. I swung the ice cream pail at it, banging the edge of the shelf and catching the tip of a bag of guacamole flavoured tortilla chips. The chips crinkled and fell to the floor with a crunch. The mouse stopped, sat up on its hind legs, took a quick look at us, about-faced, and scurried behind a wall of curly noodles, piled neatly in groups of four.

I knew it was now or never. I ran forward and dumped the pail over the noodles and mouse. Trapped, the mouse pawed frantically at the plastic. Witless, I thought of how one's mind and thoughts change from moment to moment, or even from second to second, like a flowing river, the present thought flowing to the next thought. I fleetingly thought of dropping the pail and moving to Las Vegas, but after instantaneously calculating the impracticality of such a drastic move, I grabbed a large can of deep-browned baked beans and plunked it on top of the pail.

The yellow cellophane packaging of the curly noodles crackled as the mouse clawed for some avenue of escape. Even with the can of beans securing the pail, the maniacal thrashings of the miniature Tasmanian rodent devil began to shift the pail. I picked up a jar of calorie-reduced triple-berry jam and set it on top of the pail. The pail stopped moving but the inside still resembled a food processor, pureeing bananas, skin and all. I turned to see Doris's ecstatic admiration at my success, but she was nowhere in sight.

"Doris!" I yelled.

"Coming!" she shouted. She appeared in the doorway of the pantry. She held a wine glass in one hand and a decanter full of red liquid in the other. "My strawberry liquor," she said, pouring some in the glass. She gulped the contents of the glass and sighed.

"Will you please curb your alcoholic tendencies until we get this thing totally secured?" I gasped, exasperated at her lack of delight in my success.

"I'm sorry, dear. I needed a drink." She disappeared briefly and returned, hands empty. "How can I help?"

"What do we do now? How are we going to get the mouse out of the pail?" I asked, hoping she would volunteer.

"You could slide the pail quickly off the shelf and hold the top of the pail underneath it," she said.

"Will that work?"

"I don't know. It's worth a try." She scurried off into the kitchen and came back with the lid.

"Strawberry swirl," I commented.

"What?" Doris asked.

"Strawberry swirl ice cream. Is that your favourite?" I asked, pointing to the lid.

"No, not really. It was on sale so I thought I'd try it. Come on, quit stalling. I'm shaking like a leaf. Let's get this over with before my legs collapse beneath me."

Doris held the lid out in front of her and crept toward the pail.

"Oh thank you Doris, you've just saved my life," I said, immensely relieved that Doris was taking charge. I could step back. My roiling stomach could subside and perhaps one day I could forget the horror of this moment.

"Oh God, what am I thinking," Doris said, aghast. She flipped the lid to me, stepped behind me and let out a huge sigh.

I caught the lid as the acid in my gut once again began its

grating churn. I listened for the mouse. All was still. Taking comfort from the silence, I edged over to the shelf. I quickly took the jar of jam and the can of beans off the upside down ice cream pail and put my hand on top of it to hold it down. I slid the pail to the edge of the shelf, at the same time holding the lid level with the shelf. I slid the pail slowly off the shelf, at the same time sliding the lid under the mouth of the pail. The mouse, sensing potential freedom, scratched and wriggled at the crack between the pail and lid. A tiny kicking foot freed itself from the pail and a tail whipped out of the pail just as I fitted the lid on. The mouse squeaked. Doris and I screamed.

"Don't let go!" she yelled.

"I've got it! I've got it!" I flipped the pail right side up. Two packages of curly noodles still remained in the pail. They crackled as the mouse pawed pathetically at the sides of the pail.

"Let's have a drink," Doris said, and ran to the kitchen.

I followed, holding the pail out in front of me. I continued to the front door, opened it, and deposited the mouse on the step, which I saw had a light covering of snow. I shut the screen door and surveyed the street, shrouded in gloom, from behind the glass. Heavy ash-grey clouds hung low in the striated sky, poised to discharge the deluge of snow in the fierce blizzard predicted by the weatherman two weeks earlier. The dire warnings rung out nightly by weathergirl seemed hollow no longer. I shut the main door, walked to the kitchen, and sat down at the table to a large tumbler full of strawberry liqueur.

Doris held her tumbler up.

"We have remained ladies and a credit to our race in the face of formidable trial," she said as a toast.

"What are we going to do with it?" I asked as I took a sip

of the sickeningly sweet liqueur.

"I don't know. You could take it as far away from here as possible. That would be a start.

Maybe we could ship it to Calgary."

"Don't you want to know its fate?" I asked as I took another small sip. The smooth fruity flavour, with the consistency of liquefied jam, warmed its way to the pit of my stomach.

"Not really, dear. Just be kind whatever you decide to do."

"Oh yes, kindness is high on my list, Doris, as I think about the future of this creepy, crawly, wiggly, slimy, hairy varmint."

"Glad to hear it," Doris said, her cheeks glowing with the effects of the alcohol. "You dispose of that little miscreant, and I'll make you peanut brittle for life."

"Is that what all those bags of brown sugar are for in your pantry?" I asked, my mind quickly whizzing through abnormal psychological options.

"Yes. I have to use it up somehow," she replied enigmatically.

Doris stuffed my coat into my arms and shoved me out the door. I grabbed the pail and carefully picked my way down the snowy steps. The air was damp with the promise of a storm, one that could go either way: high winds and driving snow, or fat wet flakes by the blanketful. I walked home briskly, making sure the pail did not bang against my coat or legs. A wave of guilt washed over me. Basically, I was carrying the mouse in its plastic prison to its, as yet undecided, death. I deposited the mouse pail outside the side door, took my sandals off, and shed my coat on the floor in the front entry.

Mice. They were a gnawing, worming, mobile malignancy that defiled everything in their path, tiny bead like droppings a foul stamp of territory claimed and trailing disease laden tails into the most intimate of areas in homes, weakening the very structure until sought out and exterminated.

I took a deep breath and exhaled nervously. What was I going to do with the mouse?

I hustled through household chores, mindful of the distasteful task awaiting me. After putting breakfast dishes in the dishwasher, a load of towels in the dryer, vacuuming the living room rug and making a note that we were out of milk, I sighed in frustration because I was still out of a plan. I changed into jeans and a long-sleeved T-shirt. I found my favourite black boots sitting on the floor of Clare's closet when I hung up a coat of hers and I grabbed them eagerly. I put my coat and boots on, grabbed my purse and took a deep breath. Then I went to get the ice cream pail.

I let the car warm up a bit and as the fan blew cold air on my legs and on the windshield, I looked at the pail on the passenger seat beside me. After a brief frenzy of psychotic scraping and crackling of cellophane, the mouse had been ominously silent.

I thought if I drove around a bit I might come up with a plan. I backed out of the driveway and headed toward the University Farm, a tract of land that had been set aside for future development. A section of the land had been earmarked for the Agriculture Department and barns, Quonset huts, stables and trailers had been built to provide hands-on education and research. I thought if I could get close enough to one of the barns, I could slow the car down and dump the mouse out on the ground. But the entrance to the farm was roped off, and I was waved away by a grounds worker who was having a smoke break.

I don't know why I was showing mercy to the mouse. I could just drive to the freeway pedestrian overpass and pitch it over the side where it would be flattened in ten seconds. I could throw it into the garbage where it would freeze in an hour. Or I could put it in a plastic shopping bag and drop a brick on it. I knew in my heart I couldn't do any of these things so I drove around the neighbourhood, searching for a humane way to rid myself of the mouse.

My mind was a blank until I hit Sixty-first Street. I jammed on the brakes and screeched to a halt inches from the bus stop. A plan was forming. It was fuzzy, the logistics not quite worked out, but I knew what I was going to do.

I had noticed that Maureen, of clumpy Doc Martens fame and parent of the obsequious Ewan, was having her furnace cleaned. On my drive through the neighbourhood, I'd noticed Fred's Furnace Cleaning van parked in her driveway. A thick hose ran from the van to the house, and the side door had been wedged open. Did I dare to set the mouse free in Maureen's house? At least then I wouldn't have to kill it. I laughed at the thought of my immature plan and wondered how much of the strawberry liqueur was doing my thinking for me. All in all it wouldn't hurt to take a look I finally decided.

I cruised slowly past the house and parked out of view around a curve in the road. I took the pail, got out of the car, and walked hesitantly up the sidewalk. The street was deserted but I pulled the collar of my coat up around my ears and slouched down into it anyway. I skulked up the drive on the far side of the van. I dropped to the ground in a petrified crouch when the front door opened suddenly and a hand reached out to get the morning mail. I peeked around the front of the van to make sure the coast was clear.

I duckwalked to the side door. The hose groaned as it sucked out the dirt from the furnace and vents. I tipped the pail over the hose and was about to take off the lid when sober second thoughts, the killers of many a great notion, started rolling in. I stepped back at the same time that the hose gave a great snort, shuddered and shifted position, causing me to trip and fall backward. As I went down, I accidentally ripped the lid off the ice cream pail and the mouse and one package of curly noodles were flung into the front hall.

I duckwalked back past the van and down the drive, straightening up when I reached the sidewalk. As I speed-walked to the car, my heart skipping beats, I was seized with a sudden terror that I would be caught. I ran the last few yards to the car, and with shaking hands, unlocked the door. I slipped quickly into the car, slammed the door shut and slunk down in the seat. I waited several eon-long minutes for the flashing lights and ear splitting sirens of the entire police force, followed by the Kevlar-vested tactical squad, tasers held firmly in their black-gloved hands, before I tentatively reached over and turned the key in the ignition.

I shifted into gear and drove slowly away with my head below the dashboard and two wheels on the sidewalk. Several blocks later I relaxed enough to sit up straight and check the rear-view mirror. No host of cop cars, following single file, with cherries flashing, followed me. The street was empty. The street was quiet.

I turned into a side road and parked. I sat in the car and listened to the motor spin and whir. It was cold inside the car and I shivered. I looked out the window. It had begun to snow. Hard little pellets hit the roof and front of the car in irregular plips. The wind had picked up. It swished through the branches of three large fir trees partitioning two nearby lots. A mangy-looking dog, a rarity in our neighbourhood, slinked smoothly across the road and into a backyard through an unhinged gate.

I visualized Maureen picking up the package of curly noodles from the floor in her front hall and looking at it quizzically seconds before noticing movement in her peripheral vision, seeing the mouse and screaming hysterically. I started to laugh. What was wrong with me? Here I was, sitting in a cold car in the middle of a strange street, laughing. I closed my eyes and rested my head on the steering wheel. It was only a matter of time before someone took me away in a strait jacket.

A solid line, neon blue, cut my eyelids in two. The woman in my dream, who had stepped on the moving sidewalk and then turned back to look at me before she was carried around the bend, flashed before my eyes. This time, as she rounded the bend, she reached out her hand to me. A cold blue light shimmered around her hand and the fingers elongated, turning white at the knuckles as the skin and bone stretched out in an effort to reach me.

I opened my eyes. I was tired. And a pain in my temples made my head ache. I wanted to be at home.

I started the car and drove home, past the older houses that needed facelifts, past newer houses that had just had one, and past houses that had just been built. People in their allotted boxes on their allotted streets in their allotted cities, living their allotted lives. Painting, adding on, taking off, roofing, trapping mice. It was all so futile.

I drove past Maureen's house and hoped that no one suspected that a tiny mouse was, at this very moment, scampering gaily over and under heating ducts and basement ceiling beams looking for the perfect spot to build a nest. I felt my throat begin to tickle and the giggles erupt. By the time I reached our driveway I was screaming with laughter.

CHAPTER 11

Cubed beef, onions, potatoes, carrots and onions sat on a plastic cutting board on the kitchen counter. I hunted for my ceramic bean pot. I hadn't used it in a while and when I dragged it out of a bottom cupboard near the sink, I saw it needed to be washed.

It was Marie who taught me to cook my stew in a bean pot. It took a lot longer to prepare this way, simmering slowly in seasonings and vegetables, but it was worth the wait to get the resulting thick dark brown gravy, which, when ladled over the flavourful meat and soft vegetables, made for a succulent dish.

I browned the chunks of meat in a frying pan at high heat in oil. I picked the crisp pieces of meat up with tongs and put them into the bean pot. I slid the chunks of onion, celery and carrot into the pot from the plastic cutting board where they lay segregated into their own personal piles. I cut the bitter ends off five large cloves of garlic, smashed them on the board, peeled off the skin, and tossed them into the pot. I poured in a can of consommé, a can of Molson Canadian beer, a twenty-eight-ounce can of plum tomatoes, a few squirts of Worcestershire sauce, half a bottle of hickory flavoured barbecue sauce, some salt, pepper and thyme. I thought of Marie as I stirred the mixture in the pot and burst into tears.

Every Saturday she would get up early and make bread. She would make ten loaves a week. It took until late afternoon before the last loaves went into the oven, along with a large pan of sugary cinnamon buns. She seemed happiest when she was cooking and would share secrets with me as I sat at the kitchen table watching her.

"You can knead the dough with your elbow if your wrists get tired," she would say, and then show me how, the flesh on her upper arm jiggling up and down as she savagely thumped the dough. "Once it rises, you can do almost anything with dough. It likes to be treated roughly."

Why would I think of her, I wondered now, as I cut a piece of tin foil to put over the top of the bean pot before I slid it into the 325 degree oven?

Dinner done, I could relax before everyone trailed in through the door from school and work. I sat at the kitchen table and looked outside, my chin resting on my hand. My head was still pounding from the strawberry liqueur and my afternoon mouse adventures.

Two little grey snowbirds swooped down from the tiny patch of dark grey sky that I could see out the top of the window. The neighbour's house and gardenshed blocked out most of the sky and the shutter framing the top of the kitchen window blocked out the rest. Just one little corner afforded a clear view of the sky. The birds dove and swirled before alighting on the fence rattling in the wind, immediately darting up into the sky and out of view, only to come plummeting down again, rounding up under the shutter. They huddled together on the inner edge of the shutter, picking at something on the ledge, their heads popping up and down like Jack-in-the-boxes, checking for danger.

"Hello," I said to them from behind the glass. "Are you coming or going?"

One of the birds looked quizzically at me.

"Because if you are going, you'd better dress warmly. I hear it's going to be cold up north this year." I tapped the window to get their attention. They stopped, and then, in unison, dropped off the ledge to the ground, and out of sight.

I decided not to tell anyone about the mouse. I would tell Doris that I threw the mouse, pail and all, into a snowbank. If she looked too horrified at my callousness, I would change my story and tell her I took the mouse to the pet store at the mall. I would check first and see if the store had pythons or snakes or any kind of animal that preferred mice as food. Or, I thought, maybe I should just tell her the truth. I knew it was something I could never ever tell Gord. He would see it as proof that I was crazy.

"Did you get the milk?" Gord asked later that evening. He religiously ate a bowl of diced fruit and cornflakes, with milk, every night before he went to bed. It was good for the digestion, he said. The side of our house could be sheared away by some great empyrean force and the nine horses of the apocalypse could thunder gallop through our living room, spewing dust and sand-coloured pebbles and leaving the stench of sweating horse and over heated metal in their wake, but if Gord was in the middle of stolidly chewing his nightly dose of fibre, he would not even look up.

"No, I forgot," I said, mentally cursing myself.

We had run out of milk that morning. Stevie had drunk two glasses of milk, leaving exactly six drops to moisten the top flakes in Gord's bowl of shredded cardboard. I had made the mistake of laughing at him, sour faced, methodically chewing the dry cereal. A curt shake of his head dismissed the idea of substituting apple juice for milk. On his way out the door he commented brusquely about my failure to keep proper provisions in the house. I laughed at this as well, to the sound of the door slamming.

"Were you too busy today?" he asked.

"I can go out and get some now," I said, trying to head off the inevitable lecture.

"That's not what I asked," he said. "I asked if you were too busy today to get some milk."

"Actually," I said carefully. "I was."

"Oh yeah? Doing what?" he prodded

"Stuff. You know. Stuff," I said.

We were standing in the kitchen. Gord had his hand on the open refrigerator door. He had obviously checked the milk supply and was planning to berate me for my slovenliness.

"Catching mice?" he asked, slamming the fridge door.

The Kleenex box, always precarious on the top corner of the fridge, fell to the floor. A picture of Batman, painted by Stevie in kindergarten and anchored to the fridge door by a weak magnet advertising a local take out pizza parlour, slid to the floor.

"I saw Doris on the way home tonight and she told me about your adventure this afternoon.

"What do you mean?" I asked, stalling.

I took the hat and glove basket down from the shelf above the coats and began digging for my gloves. I found my white mitts instead, two pairs put together for added warmth. Marie had knitted them for me. I had no idea what they doing in there. I hadn't seen them in years.

"You. Doris. Her pantry. The mouse. Doris had to tell me the story twice before I'd believe it." Gord stood in the middle of the kitchen with his arms crossed, a scowl on his face. This was never a good sign. What line of attack was he planning?

"Oh. The mouse," I said, avoiding his eyes. I tried on the mitts. They fit.

"Pay attention. What did you do with the mouse? You didn't kill it. I know you. You couldn't kill it. So what did you do with it?"

"What does it matter what I did with the mouse since you are so sure I didn't kill it?"

"You're acting weird. What's wrong with you?"

"I've got to get some milk," I said, handing him the glove basket, taking my coat from a hanger, shrugging into it and walking across the kitchen to get my purse.

"No," Gord said. "Not until you tell me what you did with that mouse. Is it a big dark secret? You're going to stand there until you tell me about the mouse. Don't move." He came over and put his hands on my shoulders. "Don't you move until you tell me what you did today," Gord warned.

"Don't order me around," I said, throwing off his hands.

I shivered, and feelings of revulsion and nausea and anger rose in me as a flash of Marie, towering over me, commanded the same. I was very aware of how angry I was, of how strongly the rage flowed through every vein in my body, adrenalin awakening and speeding my heartbeat, quickening my breath and flushing my face. I didn't need my meditation book to tell me that anger is a very powerful negative emotion that is essentially misguided mental energy.

I was still trying to grasp the theory that anger, as with all emotions, is a delusion, a distorted conception, not real, but one of many endless emotions flowing through our minds, a very powerful emotion that, because we are not in the habit of controlling it, causes much distress to us and to those around us, like it was doing to Gord and me now. We are not in the habit of trying to control our anger, the meditation book stated. We are not in the habit of trying to transform it into a positive, useful experience. We, puny humans with brains that possess awesome untapped potential were unable, for the most part, to recognize anger and deal with it in our minds instead of lashing out.

"Well?" Gord prodded.

"You remind me of Marie," I said.

"Marie would tell me to stand in front of her. She would tell me not to move. 'Don't you move until I say you can, she would say.' Like I was a dog. She was training me," I said, and then I stopped speaking. I gave full attention to a thought that was emerging, dimly, from the clouded recesses of my mind, a thought that gained in clarity with each cerebrated wave within my brain.

"Marie was training me to live a life as diminished as she had lived," I said to Gord. "Because that's what mothers do. They train you to live your life. My real mother trained me until she died. Try as she might to turn me into the cringing supplicant that was her own childhood in the convent, the best that Marie could do was force me to bury who I was."

"Hey!" Gord said.

"I'm tired of snapping to attention any time someone barks at me. I'm tired of waiting in attendance upon everyone else's commands. I'm tired of being afraid."

"Listen," Gord said, moving toward me.

"Get away from me," I screamed.

"Okay," Gord said, and put his hands up in a sign of surrender.

"I'm not going to stand here. I'm not going to tell you about the mouse. I may never tell you about the mouse. Do you get it? Do you understand? Now I am going to get some milk!" I shrieked. I burst into tears, ran past Gord and got my purse.

"Wait!" I could hear Gord calling me, seconds later, as I ran to the car.

The weather had finally committed itself and had become a severe snowstorm. A flurry of heavy flakes stuck to my eyelashes and hair. The wind blew more snow inside my open coat, nailing me sharply in the throat with stinging flicks. I brushed a clump of snow off the car so I could get at the keyhole. It was wet and cold against my hand. But it felt good.

An image of me, running naked at night through the snowbound bush, my feet breaking through thick crusts of hard snow, sinking up to my knees, my shins stripped of flesh by the jagged ice and bleeding, arms flailing as I tried to retain my balance, screaming madly as I ploughed my way through the hard packed drifts, buzzed through my head as I fumbled for the car keys, hidden in the depths of my purse.

Gord called from the side door. I looked at him and saw him stumble out on the step as he pulled his second boot on. He waved for me to stop.

I had to get away. I had to escape as fast as I could. I yanked the car door open. I inserted the key into the ignition. The car roared to life. I clicked the wipers on. They whined as they tried to push the heavy buildup of wet snow on the front windshield. I saw Gord clumping down the drive. I put the car into reverse and after a cursory check for cars and pedestrians out of windows covered with snow, backed out of the drive, shifted into first gear and fishtailed down the road. The sudden forward movement of the car dislodged a wad of snow from the rear window of the car, and as I turned the corner I saw Gord running down the road after me, calling and waving, no coat on and his boots undone.

I shook the snow off my hair. With one hand on the steering wheel, I shook the snow off the right side of my coat, and then exchanging hands, shook the snow off the left side. I dried each wet hand on the leg of my jeans and peered out the window. The wipers had cleared off most of the snow on the windshield, but the inside of the car was cold and my breath was frosting up the inside windows. I turned the defrost on as high as it would go. Cold air blasted up the air vents, condensing the moisture on the glass into a fine spray of ice crystals and up over the steering wheel into my face. A small hole of clear glass directly above the vent widened quickly as the glass warmed.

The roads were atrocious. Drifts of snow, sculpted by the winds, lay on the road like strips of twisted lasagne noodles. Snow covered patches of ice in the neighbourhood had waylaid several cars; they sat at odd angles by the side of the road, blanketed by snow. One man stood beside his car, sideways in the ditch, with his hands in the air, a gesture of surrender. The turned-up collar of his short bomber jacket provided no protection for his head, or the blonde mop of curly hair bouncing in the wind.

"Turn the wheel into the slide, not against it."

Gord's words rushed back to me. I was surprised how

many people didn't know that. Or, even if they did have that information tucked away in their heads, still gave in to the temptation to turn away from an impending accident. Gord. What was he doing? What was he thinking of me? As I inched down the street, I found I didn't care. Gord would think what he wanted to think.

At the four-way stop, the last exit from the neighbourhood, I was feeling calm, having escaped. As I turned right and proceeded slowly down a street where mounds of snow had narrowed two lanes of traffic into one deeply snow-rutted lane, I wondered what I had escaped into. I drove to the supermarket close to the junior high school and parked across the street from the store. I turned the car off and sat listening to the wind whistle softly through a crack in the passenger side window. I would buy milk, I decided. I felt calm. Routine tasks where I had to concentrate on what I was doing helped me regain my sanity. Perhaps, I thought, that was how I had lasted all these years.

The supermarket was virtually empty. I walked down quiet aisles and selected various items. One till was open, and the chatty young man in charge held up the line of four customers as he smiled and recounted the reasons why his lifelong dream of dancing in the Bolshoi Ballet had been dashed by his parents who enrolled him in hockey instead.

"Roads closed going south," he informed me merrily as he scanned my milk, whole-wheat spaghetti noodles, three cans of picante tomato sauce, a package of Earl Grey tea, one lemon lime pop, and six Turkish Delight™ chocolate bars.

"Bad night," I said.

"Road crews are going to be out all night clearing snow," he continued as he totted up my bill. "Weather advisory says to stay home where it's safe and warm. Sixteen dollars and ninety two cents, please."

I tuned the boy out. I was impatient to be on my way. The snow on my hair had melted and it ran down my neck. I felt chilled. The boy was looking at me oddly.

"Oh. Sorry," I said. I pulled a twenty-dollar bill out of my purse and handed it to him.

"Drive carefully," he said as he handed me my change and groceries.

I tossed the groceries onto the passenger side seat, grabbed the windshield scraper from the trunk, and after thoroughly brushing and scraping the outside of the entire car, I sat with the motor running, watching torrents of flakes hit the windshield, melt immediately, and stream gently downward on the glass. I was tired but didn't feel I could go home yet. I would wait until I was sure Gord was in bed. I needed to be out of the house, to drive around. But didn't the boy say the roads going south were closed? Maybe he was mistaken. I decided to go and see for myself.

After several attempts to get onto Highway 2, I could verify the cashier's information. Blocked roads with flashing signs, snow barriers created by armies of graders festooning the streets, rotund men in fluorescent work coveralls with giant X's on their fronts and backs, waved me onto detours through residential streets that left me travelling across the river and downtown. I followed the detours and lighted batons without question. Mindlessly. The workmen knew what they were doing. They were the guardians of the roadway, guiding me on to a safe path. I abandoned myself to their care and direction. I would see where the road less travelled led. I would go home when I was cleansed.

I drove at an even speed and as fast as the blizzard conditions would allow. It was still windy and snow blew in crazy circles in the air. The snow no longer resembled soggy wads of cotton batten. It seemed crisper and the sheets that swept across the front of the car were more like real snowflakes. In fact, as I concentrated on the road, it seemed more and more like I was driving through layer upon layer of diaphanous tissue. If I stopped, I thought, the layers would silently and rhythmically pile up, one onionskin film after another until I disappeared, nestled snugly in a soundless airy tomb. I was fine if I kept moving, if I kept slipping through the gauze, osmosis personified. I could see the yellow line in the middle of the highway, my torch in the dark, showing me the way.

The line became easier and easier to see. The snow suddenly stopped. I wondered how long I had been driving, and where I was. No streetlights illuminated the road and no houses provided the hopeful pinpoint of lights, connect-the-dots that signified human existence. I saw what looked to be a sign up ahead and I slowed down as I approached it. Some hitchhiker had stuck a rudimentary sign made out of cardboard "Going North" in a spindly fir tree growing by the side of the road.

I pulled over to the side of the road and stopped. I put the car in neutral and set the emergency brake. I stuck my hand into the plastic supermarket bag and took out a chocolate bar. I folded the wrapper down so half of the bar was exposed and took a small nibble out of the top. The sweetness of the chocolate next to the gummy strawberry flavour of the inside incited my taste buds. I sucked the chocolate coating from the strawberry gelatine as my tongue watered profusely. I liked to take my time when I ate a Turkish Delight™. It was my favourite chocolate bar. I could make a Turkish Delight™ last all day, nipping a corner here, and a corner there. I swallowed the first bite, the smooth sugary chocolate sliding down my throat. I took another bite and then set the bar down on the passenger seat. As I shifted into first gear and pulled out on to the highway, I wondered if I could make the Turkish Delight™ last all the way to Yellowknife.

CHAPTER 12

I looked at the three mismatched candles reflected in the large living room window of the cabin. They seemed, in their replication, to add more light to the room. Perhaps it was because the darkness outside provided a favourable backdrop that showcased the glowing sheen, or perhaps it was wishful thinking on my part. I looked at the candles again, stuck with clumps of melted wax to upside-down lids of Ogden's™ tobacco, the shredded leaves of which had been poked and tamped solidly into shiny well-used pipes and inhaled in companionable silence by grizzled old men, friends for life, who knew the value of a good smoke. The candles sat on the tiny lacquered stump that served as a coffee table. I envisioned the owner going wild with a chain saw one sunny weekend and levelling an innocent pine grove somewhere to furnish the cabin completely in wood.

The one-room chinkedlog cabin was a pre-fabricated twenty-foot square pine unit, hauled no doubt, to Yellowknife on a big rig. The walls had been carelessly slathered with a clear protective wood resin that had dried mid-drip on many of the logs. The floors were heavily varathaned pine planks. Wide and natural, they had seen better days, but an intense scrubbing with a non-abrasive brush and soapy floor cleaner would erase the many years of indifferent care they seemed to have had. Three four-foot metal shelves had been fixed to the wall above a small kitchen counter that contained a built-in sink, a plastic cutting board, and storage space under the counter which was hidden behind a grimy, threadbare blue cotton tarp. The kitchen area stood in the corner opposite the door.

A pine woodbox stood to the left of the door. On the wall above the woodbox was a big irregular shaped piece of pine with a picture lacquered on to it. It was a winter scene. A fluorescent pale blue deer, with a rack of pale blue antlers the size of a car and one blue foot raised, stood thoughtfully in the middle of a white forest with blue trees. Past renters, or even the owner himself, had etched numerous guns into the lacquer. They protruded from the trees in the forest, pointing directly at the deer's head. A ratty rabbit skin with several bald spots hung over the woodbox to complete the outdoor northern woodsman motif.

The woodbox served a fairly modern woodstove, placed in the opposite corner of the room from the kitchen area. A large picture window had been placed low to the ground and along the wall between the stove and the woodbox. A lumpy sofa bed sat in the middle of the room facing the window. It was on this sofa that I sat, contemplating the candles.

It was my third night in the rented cabin, at the end of the road on Latham Island, in Yellowknife, Northwest Territories. I had arrived in Yellowknife three days earlier around noon. Through crackling radio waves, the weatherman had reported that it was minus-thirty Fahrenheit with an expected high of minus-twenty-eight.

Winter. It had grasped this Precambrian land and would not let go for eight long months. I had forgotten what real cold was. It had risen with the sun as I drove the last fifty miles into town. Ice crystals hung in the air. Frozen.

That first dawn began with a slight lifting of the pitch-dark night. The weak sun, rising from below the black-lined horizon sent a deep purple hue announce its coming. A rich plum tint stained the sky briefly before it gave way to streaks of salmon pink. It was the pink that mingled with the tangible Arctic front that made it seem like I was driving through cotton candy air. And then it was there. The sun. A great big orange ball. It was brilliant. But only for a second or two. Literally. The sun in winter in the North. It soon faded behind a pale cloud cover and stayed there. Indirect lighting by Mother Earth.

The road was bumpy in spots, with crater-like potholes padded with snow. It had snowed a lot. The trunks of the shrunken trees were nowhere to be seen, and boughs were weighted down with snow. Large rocks poked out here and there, eruptions in the white. Closer to town I noted movement on the road. Bustling. I slowed down my already moderate speed, apprehensive at first, but then breathed a sigh of relief to see small flocks of fat ptarmigan waddling across the road.

Northern birds, they turned completely white in the winter, except for black markings on the tail, which could only be seen when they took low flight. They don't take flight often, preferring to glide on snowbanks and drifts, like penguins. Several rabbits, pure white as well, jumped out of the bush, but when they saw the car, they turned tail and hopped quickly away over a rise. I saw the airport's red beacon blinking soon after and knew I had arrived, my misgivings about my decision to drive north, forgotten.

A sense of relief enveloped me as I drove into town, partly because I had worried that the car would break down on the deserted highway or that I would freeze and be eaten by gangs of marauding wolves. For the entire trip, I'd felt like an escaped convict in a stolen car. As I drove past the airport I saw that an old floatplane, in what looked like its original condition, with battered pontoons, faded paint and wings that sagged a little from all those happy years of soaring over ponds of muskeg and galloping herds of caribou, had been mounted on a sturdy triangular metal base. It was surrounded, realistically at this time of year, by chunks of wind-carved snow.

An industrial area had been built up in my absence and I was surprised to see that "suicide rock," a hairpin curve sculpted around a large jutting granite hill halfway into town had been blasted away. An easy curve had taken its place. Houses, with chimneys chugging smoke, crammed both sides of the road, providing a comforting welcoming scene. I felt like I had made it, home free.

I drove to the hotel, found the public washrooms and freshened up. I was bone tired from having driven eighteen hours straight north and saw the dark circles around my eyes, the black eyes of the loser in the championship boxing match, I thought, as I peered wearily in the mirror.

It was too early to check in to the hotel, the cheery hotel clerk with the shiny, swinging blunt-cut hair told me, so to kill time before I could throw myself on a firm bed and go to sleep, I went shopping. In a fit of nostalgia, I bought a pair of hide mitts, gauntlet style, with a colourful braided string that went around the neck, red embroidered roses with dark green stems on the backs and fox fur at the tops. They cost as much as a new winter jacket would for Stevie, in the city.

I charged them on my Visa™. It was probably the mitts, I thought, that convinced the owner of the cabin I subsequently rented, that I was one of those rich city women who could be easily swindled. I saw the advertisement on the counter at the clothing store I bought the mitts in. It read, "Winterized Cabin, Cheap." I asked the salesclerk about the ad and, as it happened, the owner worked part-time in the back of the store unloading and stocking merchandise. She called him out to the front of the store, and we struck a deal.

"Eighty a night," he said, a toothpick doing a dance at the side of his mouth.

His name was Ray, and I, at five-foot five, had a good three inches on him. He looked to be about fifty years old, with shiny hair slicked back. He had an inordinate number of wrinkles around his eyes, probably because he squinted a lot. Squint. Relax. Squint. Relax. It looked like he was forever trying to focus.

"Is it near here?" I asked. I liked his rawhide coat, with its beadwork and fringe. It would go nicely with my mitts, I thought.

"On the island," he replied.

"Near or far island," I asked. The toothpick stood still in his mouth. He took it out and looked at it.

"You from around here?" he asked, alert.

"Born and raised. I'm back for a visit."

"Far."

"How far?"

"How long you been gone?"

"The far part of the island was called Rainbow Camp way back when."

"Long time. It's called N'Dilo now. Got a proper bridge too. Not that old wooden thing."

"Eighty a night, eh?" I couldn't believe I'd said that. It was funny how easy it was to slip into the jargon. "Eh?" It was a word I tried to keep out of my children's vocabulary. "And what do I get for eighty dollars a night?"

"A hell of a nice view."

"And?"

"A hell of a nice cabin. Completely winterized. All the amenities of home. A cord of wood out back, already cut."

The sales girl behind the counter laughed.

"It depends a lot on where your home is, don't you think, Ray?" she asked grinning.

"I'll handle this, Sheila, thank you," Ray said.

"Don't rip her off, man," Sheila said, shaking her head. "Geez."

"All the amenities of home. Like what?" I asked, wondering if I should drop the whole thing and register at the hotel.

"Come on. I'll give you a good deal. Seventy bucks a night," Ray whined.

"Indoor plumbing?" I asked.

They both laughed.

"Stove? Fridge? Bed? Walls? Or is it a lean-to?"

"Okay. Okay. Fifty a night. What are you talking about? It's a fully winterized cabin, with walls, a bed, blankets, water, fireplace, wood, lots of wood. I just chopped a load of wood. Enough wood for two weeks at least. My nephew was going to go and stay there this weekend if it was free. Great view, too. No kidding."

I looked at Sheila.

"If it was free," she laughed.

Ray ignored her. He put his arm around my shoulder and led me away from the counter, out of Sheila's hearing.

"Okay. I'll level with you. It's pretty basic. Got a stove, pull-out bed, blanket, dishes, water. I did chop wood. The outhouse is deluxe and it's not that far from the house. Throw your coat on, nip out, do your thing, nip back in. A lot of people wouldn't have it any other way." He tried to look convincing.

"Who?"

"Who what?"

"Who do you know that would rather have an outdoor toilet at forty below than an indoor one?"

"I mean in the summer. They like it in the summer. They can commune with nature, that sort of thing."

"But it's winter now."

"Technically, not yet."

"For a basic cabin where I would have to get fully dressed every time I hear nature call, I would pay thirty-five dollars a night."

"Done," Ray said it so quickly I wished I had offered fifteen.

I paid Ray for three nights. Cash. He gave me directions and said he would drop around in three days to see if I needed anything.

The cabin was situated on the north shore of the island, nestled at the edge of a small copse of fir trees. The back of the cabin faced the driveway, which was snowed in. I had to park the car on the side of the road. As I carried the two bags of groceries I bought at the supermarket in town through the knee-deep snow, I could see that the view of the lake and town across the bay was very pretty indeed. The door to the cabin was unlocked, as Ray had said it would be. Cabin owner's law. Leave it open for someone in need.

A quarter inch of green candle swam uncertainly in a lid full of hot wax, the wick flickering a few seconds before being engulfed. The tobacco lid, full of molten wax, looked like the odd man out on the stump. I thought about sticking a new candle into the wax before it hardened. An old cardboard box in the cupboard above the sink was filled to the brim with new and partially burned white candles. There was no need for electricity in the summer with twenty-four hours of daylight, and any time hunters inhabited the cabin they would undoubtedly bring kerosene lamps with them.

It was easier getting used to the candles than it was getting used to no heat. I awoke the first morning to a frigid room, the air exhaled from my mouth condensing the instant it left me into a small white cloud. After that I served wood to the stove like a slave to an exacting taskmaster. I did my cooking in the one cast iron frying pan provided so thoughtfully by Ray. No plates or saucers meant that I ate out of the pan with the teaspoon that I'd found in the knife and fork drawer. I opened my canned ravioli and chili with a beat-up can opener screwed to the wall in the kitchen area. Five mugs came in very handy.

Ray said there was water and there was. In a rain barrel outside the door. It was full, I gave him that. But it was also frozen. I had to chip it out, with the axe that I would have gladly chased Ray around the yard with, melt it in the pan and pour the resulting water into mugs. Ray. Every renter's nightmare landlord.

But I was okay. The day-to-day mechanics of trying to stay reasonably comfortable in this rustic setting kept my mind off what I was really doing in an isolated cabin on the north shore of an island just outside of Yellowknife. During the long drive to Yellowknife, I'd refused to think about what I was doing. I'd pushed it from my thoughts. But now I was here. At the end of the road. Literally.

What did I do now?

A second candle flared briefly and went out. The middle candle had maybe an hour of burning time left. I sat watching it twinkle out from the confines of the blanket on the pulled out sofa bed. I still had the wood in the dependable stove, humming and crackling me softly to sleep, for company.

I'd put off going to the woodpile because it was so cold. Trips to the outhouse were even less pleasant than I could ever have imagined and the thought of wading through snow drifts to pry armfuls of frozen logs from the messy heap in the yard was not an inviting thought. But I needed wood. Reluctantly I got up and put on my coat and boots and went outside. The cold chilled me immediately. The hair in my nostrils froze with every breath and blistered my throat. I was shaking by the time I had threaded a path to the wood.

I stopped before the mound. It was covered with blue, glistening snow. I looked up to see if it was the moon that was the cause of the light. It was not the moon. The aurora borealis, the northern lights, filled the sky. They were most brilliant on the coldest nights, and tonight they bathed the sky in electric blue, green and yellow. It was eerie in that it was almost as light as day. The yard shone under the glare of a blue floodlight. I dug wood out of the pile, kicking it loose with my foot, and carried it inside.

It took me four trips to fill the woodbox. The activity warmed me, and I decided to walk out to the road to see the spectacular light show better. Although I knew that sunspots, which spit out solar flares into space and cause magnetic storms in the Earth's magnetic field are the real cause of the auroras, the fanciful side of me warmed to the old Inuit tale that says the northern lights are either spirits playing ball in the sky with a walrus skull or flaming torches carried by deceased souls guiding travellers to the next world.

The auroras flared and faded as they moved across the sky. And then they were gone. I savoured the stillness for a moment and turned to walk back to the cabin. A movement in the bushes by the woodpile made me pause. A trill of fear ran through me. Wolves. I froze, not knowing whether to remain immobile or to run. I heard the noise again and decided to run, keeping my eye on the woodpile the entire time. Several steps into my flight I stopped and screamed. A gigantic apparition leaped out from between the woodpile and the cabin. I ducked and felt a stab of pain as I fell backward onto to my hip into the snow.

It was a deer. A blue deer in mid-jump, outlined in electrified bolts of neon blue that dispelled jerkily into the night as it ran down the road, its hooves crunching in the snow, creating echoes, staccato drumbeats that rose, revealing my hiding place to the stars. It looked exactly like the deer in the lacquered picture on the wall in the cabin. Had I really seen it or was my imagination working overtime?

I gasped and scrambled to my feet. I had thrown my arms back to help break my fall and my hands and wrists were wet. I stuck them in the pockets of my coat and stumbled into the cabin. I leaned against the closed door. I took my hands out of my pockets and stared at what was clutched in them. I held the white mitts that Marie had knitted for me when I was a child. I threw them on the ground. All the emotions I had been able to repress since my arrival in Yellowknife welled within me. I started to cry. A profound sense of despair sapped my strength.

I went to sit on the sofa to reflect upon my fate.

I was alone. I had always been alone. I could live with that. Not belonging. Always on the fringe of life. I had grown to prefer it, in a way that I couldn't explain. But I couldn't live without love. No one could. I didn't care how trite it sounded, or if it was the oldest cliché in the book. I hungered for the loving touch of my mother. I was dying from the lack of it, dying of starvation.

I had been imprisoned as a child in a fancy cage of wood. No expense had been spared in creating the illusion of happiness and freedom. Ironically, from my perch within the bars, I learned that everyone but me could have love, and when I escaped into adulthood, my capacity to accept and give, but mostly, I think, to accept, the same, had been so shrunken and reduced that being a part of the universal experience that binds one human being to another, that of giving and receiving love, didn't even occur to me to as a possibility. Was the loneliness, the isolation of being alone, the deprivation of the human touch, the emotional touch, a way of preparing for death? Maybe that was why I was here. Maybe the brilliant aurora I witnessed was a clue. I had come home to die.

The fire snapped quietly as the glowing embers sank into the hill of ash in the bottom of the grate in the stove. Because I had let it burn so low, I would have to rekindle it before putting logs of any size on it, or it would smoulder and go out, I thought. I went to the woodbox and dug around for splinters at the bottom of the box. Taking a handful of wood chips over to the stove, I knelt in front of the open cast iron door, dropped all the chips on the floor, and held one match-sized piece of wood over the coals. It burst into flame immediately and I flung it down, my hand singed. I fed the fire with wood chips until there was a steady stream of little flames licking the air. I put four larger sticks on top of the mini-blaze in a square shape, and when they caught fire I added two small three-by-ten inch logs, side by side, to the flames. As I watched the dry wood catch fire, I thought of a story my mother once told me.

We had been visiting our grandfather in his cabin on the island, one of a few cabins at the time. In summer, he had to canoe over to the mainland as no bridge had yet been built, and in the winter he used a trail over the ice. One frigid afternoon, she had decided to leave us with our grandfather and walk across the frozen snow-covered water to the Hudson's Bay Company store. She had met some friends there unexpectedly, and stopped to chat. It was late when she started home, the bitter cold accompanied now by a howling wind and blowing snow.

I remembered her description of walking back across the ice. Black patches of windswept ice merged the sky and land into one, and the feeling of walking in space had filled her with dread. She had been afraid that something would emerge from the murky depths of the frozen ice or swing down from the pitch sky and grab her. She wandered, lost, as snow blew and drifted. That's what snow did in a storm. It drifted. And it led my mother clear out into the middle of the lake. I didn't remember how she found her way back to the cabin. I just remember her alone on the lake.

The wood burned fiercely. I stuffed three more logs into the stove. I watched smoke curl up around the sides as they were warmed. I shut the door of the stove to help direct the smoke up the pipe and went to sit on the sofa. My head throbbed from being too close to the heat and my own disturbed state of mind.

I got up and walked over to the window. I cupped my hands over the glass. It was cold on my palms. The lake was not visible through the trees and the dark. I knew an ice trail existed from the island to the mainland because during the day I had seen figures in the distance slowly making their way across the icing of the lake. I felt my heart thundering in my chest. I was afraid. What if that was why I was really here? To die.

I paced the room feverishly and then threw myself on the sofa. I was exhausted and fell into a fitful doze, surrendering to the jumbled images that pulled me under. Which recollection would it be this time? It didn't matter. I would take them as they came.

I had been imprisoned. Several other people, whose faces I could not see, and I, had been forced into a small bamboo hut in a jungle camp. The hut was set on stilts in the middle of a compound and was guarded round the clock by men with semi-automatic machine guns.

The roof of the hut was poorly thatched, and bugs of all types and sizes dropped regularly from the rafters onto the reed mat that was my bed. I knew every inch of my small prison. I knew what I would get to eat and what my rice bowl looked like. I knew the boots of the commander coming to periodically check on his prisoners. I knew my silent resolve not to give in.

I tried to focus on the wooden rice bowl with the crack on the bottom, so I could identify it from the others put outside the door at mealtime. I tried to linger on the meal, wiping out each grain of rice with my fingers from the curve of the bowl. I liked to feel the sticky inside of the bowl after the food was gone and hear the *chik* of it as I set it down on the bamboo tray that was whisked away every day by unseen hands.

I needed to reaffirm my existence. Each meal was potentially my last supper. One night it dawned on me that if I didn't escape, I would be killed. I would die, shrivel up on my filthy mat, as one of the others across the room had begun to do. I would become brittle, curled, and hard, slipping through the cracks in the rough bamboo planked floor into the thick muck on the ground, where I would sink noiselessly into its depth.

I waited until night, having made up my mind to die in a blaze of bullets rather than to give in, to be lost. When I first thought to confront my captors, I decided I would throw open the door, announcing my intent, defiant, challenging. I would stand there, on the six-inch step, my arms spread, waiting for the first bullet to hit me. And I would pray that when that bullet hit my chest and I exploded, bits of bloodied flesh shooting out in front of me, the rest of my body smashed against the flimsy bamboo hut, that I would die quickly, like the switching off of a light.

I would stand there, on the step, my arms spread, waiting. And as I waited, tensed and shaking, I opened my eyes just a little, and through the slits, I saw that many of the soldiers were shirtless, some wearing their suspenders hanging down the back of their pants, and others mopped their necks with yellowy-grey handkerchiefs, soaking up the intense jungle heat. I looked down at the disorganization, the incompetence, the slack army which I thought had been so carefully guarding me, encircling me, their living hostage, to kill at their will.

And the dream began to change. I no longer felt it was an inevitability that my captors would win over me. I was still defiant, challenging, and I still went out onto the step. But I was quiet. I let the soldiers see me, get used to me. They would look up at me from their games of Mah Jong and poker and sneer and spit into the mud. I would sit still on the step, my arms wrapped around my knees. I would pretend to look at the sunset, or the rain clouds gathering, but all the while I was memorizing the compound, looking for a hole, devising a plan, plotting my escape.

One night I heard the soldiers mobilizing and I knew the time had come for me to escape. I tried to convince the others to come too, but they shrank from me, shaking their heads. I cut a hole in the bamboo hut on the wall that faced away from the compound. I ran to this flap, quietly lifted it and slipped through. The cool night air made me shiver. I could smell the damp and looked at the sky. Heavy black clouds churned above and a cutting wind sprang up. I was seized with fear and tears welled up in my eyes, my throat constricting.

And then, my faith and I leapt. Like a cat, I pounced, my thin cotton top clinging to my breasts, my legs drawn up under my body. The first spurts of rain spat at me as I fell, landing with a splat in the muck. I felt as if I was swimming in a vat of Kaopectate. I scrambled to my feet as ear-splitting claps of thunder and thick snakes of lightning illuminated the sky. I stood, framed by a flash of light, as the first bullet whizzed past my head.

I began to run, slipping in the mud, scraping my knee,

feeling the pain and absorbing it, and then clawing up a rain-slicked rise, grasping at clumps of grass, pulling myself up. The rain, driving now, was beating on my head and shoulders, blinding me, stinging my arms and thighs. When I reached the barbed wire fence, I grabbed it with both hands, squeezing the barbs into my palms as I wrenched the wires apart. I thrust my head through the tiny hole, scraping my neck, my shoulders, feeling the barbs digging into my hips, giving me a particularly deep gash on my left side. My skin was alive with pain, but it was the pain of accomplishment and victory. The rain became a welcoming wash. I lifted my face up to it. Then, hearing shouts and rifle shots behind me, I ran into the darkness.

I stumbled through black, rain drenched jungle, trees whipping my face, tripping on exposed roots and crashing to the ground. Surprised animals flew into me with a horrifying thud, their padded claws catching my hair, legs and hands. I ran blindingly at first, frantically, fearfully trusting that each step would not plunge me into a hole where I would be lost forever. But I also ran with hope. I saw an infinitesimal silver speck right in the middle of my heart and I fixed on it. I refused to think of the possible consequences of my failure. I began to see an end. I began to see that I really could escape my captors. There really was a way. If I could reach the imaginary line, I would be safe. If I could get to the other side of my dream, I would be granted a pardon. I could live.

I almost made it to the line, which in my dream, had become a thin, blue neon stream, wavering in the distance. I tripped on a root and was shot as I fell. I felt the bullet enter from behind: the pain in my leg immediate as the tissues registered shock at the sudden assault. I dragged myself over grass and roots in muddy slime, using them to scrape myself along the ground. I began to cry as I inched forward. I had come so close. I heard the soldier approach as I lay, face down, near the line. My face rested in the mud, grating against my cheek. The commander stood over me and I tensed, waiting for the impact of the bullet. But, incredibly, he paused.

The rain had stopped. I could hear the drops falling from the leaves of a nearby bush in a steady drip. I heard him fumble with his clothes, searching for something. Drops of water hit the mud . . . *pht . . . pht . . . pht.* And then, the strike of a wooden match against the side of a box. I sprang out, fingers splayed, grabbing the line. I had expected it to be sharp, wire cutting into my hand. But it wasn't. It was soft, and wet, and cold. My hands clawed for the neon blue barbed wire fence.

I was screaming. I couldn't grip the wire. I held on to it, to brace myself against the impact. It kept slipping through my fingers, which were becoming numb from the cold. My body was cold too. Very cold. Had I already been shot? Was life leaving me? Was that why the air was so cold? Like winter. I began to dimly comprehend that the horror of the nightmare was not real.

I heard a wolf howl. In the jungle? I heard another wolf, and then another. Their howls drew me out of the semi-conscious stupor that I was floundering in, into the realization that I was alive, and alone, in the middle of the ice trail that led to the mainland. I was no longer sitting on the sofa, in the cabin. I was half lying, half sitting on the dark, iced path, crunched up wads of snow in my freezing palms.

I must have run out of the cabin at some point, I thought hazily. I could see the mainland where the lights of the houses curved along the U-shaped bay, twinkling faintly. Turning my head I saw fewer points of illumination coming from the island. I couldn't tell which cabin was mine. I remembered the candle on the stump and doubted that it could be my guiding light home.

I stood, stiffly. My body was numb but I did not feel cold. I knew that was a bad sign but I didn't care. I concentrated on my heart beating behind an armour of ice. I looked up at an aurora borealis swathing its way across the sky toward me, shimmering brilliantly. Curtains of light, dancing sprightly against a black universe, whirled into a glistening corona of yellow and blue directly over my head, exploding outward, and leaving a trail of phosphorescent dust in its place. I was drawn by the vibrant intensity of each minute flake as it hung in the air around me, the sparkles giving way to spinning stars that swelled and grew, and clustered around a small ray of light that dilated smoothly. I squinted to see an object at its centre.

A white moccasin, the top of which was embroidered with pink roses and curly green stems, encased a descending foot. A robe of purest white, and then, the deep brown wells of my mother's eyes. The vision, surreal, smiled and reached out to enfold me to her breast, and I felt the love of a mother for her child for the first time. Again. It had begun in the womb and lasted beyond death. Beyond time. Love. It flowed through me to my very core. I shed the shield of invincible will that had protected me until now and I laid my heart bare, to be healed. The armour of ice shattered, softly.

A flush of warmth surrounded my ankles, tingled at my knees and spread through my thighs, making me feel slightly queasy as it permeated my abdomen and stomach. It hardened my nipples and crept up my neck and flushed my face, pouring down my arms, the tips of my fingers pulsing. I ran my fingers through my hair, igniting it, and then I pressed them down my neck and breasts and thighs.

A gust of cold Arctic wind swirled around me, but the heat emanating from within me, warmed it, scented it, somehow, so that it curled away from me condensed, and glowed a silvery pink. Hope burst forth, like a torrential rain sweeping a clean and sure path to its designated end. Silently, yet from the very centre of the heart that had always held one pinpoint of hope, just in case. I felt my heart for the first time, I thought, startled. Pounding, booming, pulsing out pure oxygenated blood, reviving, regenerating. I wanted to rest my head on her breast forever, continuing to receive the transfusion of life.

But she was gone. My teeth chattered uncontrollably as I opened my eyes to see the last gleam of the aurora in the night sky. A trail of pink floated in its wake like the lost tail of an errant kite.

How could I have forgotten that I was loved? What time of day was it when my memory lapsed? What was I wearing? Who was standing near me, witness to the life snap out of me? It was so simple. My mother loved me. She gave me life, not once, but twice, the second time this night. There was no question. The love between a mother and her child was innate, timeless, forever. I marvelled at the concept.

A blast of wind slapped my body and I gasped, filling my lungs with the coldest, freshest breath I had ever taken, a not too subtle cuff from Mother Nature to tell me that I was alive and if I had any wishes to stay that way I had to get moving. As I peered through the night in an attempt to discern which spot of light on the island I should be working my way toward, an unearthly scream rent the air. I thought of wolves or sled dogs on the loose and I began to panic. I needed to make my way to one of the lights on the island, any light, quickly, before the fleet footed canines caught my scent, outstripped my blundering through the snow, and ripped the flesh off my bones faster than a bubble could escape the startled lips of an insipid angelfish when plopped in a tank full of piranha. But then the pitch of the screams changed.

I turned in their direction. What I first thought was the sound of the frantic howling of a pack of carnivores racing across the bay to finish me off actually sounded like the high-pitched whine of a chainsaw. The sound grew louder by the second. I squinted. Lights from two houses seemed particularly bright. It was as if they were bobbing and weaving their way toward me. Understanding dawned suddenly and too late. The beams were connected to a big black block of steel that hit me with such force that I catapulted into the air. As I sailed upward into the atmosphere, I became conscious of an excruciating pain in my right foot. As I began my descent, and just before the black engulfed me, I laughed as I realized I had just been run over by a snowmobile.

CHAPTER 13

I opened my eyes to verify where the pain was coming from. It was throbbing, pulsing, agonizing pain. I was right. It was my foot. My right foot, which was propped up on something hard and stuck out of a pink fuzzy blanket that covered me up to my chin. A threadbare striped hand towel that Ray, the landlord, had mistakenly categorized as "linen," and which I used to wipe my face after I had melted enough ice from the water barrel to wash my face, was wrapped around it. I ached all over. I searched for a spot on my body that did not cramp and spasm any time I twitched, but could not find one. I tried to sit up, but my body was welded to the sofa bed. And to make matters worse, a toothpick appeared, halting two inches from my face, with Ray attached.

Ray. I fluttered my lids closed, rolled my eyes up under my lashes in what I hoped was a realistic portrayal of someone slipping back into the world of the unconscious. I needed some personal space and time to accept the pain and find a way to deal with it and finding that place of calm and acceptance did not include harassment by Ray. I inhaled as deeply as realistically possible under the circumstances and exhaled slowly, imagining all the pain leaving my body with each exhalation. I tried to develop a mindful motivation for the meditation I was attempting, but the eyes of the holy man featured on the front cover of my meditation book kept intruding upon my efforts to bring my mind to a clear and quiet state. They were bizarre, heavy lidded, and half open; they stared somnolently at nothing.

He had relinquished all that was human to achieve nirvana. That was the reason for the comatose expression on his face. He was a shell of his former self. He had spiritually "made it," attained the most exalted state of enlightenment, the elimination of all negative aspects of the mind and the perfection of all positive qualities, and had come into his own Buddhahood. I, on the other hand, wished for true happiness but did not know how to find it and wanted to end my suffering and yet did not know how.

Ray's face appeared again. "You alive?" he asked, chewing on his toothpick furiously.

"The jury's still out on that one," I managed to croak. My lips felt thick and dry.

"Good news. Your foot's not broken. Swollen. Whoa. Swollen like a sausage that's been sitting out in the rain for two days. But not broken. Sprained a bit, maybe. Got the doc who lives in the cottage a few doors down, you know, the one with the big deck built out over the rocks and that big old ugly sculpture sitting on the end of it ready to fall off. Yeah. I got him to come over and take a look at it."

"And?"

"Yeah, well, like I told you, he checked you over real good. Twisted your foot this way and that until I thought I was gonna puke, and then he says it's just sprained a bit. Good thing you were out cold when he wrenched on it. Hoo boy, that was spectacular. You could be on that TV show, you know the one where they show all these people doing things and piling themselves big time."

Ray's voice came to me from different points in the room. He was pacing. I could hear the floor squeak by the woodstove and then again by the door.

"The doc said to elevate your foot and ice it. So I propped it up here on the sofa, and the doc wet the towel and wrung it out in some snow and wrapped your foot in it. I'm supposed to wrap it again when the towel gets warm. Can you hear me?" he asked loudly. "You had an accident."

"Really? I would never have guessed."

"You got run over by a snowmobile."

"It felt like a bus."

"Heh, heh, heh," Ray laughed obligingly.

"Who ran me over?" My throat was dry too.

"You see. There are two trails out there. One for people and one for snowmobiles. That's why you were hit. You were walking on the snowmobile trail."

"What happened to the dogsled?."

"What?"

"Dogsled. Where are the dogsleds?"

"Oh. Yeah. Gone. Mostly. Snowmobile is the modern mode. Faster. Can haul a lot more than dogs. The only drawback is that if you run out of fuel, you're sunk. And that's a pretty big drawback if you ask me. "

"Too bad."

"Yep. We all wish for the good old days, eh? Hey, you want to tell me something?"

"What?"

"What were you doing out on the lake in the middle of the night? You had no coat on, nothing."

Ray seemed like a nice guy, but I was afraid to start spouting off to him about the innate umbilical cord of love I had just re-established with my long dead mother. He would think I was crazy.

I started to cry. I put my hands on the sides of my head in an attempt to stem the crashing headache that was developing. I was tired of living my life as a walking cliché. I was tired of striking the servile pose, minimizing myself so as not to attract any undue consideration and apologizing, constantly, for existing.

"What were you doing out there in the middle of the lake in the middle of the night?"

"I was thinking about a nightmare I used to have about being chased," I finally said. "I must have gotten too involved in it and it freaked me out and I ran out onto the lake. I didn't even realize that I had no coat on, but you know Ray, it didn't matter at the time, because I had a vision that I saw my mother come down from the middle of a northern light. She said she loved me, Ray, and then she disappeared and I was hit by a snowmobile two minutes later. There. Now you know."

Ray sat down on the tree stump coffee table. He took the toothpick out of his mouth and flicked it away. He ran his tongue back and forth quickly over his front teeth a few times as he thought over my confession and sighed.

"So you had a vision, eh?" he asked. "Cool. Weird. But cool."

"You believe me?" I asked, incredulously.

"It's a possibility," Ray replied.

"Oh," I said, surprised at his casual acceptance of my statement.

"My grandma has them all the time. Sometimes I think

she fakes it, though, to scare me. But for the most part, yeah, I believe in them."

Validation. And from a most unlikely source. It felt natural to accept it.

"Was it a hit and run?" I asked, groaning under the pain of the headache. I pulled the pink fuzzy blanket over my head to shut out the light.

"Hit and run," Ray said, "That's a good way to put it. I hit you with my snowmobile and then I run you over here to the cabin. Heh, heh, heh."

"You hit me?" Somehow it didn't surprise me.

"You were on the wrong trail. Hey, come on. I brought you right back here. Got you checked out right away by the doc. Won't be more than a day or two and I'll find your boot too."

"You lost one of my boots?" I moaned. "I've had them forever."

"Hey, what can I say? It must have flown off when you went flying through the air. Man you went flying. But don't worry. I said I'll find it for you. If I can't, it'll turn up in the spring. Probably, anyway, if it doesn't sink first."

"You better get out there today and find it. I mean it, Ray," I said threateningly from under the covers.

"You won't be needing it for a few days anyway," he said. "It's the boot from the foot you sprained. Heh, heh, heh."

"Ho. Ho. Ho." I said sourly.

Ray got up from the coffee table and began pacing. I folded the blanket off my face and tried to get Ray in my sights.

"Listen," he said as he walked around to the side of the sofa and looked down at me. He reached behind his ear, pulled out a toothpick and inserted it in his mouth. The toothpick began its familiar two step across his closed lips.

"You can have the place for free until your foot's better. And if you need anything in the meantime, you can just ask. I'll get it. On me. Okay? Cuz that's the kinda guy I am. Considerate. My grandma even said so once."

I looked at his worried face and realized why he was being so nice to me.

"Afraid I'm going to sue you, Ray?"

"What, are you kidding? It was your fault, man. You were on the wrong side of the trail. Lawyers are expensive, you know."

"My husband is a lawyer."

"Someone married you?"

I laughed in spite of myself at Ray's remark, and it hurt a lot.

"You still have to prove it in a court of law, you know."

"Bring me a snowmobile safety rule book. I'll bet I could find a few lines about driving with undue care and attention, about running people over, especially at night. Yeah. I'll bet there are a few choice phrases detailing how a snowmobile should be driven at night."

I had raised myself up on my elbow during this tirade, forgetting my crippled body and sprained foot. I shrieked at the stabs of pain shooting through my body like jolts of high powered electricity and flung myself back onto the sofa with a groan.

"Okay. Okay. I admit I was going a bit fast. I was coming to give you that blanket you got on there. And I was coming to get some money from you. But not now, not now. Don't worry." Ray sidled around the sofa and looked at me speculatively.

"Even though I sure could have used it. My mother's sick and I was going to help her out a bit."

"Oh my god, Ray. Let me guess. Your mother is going in for a big operation and she might not live. My thirty-five bucks are imperative to her survival. I have to say I think I've heard it all."

"Well, she'll live, but she could use a few bucks."

"Oh come on, Ray. You wouldn't even be here if you didn't think I had a case. So let's cut the crap and deal. Right now." My lips cracked in several places as I spit the words painfully out. I would settle for a half used tube of Ray's lip balm, germs and all, and be happy.

"Okay. Name it," he said with a sigh, now in familiar territory.

"I want some type of fast food hamburger, fries and a large Coke.™"

"What?" Ray asked in disbelief.

"You heard me. And the operative word is fast. I am sick and tired of cooking in the one stinking frying pan you so generously provided and eating my food with a teaspoon. I want napkins and lots of those little packages of ketchup. I get real surly if I don't have enough ketchup for my fries." Eating the greasy, salt laden fries with my split lips might smart a bit, but I was willing to endure a little discomfort in exchange for real food. Or semi-real food.

"Well, okay," Ray said, looking at me suspiciously. "Is that it?"

"I want a pot, Ray, to melt some bloody water in. I don't enjoy melting it in those mugs you've got in the cupboard. And I want a plate. Extravagant, eh? I want a plate, a knife, and a real honest to goodness towel to wipe my face with after

I've melted the damn stuff." I threw the "damn" in just to show I meant business.

"You'll get it today," he said, relaxing visibly. I could see he thought I was a pushover.

"And?"

"And?" Ray asked.

"I want a portable toilet, and I have to say I really love your coat."

"What?"

"I love it Ray, and it would go so nicely with my new mitts."

"What? No way. You are crazy. No way you are getting my coat. My mom made this for me. Forget it."

"I thought she was sick?"

"What?"

"I thought your mom was sick. I thought she was on her deathbed."

"It cost a lot of money, man," he said, still resisting.

"Fine. Through your own carelessness, which you yourself admitted, you ran me over, Ray. I've got a sprained ankle, or worse. I can't get it checked out for a while, during which time you expect me to melt water over the stove in a frying pan because you misrepresented your accommodations." Gord would be proud of me.

"I'll track down a porta-potty for you but there is no way you are going to get this coat." Ray looked defiant.

"I don't want your coat. I'm sorry. I think I must be going a bit nutty from the pain. I would appreciate the food and the indoor toilet, though. I have need of both."

"I'll go then." Ray shrugged deeper into his coat and zipped it up. He took the snowmobile keys out of his coat pocket, paused, reached into his pocket again and took out a small-Zip lock plastic baggy. He handed the bag to me. "I almost forgot. My grandma sent you some dried caribou meat. She says she thinks we're related."

"Really?" I asked, interested.

"Yeah, well, don't get too excited about it. It's a favourite pastime around here, trying to find some connection. I made the mistake of telling her that you used to live at Rainbow camp and now she's not going to get a wink of sleep until she and her decrepit old friends figure out who your mother was."

"I'd be happy to tell her whatever I can," I said.

"You can give me the info. I could use some leverage with her right now. I gotta go. I don't want to be out on the lake at night again. You can fill me in when I get back with your food," Ray said. He saluted me and was gone.

I looked out the window and saw Ray manoeuvering the snowmobile down the path to the lake. He was partially standing, his shoulders heaving left and right as he guided the machine. The white expanse of lake that I could see from the sofa was fading to a grey wash under the wan afternoon light, turning Ray into a dancing silhouette as he bumped over shoreline moguls. Soon I would be munching salty fries by candlelight, I thought, and then groaned inwardly when I glanced over at the three lumps of melted wax in the tobacco lids. I would have to mobilize myself and get to the kitchen cupboard somehow to replenish my light source.

A crinkle reminded me that I held the well worn Zip-lock baggy that Ray had tossed to me before he left. Through the plastic I could see several pieces of dried caribou meat, hard as a rock and dry as a bone. The backstrap, or tenderloin of this northern animal, killed for food, not sport, was sliced from a still warm body, carried to a sturdy rock or cutting table and with the sharpest knife possible, was cut horizontally and folded out, cut and folded out, until a thin sheet of meat was ready to be laid carefully on a slanted drying rack, high enough above the "green" wood smudge below so as to slowly smoke the meat, not cook it. And when the dense smoky air had curled up and around the meat long enough, gently drawing out any moisture so the caribou attained the look and consistency of a piece of driftwood, the final testimony to whether the drying process was complete was to snap a piece in two, and if fine, powdery splinters of meat fell from the split ends, the meat was ready to eat.

I opened the bag and took out a small piece of dried caribou. I snapped it in two and several tiny flakes of meat fell onto to the blanket. I put a piece in my mouth and began to chew. It was definitely dry, so dry that after chewing through the initial wax like outer coating, it almost melted on my tongue. There was no appreciable taste to it, but I knew of its life-giving qualities, of how, once preserved, it could last for years, stowed away in some secret hidden cache by a hunter or a trapper, marked with a stone or a crudely fashioned cross, and when the hunter, trapped by a sudden snowstorm and having lost his way, remembered the cache and made his way to it, spotted the cross, weathered and worn, unearthed the bundle he had buried and, in a makeshift snow shelter waited for the storm to pass, consumed the jerky and was sustained by it.

I put the second half of the dried meat in my mouth and chewed. I did not know what piece of information about my mother I could pass on to Ray's grandmother that might give her a clue as to my history and whether or not she had a part in it. I could not think of one precise detail that would provide a sudden gasp of recognition, a memory fast-tracked to the forefront of her mind, brightening her face with a smile at the sudden remembrance, and changing the *idea* of my mother into a real memory; a memory tinged with sadness, for me, perhaps, as she thought of a small innocent soul standing alone, before life.

Yes, I stood alone.

At Marie's command, I had packed up my memories, like love letters folded and tied with a thick red ribbon, the ends flying free as the packet is pressed into a shoe box and stuffed on the top shelf of the spare bedroom, not forgotten, but stored away for future reference. Marie wanted to love me, I think, but there were conditions on her love, something innocence does not understand, and in defence I drew a shield around myself, protecting my young heart from harm, and I let no one in.

I sighed. My back was stiff from lying on the lumpy sofa. I tried to shift onto my side but my dead weight body would not budge.

"I need to move," I said aloud to myself. "I need to get up off this sofa and go to the kitchen counter and get some candles so I can see. Of course, I will be risking immediate, agonizing pain to my entire body, but hey, I can take it."

I peered through the dusk filled room and sighed, and before I could calculate the depth of discomfort I would feel, I gritted my teeth, threw off the pink blanket, hoisted my body up to sitting position and swung my foot down to the floor in one great motion. I howled as the pain registered.

Holding on to the stump coffee table with one hand and the sofa with the other I dragged myself to my feet. Favouring my swollen foot, I limped to the kitchen cabinet that held the box of candles. I opened the cabinet door, grabbed several candles from the box and then, breathing heavily, rested my elbows on the counter. I bent my right knee and lifted my throbbing foot off the floor.

"Ouch," I said and glanced at the sofa, mentally calculating the number of jarring hops it would take before I was once again reclining on its lumpy cushions.

I could extract a million precise moments from my own personal storehouse of memories, I thought, as I ran my hands over the rough counter top, pressing my roving fingers lightly into small sharp notches, deep knife cuts and an uneven finish in the wood where the varathane had scaled away. I was free to pull an unlimited number of images from the files stored in my faultless memory, drawing out each and every remembrance, thread by thread, to be examined in the light of day, now, instead of furtively, secretly, behind a face of stone, I speculated, as I rolled a smooth, waxy candle between my fingers.

And any time I needed to, I could call to mind slipping in beside my mother, back side first, snuggling against the warmth of her chest as she lay on a small cot by the kitchen door so she could better watch a feverish Ben. She would shift slightly to make room for me, turning on to her side, her chin coming to rest somewhere near my ear, where I could feel her breath on my cheek, and I could feel her arms slide around me. And taking my hands in her own and clasping them together, she would ask me sleepily if I had said my prayers and she would tuck my hands in prayer-form under my cheeks to more easily catch an angel's ear.

It was the one gesture, the one pure thought that showed me where my history had begun and finally, where my place was in it. In a sense, I had come full circle and could begin again, limping, literally, into the future.

The cabin was silent.

Still leaning on the counter, I rummaged awkwardly in my pocket and drew out a crumpled book of matches. I stood, my foot still bent at the knee, and struck the match on the closed cover, watched it flare, and then held it to the wick of a candle. I waited until the wick caught, fluttered and grew steady, and then I blew out the match. A faint scent of sulphur curled up with the smoke of the dead match. I held the candle out in front of me and set my injured foot gingerly on the floor as I girded myself up for the return journey to the sofa. Several booming knocks on the cabin door caught me by surprise and I gasped and jumped at the unexpected sound.

Ray.

I waited for the door to fly open and for Ray to stumble in. But he did not and all was silent.

Holding the candle before me, I watched the pale yellow tail of flame smooth out to a golden point, reveal the blue surrounding the wick, and then stand tall again, the process repeated in a slow jerky fashion as I limped painfully to the door. Keeping my eye on the flame I swung the door open and let it bang against the wall. I quickly put my free hand up to protect the flame from the rush of cold air sucked into the room from outside. Only then did I look up to see some human form hidden behind a large box with a colour photograph of a portable toilet on the side, a smaller open box on top of the toilet box with plates and utensils sticking out haphazardly, and a yellow plastic foodstore bag with a package of spaghetti sticking out of it.

"Ray?" I asked. "That was fast."

A small head wrapped in a Russian style fur hat poked around the side of the box. The forehead flap was down, and the earflaps had been unsnapped and were securely fastened under my visitor's chin. All I could see was a nicely shaped nose and pink bow lips.

"No such luck," laughed a female voice. "I heard Ray was renting the cottage. It is a somewhat unusual occurrence at this time of year. Anyway, I took most of the inside gear home this past fall. I think all I left were candles."

"Yes. There are a lot of candles."

Who was this woman? Had Ray sent her to take some of the heat off of him? I would admit her now but only because she might have brought me some food.

"Come in," I said. "You can put everything wherever you want."

"Thanks."

The tiny woman scurried into the room and dumped the boxes on the kitchen counter with a grunt. Then she turned and nodded to me in satisfaction.

I grabbed the door and shut it. I leaned against it to take some of the weight off of my foot.

"Thank you," I said. "Are you Ray's wife?"

"Oh God no!" The woman shuddered in mock horror and laughed. "I'm his sister-in-law. We share ownership of the cottage. Did Ray bring any water in for you?"

"No. The only thing Ray has brought for me is his charming personality and a sprained ankle. It's been quite rustic so far."

"A little of Ray's personality goes a long way. Believe me I know." The woman shook her head. "Forget what I said. That was uncharitable of me. I know that deep, deep, deep down in Ray's murky old soul there's a nice guy trying to get out."

The woman unsnapped her hat and pulled it off her head. She shook out her black shoulder-length hair and looked at me. It was a friendly familiar smile.

"Ray is supposed to be visiting me later today," I said, wincing as a stab of pain shot up from my ankle to my knee.

"Can I help you sit down?" The woman looked at me worriedly.

"Please."

My ankle was throbbing alarmingly and felt like a dead weight at the end of my leg. It needed to be elevated immediately.

The woman leaped to my side.

"Here. Put your arm over my shoulder and take some of the weight off your foot."

I studied her face as she lifted my arm and placed it on her far shoulder. She held it there with her right hand and wrapped her left arm around my waist. Several painful seconds later I was once again ensconced on the sofa, my ankle tucked comfortably on the pillow.

"Better?" She asked.

"Much. Thank you," I said, staring at her.

"I should go. I hope your ankle mends soon."

She looked at me as if she wanted to say something but then changed her mind and turned to leave.

"Wait." My heart was pounding. Could it be?

"Yes?" She looked at me expectantly.

"Wynn? " I asked. "Is that you?"

"Yes. It's me."

She looked hopeful and apprehensive at the same time. "Is

that you?"

"Yes," I said. "It's me."

We smiled at each other awkwardly.

"I wondered what this moment would be like," Wynn said as she reached out to embrace me. "I was giving up hope."

"I was too," I said.

I held her at arm's length and searched her face for telltale signs of a hard life: vacant eyes coupled with an air of resignation that accepted defeat in all things. But I could see none. Yes, her shining black hair was peppered with grey, and a fine spray of wrinkles surrounded the corners of her eyes. She was thin, and I could sense a slight alertness about her. I recognized that she, too, had cause to be wary more often than not, on whatever road had brought her here to me. The quiet, defiant spark that I knew so well, shone brightly as she smiled up at me, and tears welled in her eyes.

I didn't cry. I was too happy. I wrapped my arms around her in a comforting hug that lasted for quite some time.

Then Wynn got the boxes of candles out of the cupboard, placed them around the room and lit them all. She sat opposite me on the sofa, holding my injured ankle on her lap. And within the minor flickering blaze that surrounded us, we were warm and content as we talked deep into the night.